"I didn't want to tell you like this, Lee. But I'm Malone. I've come back."

"No." Ainslie shook her head. "No, Malone's dead. You're someone called John Smith, and right from the start you've come up with one crazy story after the other. You're not Malone. I buried Malone."

"Ask me anything about our time together." His voice was edged. "I remember it all."

"He made me a promise. You can't know about that." Ainslie heard her own voice as if it was coming from a long way away, through the enveloping mist of pain.

"I promised you I'd never leave you the way you'd been left before. You'd had a nightmare, and I heard you crying out in your sleep. I held you and you told me about your dream." His eyes were dark as he grabbed her wrists. "Don't you get it, Lee? I didn't break my promise to you. I've come back., dammit!"

Dear Harlequin Intrigue Reader,

May holds more mayhem for you in this action-packed month of terrific titles.

Patricia Rosemoor revisits her popular series THE McKENNA LEGACY in this first of a two-book miniseries. Irishman Curran McKenna has a gift for gentling horses—and the ladies. But Thoroughbred horse owner Jane Grantham refuses to be tamed—especially when she is guarding not only her heart, but secrets that could turn deadly. Will she succumb to this *Mysterious Stranger?*

Bestselling author Joanna Wayne delivers the final book in our MORIAH'S LANDING in-line continuity series. In *Behind the Veil*, we finally meet the brooding recluse Dr. David Bryson. Haunted for years by his fiancée's death, he meets a new woman in town who wants to teach him how to love again. But when she is targeted as a killer's next victim, David will use any means necessary to make sure that history doesn't repeat itself.

The Bride and the Mercenary continues Harper Allen's suspenseful miniseries THE AVENGERS. For two years Ainslie O'Connor believed that the man she'd passionately loved—Seamus Malone—was dead. But then she arrives at her own society wedding, only to find that her dead lover is still alive! Will Seamus's memory return in time to save them both?

And finally, we are thrilled to introduce a brand-new author—Lisa Childs. You won't want to miss her very first book *Return of the Lawman*—with so many twists and turns, it will keep you guessing...and looking for more great stories from her!

Happy reading,

Denise O'Sullivan
Associate Senior Editor
Harlequin Intrigue

THE BRIDE AND THE MERCENARY

HARPER ALLEN

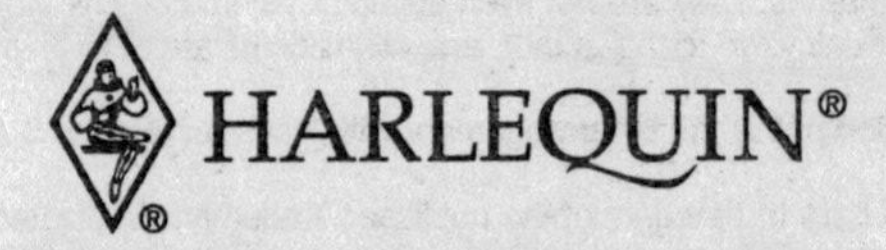

TORONTO • NEW YORK • LONDON
AMSTERDAM • PARIS • SYDNEY • HAMBURG
STOCKHOLM • ATHENS • TOKYO • MILAN • MADRID
PRAGUE • WARSAW • BUDAPEST • AUCKLAND

ISBN 0-373-22663-2

THE BRIDE AND THE MERCENARY

This edition published by arrangement with Harlequin Books S.A.

Visit us at www.eHarlequin.com

Printed in U.S.A.

ABOUT THE AUTHOR

Harper Allen lives in the country in the middle of a hundred acres of maple trees with her husband, Wayne, six cats, four dogs—and a very nervous cockatiel at the bottom of the food chain. For excitement she and Wayne drive to the nearest village and buy jumbo bags of pet food. She believes in love at first sight, because it happened to her.

Books by Harper Allen

HARLEQUIN INTRIGUE

468—THE MAN THAT GOT AWAY
547—TWICE TEMPTED
599—WOMAN MOST WANTED
628—GUARDING JANE DOE *
632—SULLIVAN'S LAST STAND*
663—THE BRIDE AND THE MERCENARY*

*The Avengers

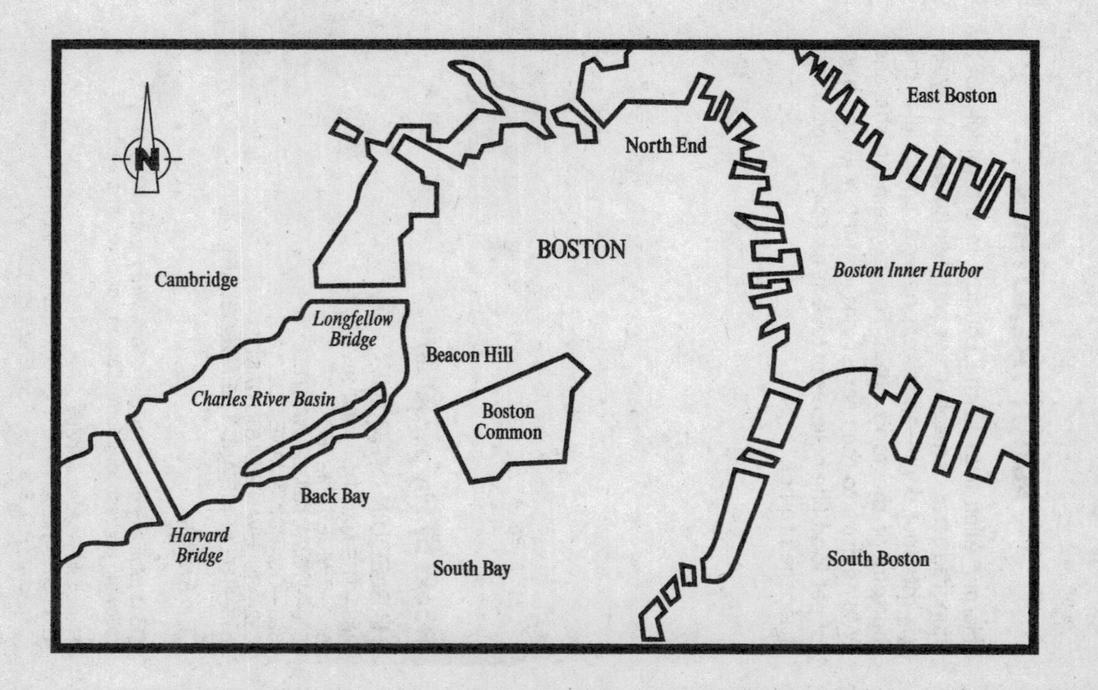
N
East Boston
North End
BOSTON
Boston Inner Harbor
Cambridge
Longfellow Bridge
Beacon Hill
Charles River Basin
Boston Common
Back Bay
Harvard Bridge
South Bay
South Boston

CAST OF CHARACTERS

Ainslie O'Connell—Two years ago she buried the only man she would ever love. But when she glimpses a stranger on the way to her wedding, she's almost certain Malone has come back from the dead....

Seamus Malone—He was killed by a sniper's bullet. Wasn't he?

Terrence Sullivan—Ainslie's P.I. brother, Sully knows that the man she loved hid a dark past. But does the man who looks like Malone have an even more dangerous secret?

Pearson McNeil—Older than Ainslie and slightly stuffy, he's offered her his hand in marriage. Being jilted at the altar wasn't part of the deal.

Brian McNeil—He's angry at the way Ainslie has treated his brother. But is his anger a cover for a more deadly intention?

Paul Cosgrove—He was Malone's partner when the two of them worked for the mysterious "Agency," and he saw him die. Now his own life seems to have fallen apart.

Noah Watkins—He's tracked the international assassin called the Executioner for two years. When he finds him he'll kill him without a qualm.

The Executioner—He's responsible for too many deaths to count, and his identity has remained a secret. But does he himself know who and what he is?

To Sean Cole with thanks.

Prologue

They made little shovels especially for this, Ainslie O'Connell thought in dull wonder, taking it from the man beside her and grasping it by the handle. Who would have thought it? The shaft was of oak, so smooth that it felt like silk instead of wood, and the blade itself gleamed like polished silver. It was almost too pretty to use.

"You don't have to do this if you don't want to, Lee." The low voice at her shoulder was thick with emotion. She looked up.

"No, I'm okay." She looked down again at the shining shovel, the heap of brown loam at her feet. "But I'm not really sure how this works. Am I supposed to take a full shovelful, or is it just kind of symbolic, Paul?"

"It's only symbolic, Lee." His tone was edged with sadness. "Get a little dirt on the tip of the blade and then throw it onto the coffin. They'll cover up the rest of it after we leave."

"Oh." Ainslie frowned in understanding. "Okay." Hefting the delicate implement in her hands, she started to slide the blade into the pile of earth, but then she stopped. "Do they leave the flowers on top of the coffin? They don't take the flowers off before they bury him, do they?"

"No. The flowers stay with the coffin. The roses are yours?"

"Red roses." She nodded in agreement. "Red roses for true love. That's why I chose them. They're really beautiful, aren't they?"

"Yeah, they are, sugar. He would have liked them." Paul Cosgrove's hand wrapped around the shovel handle next to hers, his skin almost the same color as the oak, the white sliver of shirtcuff protruding from the somber gray of his suit sleeve a snowy contrast to the brown earth and the dull red fire of the roses. "It's time to say goodbye, Lee. That's really what this symbolizes."

"Oh, I don't think so." She gave him a startled look, shaking her head. "I'm not ready to do that. I don't know if I'll ever be ready."

Her gaze clouded in confusion, and she let go of the shovel. Her gloved fingers touched her forehead. "Is this really happening, Paul? Do you think there's any way this might be some kind of a bad dream?"

The man watching her sighed heavily, a flicker of pain passing over his features. Instead of answering her, he leaned forward, plucked one of the blood-red roses from the arrangement on the polished mahogany lid in front of them, and handed it to her. Ainslie took it from him, her eyes wide.

"Can you smell it?" he asked softly.

She brought the flower up and took in a deep breath, her lashes drifting onto her cheekbones as she did so. Yes, she could smell it, Ainslie thought. The scent was intoxicating—wine and perfume and a lover's kiss all swirled together in one heartbreakingly lovely scent. The cold petals felt like velvet against her lips.

And then she knew. Her eyes flew open and met his.

"But...but I *loved* him, Paul!" she whispered, her voice

cracking in urgency. ''You don't understand—he *can't* be gone! I *can't* have lost him!''

''You didn't lose him.'' The big man took the rose gently from her and handed it to the woman standing slightly behind them. He placed Ainslie's hand back on the shovel. ''You didn't lose him, Lee. He'll always be in your heart.''

Unresistingly she let him slide the tip of the spade into the crumbling earth. When the two of them had lifted the shovel, he let his hand fall away. With a suddenly frightened glance at him she saw his encouraging nod, and slowly turned her attention back to the task in front of her.

The silver blade held little more than a palmful of dirt, but that was enough to dull its shining surface. It was pretty, and delicately crafted, but in the end it was only a shovel, Ainslie realized. And Paul could say what he wanted about symbolism, but his words were just a comforting lie.

There was nothing symbolic about what she was doing. She was filling in the grave of the man she loved.

She straightened, her shoulders thrown back and her feet planted slightly apart for balance. She felt Paul's hand on her arm and shrugged it off almost angrily. Bringing the shovel up, she held it over the lowered coffin and tipped it sideways.

The clod of earth fell onto the polished lid with a terrible thudding sound. On the other side of her she heard the priest sigh and then begin intoning words she'd heard in movies and read in books, but that she'd never really listened to before.

''Ashes to ashes, dust to dust—''

''He's not in there, you know,'' Ainslie said loudly. ''I think I'll go home and wait for him. Celeste, can I have my rose back, please?''

She grabbed the flower from Paul's startled wife, and began to push her way through the black-clad crowd. She took three determined steps.

Then she fainted and Paul, darting forward, caught her.

Chapter One

"I look like a blob of pistachio fudge in this stupid dress, Aunt Lee. And when am I ever going to wear green satin shoes again in my *life?*"

"Next St. Patrick's Day?" Ainslie gave her fourteen-year-old adopted daughter an unsympathetic glance and looked out the limo window. "Jeez, it's a real October breeze out there. I hope this darn crown thing stays on."

"It's not a crown, it's a headpiece," muttered Tara, flopping back dramatically against the seat. Then she relented, peering at Ainslie through silky, for-this-occasion-only, mascaraed lashes. "Don't worry, Aunt Lee, it'll stay on. You look beautiful—the perfect bride."

"Please." Ainslie's voice was gruff. "I don't feel any more comfortable in this getup than you do. Why I couldn't have worn a simple suit and tied the knot at city hall, I don't know."

"Because Pearson's rich and stuffy and comes from one of Boston's oldest families, maybe?" Tara looked immediately stricken. "Sorry. But he *is* an awful lot older than you, and he does seem to care about doing the right thing all the time. Doesn't that bug you just a little?"

Ainslie framed her answer carefully. "Sometimes, pumpkin. Just like sometimes I guess it bugs him that I still run the gym downtown and manage a couple of the boxers. But he loves me and he wants me to be happy, so he makes compromises. And I want him to be happy, so I compromised on this wedding.''

''Compromised?'' The teenager snorted. ''What did he want originally, if this was the compromise?''

Tara had a point, Ainslie thought. In a few minutes they would be pulling up in front of St. Margaret's Cathedral. There would be a red carpet leading up the stone steps to the massive church doors, and police had apparently been hired to hold back the crowds of spectators that were expected.

It was one notch down from a royal wedding, except for the bride, she told herself glumly.

''I know you like Pearson well enough,'' she said reasonably. ''If anyone's supposed to get cold feet at this point it's me, not my bridesmaid, for heaven's sake.''

''I know.'' Tara fiddled with the ribbons on her wrist. ''But I'm worried you're getting married to him mainly for my sake. You aren't, are you, Auntie Lee?'' She looked up at Ainslie, her smooth young features troubled. ''Because if you are we could stop it right now. We could tell the driver to turn around and you could phone Uncle Sully at the church and—''

''Sweetie, calm down!'' With a little laugh, Ainslie leaned over and clasped both of Tara's hands in hers. She met the suddenly brimming eyes with a mixture of love and concern on her features. ''Of *course* I'm not getting married just for your sake. Where in the world did you get that idea?''

''From Uncle Sully.'' Tara's flooded gaze widened in alarm and she hastened to elaborate. ''Well, not exactly. I overheard him talking to Bailey about it. He said Pearson might be an old stick in the mud, but that your main concern was making sure I had a stable home and a father."

"Your uncle Sully has no idea what he's talking about," Ainslie said tartly. "Listen to me, pumpkin, and listen good. I'm marrying Pearson because I want to marry Pearson. In fact, you were the reason I didn't accept his proposal when he first popped the question."

Tara looked dubiously at her, and she gave the girl's hands a little shake. "Scout's honor. I wanted to be sure you felt comfortable with this, too."

"I guess I do, really. It's just that he tries so hard to be nice all the time—buying us presents, telling you there's no need for you to keep working at the gym." Tara stuck her bottom lip out stubbornly and suddenly she looked very young, despite the mascara. "What does he have against boxing anyway? He never comes to the ring."

"He's old-fashioned enough to think that boxing's a man's sport—and even then he wouldn't be caught dead at the fights." Ainslie sighed. "I'm not going to make myself over into some society matron, if that's what you're worried about. We O'Connell females are a rough, tough breed, and Pearson knows that." She slanted a quizzical gaze at Tara, and the outthrust lip curved into a reluctant smile.

"I'm sorry, Aunt Ainslie. I didn't mean to spoil your wedding day. I just wanted to be sure you were happy."

"I'm happy," Ainslie replied promptly. "I'd be happier if I hadn't let the saleswoman talk me into this ridiculous outfit. I look like Marie Antoinette dressed up as a shepherdess, for heaven's sake."

"Yeah, kind of," Tara said judiciously, tipping her head to one side and then dodging Ainslie's mock slap with a giggle. She sobered again. "But you do love him, right? Like Uncle Sully loves Bailey?"

She'd never lied to Tara, Ainslie thought regretfully, but there was no way she could answer that particular question with the truth. She fudged, telling herself it was in a good cause.

"O'Connell women only fall in love once, and that's it for the whole of their lives," she said. "Do you think I'd be marrying Pearson if he wasn't the one?"

"I guess not," Tara said slowly. She kept her gaze fixed on Ainslie's for a second longer, as if looking for reassurance. Whatever she saw there seemed to satisfy her, and she straightened in her seat. "We're almost there, Aunt Lee. Are you nervous?"

"I'd ten times rather be going into the ring to face Holyfield. Does that answer your question?" Ainslie put her hands gingerly to the headpiece to make sure it was straight, and managed to pull her veil sideways just as St. Margaret's hove into view.

"Great," she muttered. "By the time we drop you off at the side entrance I'll be looking like a—" She blanched. "Oh, my God, it's worse than I thought it would be. Look at all those people! Don't they have lives?"

Oblivious to the fact that the limo windows were heavily tinted, Tara regally tilted a palm back and forth until they turned the corner and left the crowd behind. "Wow, this might actually be fun. There's that cute usher getting off his motorcycle in the parking lot."

"Don't even think about it. Motorcycles are dangerous—why do you think I stopped riding them?" Ainslie said distractedly. "Okay, pumpkin, this is where you get out."

Tires crunching over the gravelled parking lot, the limousine rolled to a stop, and almost instantly the uniformed driver was at their door. As he opened it Tara threw her arms around Ainslie impulsively, hugging her tight.

"I love you, Aunt Lee. If you're happy, then I'm happy."

How many times had she held this precious gift of a daughter close? Ainslie wondered, her own eyes tearing as she fiercely hugged Tara back. When her cousin Babs had died of leukemia, leaving the seven-year-old daughter she'd had out of wedlock in Ainslie's care, she'd already been head over heels in love with the little girl. All the O'Connell clan had adored the child, and even Ainslie's half brother Terry Sullivan had taken one look at her and handed her his heart. Tara had never wanted for love, and she had given it back in return.

But she hadn't ever known the permanent presence of a father, and sometimes Ainslie had worried about that. Pearson would fill that void, she thought, giving Tara one last too tight squeeze.

"I'll see you in there, pumpkin," she said, clearing her throat and blinking rapidly. "I guess I'd better go run the gauntlet now. If your uncle Sully isn't waiting for me on that darn red carpet, I'm going to have his hide."

"He'll be there." Tara stepped out of the car, and then popped a thoughtful face back in. "Unless Megan Angelique picked today to be born. Bailey said she's been feeling like the Goodyear Blimp these last few days."

With a quick wave she turned and ran to the side entrance of the church, where Ainslie could see a knot of females already waiting for her. The O'Connell women, she thought fondly, catching a glimpse of her aunts Cissie and Jackie before her view was cut off by the driver closing the car door. A moment later the limo pulled sedately out of the parking lot and onto the street.

Ainslie folded her hands in the creamy satin and lace of her lap and chewed nervously at her bottom lip, wishing the day was over.

Immediately she felt a pang of contrition. Pearson had meant well when he'd arranged their wedding. He came from a different strata of society than she did—not to mention a different generation, she admitted honestly to herself—and this was the way things were done in his circle.

So how come when he finally decided to marry he picked a single mom twenty years his junior and an ex-boxer to boot? she wondered as she'd so often done before. But she knew the answer to that—at least, she knew the answer he'd given her.

"Don't sell yourself short, Ainslie." He never called her Lee, which was just one more instance, she supposed, of the stuffiness that Tara had referred to. "You've got a lot going for you. You've built up that derelict gymnasium of your aunt's into a going concern, you've raised Tara as if she were your own child, and you even mended the relationship with your half brother, Terrence, despite the way his father left you and your mother in the lurch when you were a child. I look at you and I see strength. I admire that."

"As long as it's out of the boxing ring," Ainslie hadn't been able to resist adding, and his handsome features had relaxed into a rare smile.

"You can't blame a man for not wanting to see the woman he loves take a beating in front of a crowd of lowlifes and riffraff, can you?"

"I prefer to think of them as paying customers, not riffraff," she'd answered with a touch of tartness. "And I didn't exactly stand around and take a beating, as you put it. I retired a champ, Pearson. Now I coach future champs. Boxing is an empowering sport for a lot of women."

And it helped save my sanity two years ago, when I didn't know if I could go on, she might have said, but didn't. Pearson didn't know about that part of her past.

There was no reason for him to know. The girl she'd been then was dead, and the man that girl had loved was dead, too.

She hadn't lied to Tara. The O'Connell females *were* one-man women. He'd been her first love, her last love, and her only love. She'd been twenty-five years old when she'd seen Malone's coffin lowered into the cold, black earth, and she'd known that her own life had ended with his.

For a while she'd gone a little crazy, she realized now. Paul Cosgrove had been his partner, and although the government agency they both worked for was so security-conscious that it didn't even have a name, he'd bent the rules enough to tell her that Malone had been shot in front of his very eyes. Although Paul had gotten him to a hospital, Malone hadn't survived the head wound he'd sustained—a head wound so horrific that there had been no question of having an open coffin at the funeral.

But even hearing the terrible details of his death from the man who'd witnessed it hadn't helped her to accept the reality of his passing.

For three whole days after his funeral she'd sat in her darkened apartment all alone, not bothering to change out of the somber black suit she'd been wearing. Only when Paul had actually pounded on her door, demanding to know if she was all right, had she roused herself enough to tell him to go away before returning to her vigil.

Because that had been what it was. For three days and three nights she'd sat, her hands folded quietly on her lap, her eyes open wide in the shadowy gloom, waiting for Seamus Malone to come back to her. Not from the dead. She just hadn't accepted that he'd been killed. She'd been convinced it had all been some kind of insane trick.

And then on the third day she'd finally fallen into a state

of semi-consciousness—not sleep, not true wakefulness, but a limbo halfway between the two. In it she'd relived every moment she'd ever had with him, from the moment they'd first met only a few weeks before, to the last time he'd left her arms. Measured in days, their time together had been cruelly short. But time was an irrelevant yardstick for what they'd had.

In two weeks they'd made a lifetime of memories.

They'd so nearly missed knowing each other at all. On a rare impulse she'd dropped by Sully's house one night after seeing Tara off with a schoolfriend at Logan Airport. The month-long trip to Arizona had been planned for ages and Ainslie knew that the Cartwells would look after Tara as if she were their own daughter.

That night Sully had casually introduced her to his guest.

She'd stared into a pair of brilliant green eyes, and that had been it. Twenty minutes later, Malone and she had left a bemused Sullivan and had gone out to a Thai restaurant together. Two hours later they'd walked hand in hand along Beacon Street, then ended up back at her apartment and making love. The next morning, just before dawn, Malone had shakily told her he couldn't imagine life without her.

Love at first sight really happened. They'd had it, and it had lasted, right up until the end.

On their last night together he'd asked her to marry him. She'd thrown her arms around his neck tightly enough to knock him backward onto the sofa. Half laughing, half tearfully, she'd told him yes, and in the middle of their kiss his pager had gone off. Forever after, Ainslie had wondered how things would have turned out if he'd ignored it, but wondering was futile.

He'd answered the page. He'd left her apartment a few

minutes later, after one last, hard kiss and a quick grin, telling her he wouldn't be gone long. Sometime in the hour that followed, he'd been killed.

It had been her love for Tara that had finally forced her to pick up the pieces of her shattered life and rebuild some kind of existence after Malone's death. On the fourth day after his funeral, she'd stripped off the clothes she'd been wearing and stood under the shower until the hot water ran out. Then she'd pulled on a sweater and a pair of jeans, balled the black suit into a paper bag and thrown it down the garbage chute at the end of the hall. She'd returned to her apartment, taken a deep, shuddering breath and firmly closed a door in her mind.

But she still dreamed about him every night—saw those brilliant green eyes, that midnight-black hair, his slow smile. She hadn't let those dreams stop her from agreeing to marry Pearson, however. Tara needed a father. Pearson wanted a wife. And what she'd told Tara a few minutes ago had been true—he was a good man, and she cared for him. He knew she wasn't madly in love with him, but that wasn't what he was looking for, he'd told her quietly. Mutual affection, the shared goal of creating a family of their own one day—if she could give him that, he would make sure that Tara never wanted for anything.

It was something a little more than a business agreement, something much less than a love match. And she was going through with it.

The limousine whispered to a stop in front of the red carpet. Before the driver could get out, Sully, impossibly handsome in a dove-gray morning suit with tails, was opening her door for her. He looked harassed. Behind him one of Boston's finest was trying to keep onlookers away from the waist-high velvet ropes that created a barrier between the crowd and the carpet.

"What the hell was McNeil thinking?" he growled as he took her hand and helped her from the back seat.

"It's like a damn circus," she agreed, slanting her eyes sideways at the throng of bystanders just as a camera flash went off. "Let's get into the church and get this over with."

"My sister the romantic," Sullivan murmured, stepping up his pace. "You should at least give them a smile, Lee. When Pearson and the rest of the McNeil clan arrived, they were glad-handing all over the place."

"Goody for the McNeil clan," Ainslie said tightly, almost tripping on a ruffle as she mounted the last step. Nonetheless she paused just before the open oak doors, pasting a stiff smile on her face and looking out over the milling crowd.

Sully was right—the least she could do was to be gracious. After all, these onlookers were ordinary people like herself. Most of the upturned faces were smiling at her.

But not all of them.

About to turn away to step into the church, Ainslie's attention was caught by the incongruity of a figure at the edge of the crowd. Heavily bundled in an old army greatcoat, the derelict's inappropriate clothing alone pegged him as odd. The knitted watch cap pulled low on his forehead only partially concealed the unkempt hair that straggled to his shoulders. His heavy beard was dark and ungroomed. He was wearing fingerless gloves, as if it was deepest winter instead of a mild autumn day. His ramshackle shopping cart was piled high with what appeared to be odds and ends of broken appliances. Riding on the top of the pile was what looked like a pair of used boots.

Although the shopping cart provided a physical barrier between him and those nearby, it was obviously unnecessary. Like so many street derelicts, there seemed to be an invisible demarcation line around him, as if drawing the attention of someone so obviously unbalanced would be dangerous.

Except there was no fear of that. His attention was fixed solely on her, Ainslie saw with a prickle of unease.

"Come on, champ," Sully said wryly. "This is just the pre-bout warmup. The main event's inside."

He started to move forward, but Ainslie remained rooted to the stone steps, her grip on his arm tightening.

She could smell roses—smell them so strongly that it seemed as if she were enveloped in a perfumed fog. She knew her bouquet was inside the church; even if it hadn't been, it was of white lilac and lilies. Yet she could smell roses—*red* roses—and for a moment she could almost swear she could feel cold velvet petals brush against her lips.

It wasn't unease that was making her heart beat so madly, Ainslie thought, holding on to Sully for support. It was fear. She was going crazy, and she knew it.

The derelict's hair was a matted tangle obscuring his eyes, but even as she watched he wiped at it with a gloved hand. Across the crowd, his gaze met hers, and she felt the blood drain from her face.

His eyes were a clear, brilliant green. She'd only seen eyes like that on one man, and that man was dead.

Abruptly the derelict turned away, wrenching his shopping cart around on two wheels so quickly that a man in a business suit had to scramble to get out of his path. Hunched over the handles, he started pushing it down the street toward a nearby alleyway.

He was trying to disguise his height, Ainslie thought faintly. He was trying to cover his features with that appalling beard, trying to become just another invisible castoff from society with his strange assortment of clothing.

Either that, or he was exactly what he appeared to be—

a lost soul, a denizen of the streets, a man who had slipped through the cracks and who had stayed there.

But she had to *know.*

"What the hell's going on, sis?" Speaking out of the corner of his mouth, Sully tugged at her elbow, a faint frown creasing his brow as she turned to him. "Are you getting cold feet, or what?"

"Did you see him?" She forced the urgent question out from between lips that felt coldly numb. "Did you *see* him, Sully? Was it *him?*"

"See who?" Frowning in earnest, Sullivan looked over his shoulder from where a knot of ushers and bridesmaids waited just inside the oak doors. "What are you talking about, Lee?"

"I'm *sure* it's him. See—there, with the shopping cart!" It felt like a gigantic weight was pressing down on her chest, making it hard for her to breathe. Ainslie heard the high quaver in her own voice, and turned to her half brother. "Don't you *see* him, Sully?"

There was more than concern on his features now, there was alarm, and beyond him Ainslie caught Tara's dubious look. The good-looking teenager she was standing with broke off whatever he'd been saying to her.

She was causing a scene. She was causing a scene at her own wedding, and she didn't care, Ainslie thought desperately. It *couldn't* be him—but she had to know for sure. She wrenched her arm from Sully's grip and ran to the edge of the top step, leaning out over the black iron railing that framed it.

"Malone!"

Her hoarse cry was more of a scream, and with part of her mind she realized that the crowd had fallen silent and was staring up at her with avid curiosity. But she wasn't concentrating on anything or anyone but the shuffling figure in the greatcoat, now almost at the entrance to the alleyway.

"Malone!" Her voice cracked on his name, and she felt Sullivan's strong hand wrap around the lace on her upper arm. "Dammit, Malone—*look* at me! It's *you,* isn't it?"

"For God's sake, Lee!" Sullivan's voice was almost as shaky as hers. He thrust his mouth close to her ear. "Malone's dead, sweetheart. You *know* that. Let's get you inside—"

She shut out Sully's words. The veil blew across her face and she impatiently pushed it aside, feeling the headpiece finally let go. It fell from her hair and tumbled down the top two steps. It didn't matter, she thought as she watched the man in the greatcoat turn back to look at her from the entrance to the alleyway. Even at this distance she could see the pain etching his features.

There was no way he could be Malone, Ainslie thought faintly, her knuckles white against the iron railing as his eyes met and held hers for a heartbeat. No way at all. As Sully had said, Malone was dead.

It was him.

"Malone," she whispered incredulously, her hand going to her mouth. She felt the hot rush of tears behind her eyes and blinked. Joy, so sweet and sharp it felt like pain, lanced through her. Unheeded, warm tears slipped down her face.

Through her blurred vision, she caught his one last, agonized glance before he turned and pushed his cart swiftly down the alleyway, his head bowed. He disappeared around a corner and was gone.

"No," Ainslie breathed disbelievingly. "No—I *won't* lose you again. I *can't* have lost you!"

Breaking free of Sullivan's grasp, she whirled desperately away from him and ran down the steps into the crowd.

Chapter Two

''For the love of Mike, Ainslie—what were you thinking of, flying down the church steps like that?''

The little change room at the back of the church was packed with O'Connell females. Jackie O'Connell Byrne, once a flawless beauty and still sexy at fifty, raised an incredulous eyebrow at her niece.

''We've got a packed church, an organist who's started the wedding march twice, and one extremely patient groom out there. What we don't have is a bride walking down the aisle.''

''Would you like me to get Father Flynn in to talk to you, dear?'' Her face flooding with color, Cissie glanced meaningfully at the yards of white ruffles and lace of her niece's wedding dress. ''Is there...is there something you'd like to confess before you go through with the ceremony, Ainslie?''

''For crying out loud, of course there's nothing she needs to confess,'' Jackie snapped. ''Just because you're still hanging on to your virginity for dear life at forty-nine doesn't mean—''

''Shut up, the both of you!''

The gravelly roar that cut through the small room came from a wiry figure clad, like Jackie, in a silk suit. But instead of a skirt, the jacket was paired with trousers in the same sea-foam green that Tara, sitting wide-eyed a few feet away, had so vocally groused about earlier. Peeking out raffishly from under the cuffed silk pants was a pair of lime high-top sneakers.

A flicker of amusement briefly overlaid the chaos of Ainslie's thoughts as she took in the pugnacious jut of her Aunt Kate's jaw. Even as she stood there facing down her younger sisters, she seemed to bounce a little on the balls of her feet, as if she were getting ready to take on an opponent in the ring. Her boxing days long behind her, Ainslie mused, the woman once known as Kiss of Death Katie would never be anyone's idea of a sweet little old lady.

The rest of the O'Connell women had fallen silent. Raking an impatient hand through her cropped steel-gray hair, Kate's gimlet gaze fell on one of Ainslie's cousins.

"Bridie, go out and tell Father Flynn that Ainslie's just feeling a little faint from all the excitement. Say she needs a few minutes to compose herself before the ceremony."

"Lie to a priest, Aunt Kate?" Bridie sounded shocked.

Her aunt's jaw jutted out even farther. "It's not a lie. Look at the poor girl, for God's sake. Her face is like cheese."

"Thanks, Aunt Kate," Ainslie murmured dryly, then wished she'd kept quiet. As Bridie reluctantly left the room, the high-tops swivelled her way.

"Lying to Father Flynn's going to buy us ten minutes, no more, so let's hear it, Lee. Are we scrubbing this event or what? And what *was* that performance in front of the church all about?"

Performance was the right word, Ainslie thought, feeling the color rise in her cheeks under the scrutiny of her three aunts and Tara's alert glance from the corner of the room.

She'd made a complete fool of herself. She'd heard cameras clicking like crazy all around her, had seen Susan Frank, News Five's roving reporter, elbow her way toward her like a stevedore in high heels, and had felt one of her own satin shoes catch in a billowing ruffle.

She hadn't fallen for the same reason that she hadn't been able to go any farther. The crowd had just been too thick. As Susan Frank, microphone thrust out in front of her, reached her, sanity had suddenly washed over Ainslie in a cold wave.

Of course it wasn't Malone, she'd thought stupidly. *How crazy can you get, O'Connell? Malone's dead. You're running after a ghost.*

"And here we were hoping to surprise you, sis." Sullivan had given a rueful chuckle and tightened his grip on her arm. "We told Lee her favorite great-uncle, Paddy Malone, wasn't up to making the trip over from the old country, Miss Frank. His heart's not as strong as it used to be, so we didn't want to disappoint her if he couldn't make it at the last minute, but it looks like she spotted him. Come on, Lee, Paddy's already slipped in the side entrance."

If anyone could whip a choice morsel away from a shark, her half brother could, Ainslie thought now. Susan Frank had looked immediately bored, Sully had hustled her into the church and Aunt Kate had taken over from there.

But even the combined forces of the O'Connell women and Terry Sullivan couldn't hold off the delayed wedding for much longer, Ainslie told herself. Not for the first time since she'd accepted Pearson's proposal, she felt a pang of longing for her mother—a longing that had never really faded over the ten years since Mary O'Connell's untimely passing.

When Thomas Sullivan, Sully's feckless and charming father, had walked out on his second wife and his young daughter, taking his son by a previous marriage with him, at five years old she'd felt as if her world had been torn apart, Ainslie remembered. Reverting to her maiden name, Mary O'Connell had moved in with her sister Jackie's family and the O'Connell clan had practically smothered Ainslie with love. But the lack of a father had always hurt. Even when her beloved half brother Sully had come back into her life years later, his reappearance hadn't been able to completely make up for Thomas's absence.

Her aunts and Sully would always be there for her, Ainslie thought, meeting Kate's inquiring gaze. But her mother would have known without asking that she still intended to go through with this wedding. She wanted Tara to have the one thing she'd missed out on—the presence of a stable father figure in her life.

"We're not scrubbing this event, Aunt Kate." She forced a smile and smoothed down a ruffle. "You were the one who taught me to leave the butterflies outside when I stepped into the ring. I—I guess I just forgot that for a minute."

"Is that all it was, butterflies?" Her aunt looked unconvinced, and Ainslie nodded decisively.

"Plain old-fashioned bridal nerves," she said firmly, and saw the doubt in her aunt's eyes disappear. "Ladies, start your engines—or at least get your butts out of here so the bride and her chief bridesmaid can make an entrance in a minute or so."

The older woman's craggy features broke into a rare smile. "Some of the stuffier McNeils are going to bust a gut when they realize it's Kiss of Death Katie who's giving the bride away, darlin'. I can hardly wait to see their faces. Ciss, Jackie—let's get out there and raise some eyebrows.''

With the squeak of sneakers and the tapping of heels receding down the hall, Ainslie took a deep breath and turned to face Tara with the same grin she'd given her aunts still fixed on her face. ''Well, pumpkin, it's just you and me now,'' she said bracingly. ''Ready?''

''No.'' The teen's one-word answer was flatly antagonistic.

Shocked, Ainslie stared at her. In the limo, Tara's recalcitrance had obviously stemmed from a childlike need for reassurance, but there was nothing childlike about the white, set face turned to her now. Tara's gaze, as it met hers, was disconcertingly adult.

''You lied to them. I was the only one close enough to see what happened, and I know it wasn't just butterflies, Aunt Lee. You saw someone, didn't you? You saw Seamus Malone.''

Ainslie felt her own face pale. ''How do you know that name?'' She realized her hands were clenched at her sides, and with an effort she relaxed them. ''Don't tell me—your uncle Sully, right?''

Tara shrugged, her shoulders tense under the sea-green chiffon.

''It couldn't have been Malone I just saw, because he did die. I went to his funeral. I was there when they buried him. He walked out of my arms one night and he never came back. And he hasn't *now,*'' she whispered fiercely, her words not directed at the young girl in front of her. ''It's time to let him go.''

''At Uncle Sully's marriage to Bailey you told me that true love was the rarest thing there was. You said that if a person ever found it, she should never, *ever* let it go.

What if you did see Malone, Auntie Lee? Even if it's impossible, what if you *did?*"

Under the lace and ruffles, Ainslie felt as if an iron band was constricting her chest. "I didn't. And I don't want to talk about it any more, Tara," she said tightly. "Now, I'm walking out that door to get married to Pearson. Are you coming?"

For a long moment Tara's gaze defiantly held hers. Then the soft young lips quivered, and with an impulsiveness that she'd begun to display less and less often since becoming a teenager, she rushed to Ainslie and wrapped her arms around her.

"Of *course* I'm coming, Aunt Lee. It's not often a girl gets a chance to wear sea-foam green, for goodness' sake." Her laugh was uneven, but as she gave Ainslie one last crushing hug and stepped back, her smile was tender. "Besides, even with the door open, that perfume is getting to me. Aunt Cissie must have doused herself in it—she's the only one who would wear something so romantically old-fashioned as roses."

"Aunt Cissie doesn't wear perfume," Ainslie said absently. "She's allergic to it." Straightening her veil and turning to leave, she stopped, her heart suddenly crashing in her chest.

It was no ghost of a scent. Tara was right—it was overpowering, as overpowering as it had been half an hour ago, when Ainslie'd finally convinced herself that both the aroma and the man had been illusions. But now it seemed that the scent of roses was real. And Tara was conscious of it, too.

What if Malone hadn't been an illusion, either?

"Red roses for true love," she said through numb lips. "What if he's still alive? What if he's still *alive?*"

"The perfume means something to you, doesn't it?"

Tara's gaze was fixed on her, her eyes enormous in the paleness of her face. "You think he *has* come back, don't you?"

"But how *could* he?"

In an unconscious reversal of their roles, Ainslie turned to her adopted daughter. Tara wasn't a child any longer, she realized with a small start. She was a young woman, and her steady gaze was filled with a wisdom beyond her years.

"One way or another, you have to be sure, Aunt Lee. If you don't go after him you'll never forgive yourself." Tara gave her a little shake. "*I'll* never forgive you."

"But Pearson...Father Flynn...all those guests!" Was she actually *considering* this? Ainslie thought. "I can't just walk out on my own wedding! Besides, I'll run into the same crush outside as before. That Susan Frank will have a film crew right on my heels."

"Go out the back." Tara jerked her head toward the door leading to the parking lot, her voice quickening in excitement. "He went down that alley about a block away, didn't he? This street should get you there just as well as the one in front of the church, and it's quieter. No one will even see you."

Even as she spoke Ainslie was shaking her head. "Someone will notice, and in this getup I can't exactly outrun the mob. Leaving Pearson waiting at the altar is terrible enough. He doesn't deserve his wedding to be made into a public joke in all the papers."

"You're right. That would destroy him," Tara said slowly, her face clouding. Then she brightened. Darting to the small table near where she'd been sitting earlier, she bent over and grabbed something up. She whirled back to Ainslie, her palm outstretched. "Here."

Ainslie blinked at the object Tara was handing her. It

was a small plastic skull with glowing red eyes. Attached to it was a key.

"It's Bobby's." Tara blushed, and all of a sudden she was a teenager again. "Cool, huh? He was showing it to me and in all the excitement I guess I forgot to give it back to him." She saw the confusion on Ainslie's face and elaborated impatiently. "It's the key to his *motorcycle,* Aunt Lee. It's right outside—I'm sure if Bobby knew he'd tell you to go ahead and use it. After all, this is kind of an emergency, isn't it?"

Tara was right, it *was* an emergency. With any luck, this wild-goose chase could be over and done with in less than five minutes. If it wasn't—

"Get this darn veil off me, pumpkin." As Tara swiftly complied, Ainslie bent and lifted the masses of ruffles, revealing the two stiff crinolines that had made her walk up the red carpet resemble the stately progression of an unwieldy ocean liner being nudged along by a tugboat. Stripping them off, she turned back to Tara, feeling blessedly less encumbered.

"Go find Uncle Sully and tell him everything. If I'm not back in ten minutes, he's to make up some kind of story that'll save Pearson's face, okay?"

With that she was gone, running toward the yellow Yamaha that was the only motorcycle in the lot, holding her skirt high as she flew across the gravel.

SHE LOOKED RIDICULOUS, and she knew it. She also didn't care. Letting the motorcycle's revs climb as her riding skills came automatically back to her, Ainslie tore down the conveniently deserted street and into the alley. It was flanked, she saw, by a small commercial hotel, boarded up and abandoned.

She cut the bike's engine, realizing in the sudden silence

that she had absolutely no idea what to do next. Aside from the usual litter of junk and garbage, only made notable by a discarded and rotting sofa bed a few feet away, the alleyway was empty.

What had she expected? Ainslie asked herself, her heart sinking. From his odd appearance, the man she'd seen obviously wasn't completely normal, and when she'd unexpectedly focused her attention on him she'd probably frightened him. Had she really thought it possible that he would be waiting for her around some corner?

Very slowly, she reached for the key in the ignition. As she did so she caught a gleam just beyond the discarded sofa bed, as if something shiny was catching the light there.

She knew what it was even before she jumped off the motorcycle and ran over to it. Lying on its side, covered with a piece of torn plastic, was a shopping cart. Its contents had spilled out onto the ground, but right in front of her eyes was a pair of worn boots.

Looking up, recessed into the wall of the abandoned hotel, she noticed a door painted the same faded red as the brick of the building.

It was slightly ajar.

It had to be where he lived, Ainslie thought, her pulse racing. It *had* to be. Condemned or not, the place offered shelter and some kind of privacy; she knew instinctively that the man she'd glimpsed would find it impossible to bunk down with a roomful of strangers every night in a shelter. Like a wild animal, he would have a place where he could go to earth.

It would be impossible to find him in there. She hardly had time for a room-to-room search. There was only one way she could force him out.

"Malone! *Malone!*" Standing in the middle of the alleyway, she shouted the name as loudly as she could. He wasn't Malone—he couldn't be, there was no *way* he could be—but if this was his private lair, she was drawing attention to it. He would want her to go away, but she wouldn't—not until she saw him face-to-face.

"Malone, I know you're in there!"

For some reason she knew the stranger wouldn't hurt her if he did appear. He'd definitely been odd, but there'd been nothing threatening in his oddness. Again she saw the flash of anguish she'd seen in those green eyes that had been too much like Malone's. The memory was so clear that again her heart leaped crazily.

"Malone!"

"Stop shouting! Dammit, lady, you're going to lead them right to me!"

The hoarse warning came from directly behind her. Whirling around in shock, Ainslie stared at the big man in the army greatcoat standing only inches away.

The bottom fell out of her world.

Dark hair fell to his shoulders, and most of his face was obscured by a heavy growth of beard. His skin bore the weathered tan of someone who spent most of his time in the elements, and there was a smear of black grease high on each cheekbone. But through the tangle of hair that fell over his forehead she could see those eyes.

She tried to take a step toward him, but her limbs wouldn't work. "Malone—it really *is* you!"

This time when the hot tears streamed down her face she made no attempt to wipe them away.

"They told me you were dead, Malone! They told me you were dead, and I didn't believe them, but when you didn't come back to me I thought I'd lost you forever!"

The words tumbled out of her almost incoherently, and the ice that had surrounded her finally broke. With a little cry of incredulous happiness she rushed to him, wanting only to feel his arms around her, his heartbeat close to hers.

Swiftly he stepped back out of her reach. His eyes narrowed and his whole body seemed to suddenly tense.

In confusion, Ainslie met his gaze, and as she did, the wild joy that had been flooding through her instantly turned to sharp fear.

He was looking at her with no recognition at all. Those green eyes were blank and shuttered.

"Malone?" she breathed tremulously. "Malone, what's the matter?"

"My name's not Malone, lady." His answer was unequivocally antagonistic. "And I've never seen you before in my life."

Chapter Three

Ainslie stared at the man in front of her.

For a long moment his eyes, narrowed in suspicion, remained locked on hers. Then his shoulders stiffened under the tattered coat and he darted a quick glance down the alleyway before turning back to her.

''Did you lead them here?'' His question was more of an accusation. It was so unexpected that she was jolted into a reply.

''Of course not.'' She caught herself. ''Lead *who* here?''

''*Them,*'' he said impatiently, as if she were being deliberately obtuse. He looked down at the other end of the alleyway and then seemed to come to a decision. ''Maybe you didn't, but they're coming anyway. They must have seen you. We'd better get going.''

He moved quickly for such a big man. Before she realized his intention, his hand had wrapped around hers and he was pulling her toward the door to the abandoned hotel, and at that, her numbness dissipated.

''No.'' She tried to disengage her hand, but his grip was too strong.

It was true, then, she thought with dull clarity. He wasn't Malone, despite the shock of recognition she'd felt when she'd first seen him, despite her certainty of a few minutes ago. He was exactly what he appeared to be: a derelict, a man of the streets with more than a few problems of his own, although of the two of them, she wasn't sure who was the crazier. Suddenly the full import of what she'd done slammed into her.

What had she been thinking?

If she hurried, she could be back at St. Margaret's before Sully told the assembled guests the bride had gone AWOL.

She tugged at her hand again. "No," she said gently. "Whoever they are, they're not after me. I should get back to my own world now."

She didn't know why she'd phrased it like that, only that it seemed right. She looked up into the tanned, heavily bearded face, seeing him for the first time as the man he was, not as the man she'd so desperately and illogically wanted him to be. A pang of sadness stirred in her. She'd been right about one thing. The expression she'd thought she'd seen in those eyes *was* anguish. He was looking at her as if the very sight of her caused him immeasurable pain, and maybe it did. Maybe she reminded him of someone, too—a woman he'd known, a girl he'd loved, the life he'd lived before everything had spiralled out of control for him.

"I'll decoy them away from you." She kept her voice soft. "A bride on a motorcycle would be enough to distract anyone, and that'll give you a chance to get to safety."

Her attempt at reassurance didn't have the effect she'd intended.

"No!"

The explosiveness of his answer was shockingly loud in the quiet alleyway, his voice amplified by the narrow brick walls of the buildings. Ainslie felt a twinge of nervousness, but almost immediately she realized that her unease wasn't a result of his unexpected reaction.

The alleyway *was* quiet. They were in the middle of a busy city—surely it wasn't natural not to hear *any* signs of life. Now that she thought about it, she realized she hadn't seen so much as a stray cat since she'd driven in here.

She gave herself a mental shake. The man's fear was contagious. This time when she tried to pull away from him, she put more force into it.

Still he wouldn't let go.

"It's too late. They have to know you're with me, and they won't allow you to leave now. Come on. Maybe if we hide, they'll keep on going."

He was more than just troubled. He was paranoid. Whoever *they* were, he'd credited them with almost supernatural powers. Now her uneasiness *was* because of him.

Don't upset him any more than he is already, for God's sake, she told herself sharply. *Keep everything calm and low key, and just walk out of here.*

"Even if they do come after me, they can't catch me on that." She nodded at Bobby's motorcycle, garishly yellow against the crumbling wall. "It'll be better if we split up and—"

"Dammit, they'll kill you!" For a moment reality faded again. He even *sounded* like Malone, Ainslie thought faintly—except Malone had never spoken to her with such fearful urgency. "Don't you get it? These people are ruthless, Lee! We can't let them find us!"

Jerking her roughly toward the door, he shoved her inside and then pulled it shut. Ainslie heard him fumbling in the dark for something, and then the blackness was suddenly illuminated by the beam of a flashlight.

"Up those stairs," he whispered hoarsely. "Hurry!"

She didn't move. "What did you just call me?" Her voice sounded strange to her own ears. He looked impatiently at her, his beard and the tangle of hair falling across his eyes shadowing his face.

"I said take the stairs. Come on, we have to get to the third floor!"

"You called me Lee. How did you know my name?"

"Dammit, we're wasting time! They're coming for us!"

Grabbing her roughly by the arm again, he started up the stairs. The faint beam of the flashlight bobbing eerily ahead of them, Ainslie found herself stumbling up the first few steps. She felt her shoe catch on the trailing hem of her gown and heard it rip slightly before she could release it.

"Watch the fifth step. It's loose." Frowning, he looked over his shoulder at her, not slowing his pace or loosening his grip. "What the hell are you wearing, anyway?"

"It's a wedding dress." At the *Alice in Wonderland* turn to the conversation, she felt as if her final connection with the sane world on the outside had just been severed. "I was supposed to be getting married today, remember? You saw me going into the church."

"Oh." There was a note of uncertainty in his voice, and she wondered if he did remember. They reached the second floor, turned a corner, and continued upward. "Well, I guess the wedding's off now," he grunted dismissively, hauling her up the last few steps.

They were on the third floor, the flashlight wavering over a dusty, patterned carpet that ran down the hallway in front of them. As her abductor—*of course, he thinks he's my rescuer,* she told herself grimly—dragged her swiftly along the seemingly endless hallway, on either side she saw numbered doors, forbiddingly dark rectangles set into the peeling walls.

He'd called her Lee. She was sure he'd called her by name, although at this point she realized she couldn't be sure of anything. But she'd heard him, she knew she had, and the only way he could have known it was if—

If he'd read about the wedding in the papers, she told herself sharply. *If he'd heard someone outside St. Margaret's mention it. For God's sake, the events board on the church lawn lists the names of the bride and groom when there's a wedding being held. He could have seen that.*

Except somehow those explanations didn't seem very convincing. Whoever he was, he lived in his own world—the world of him and *them.* The danger he perceived all around him was imaginary, of course, but to him it was real and immediate. He focused on it exclusively. Nothing else existed for him.

Which was fine, if that was the way he wanted to live his life. Except now she'd been drawn into his paranoia.

Whatever excuse Sully was making for her right now, it couldn't be more outlandish than the situation she was in, Ainslie thought. She couldn't allow this to go any further. As he came to an abrupt halt in front of one of the doors, she found her voice.

"I'm not going in there with you." She was shaking, she noted dispassionately. "I don't know who you think is after you, but I know that if you don't let me leave, people are going to start looking for me. As soon as they see that motorcycle outside, they'll know I'm here. You don't want to spend tonight in a jail cell, do you?"

With the hand that wasn't holding hers, he fished for something inside the open collar of the ragged shirt he was wearing under the greatcoat. Ainslie saw it was a length of string with a number of keys attached to it.

"They're here."

She was close enough to him to feel the sudden rigidity in his muscles. In the act of unlocking the door, he froze in a listening position, his whole demeanor one of tense alertness. Despite herself, she froze, too.

"I don't hear any—" she began in a whisper, but then stopped.

Had she heard something? Unconsciously holding her breath, and realizing that her unlikely companion was doing the same, she listened intently, straining her ears to catch the slightest sound. She heard it again, and this time she knew what it was.

Three floors below them, someone—or was it more than one person?—was coming up the stairs. The footfalls were muffled, as if the intruders were trying to approach as quietly as possible.

"Two. Three..." Counting out loud almost inaudibly, the big man was staring at something above his head. She followed his gaze and saw a tiny red pinprick of light appear just above the door. "Four." He looked up for a second longer. Under the beard, his mouth was set in a tight line.

"Four of them." He saw her confusion. "Something I rigged up under that fifth stair," he said briefly, unlocking the door. "The light goes on inside the room, too, so I know if someone's coming. Hold on, I've got to disable something."

Cautiously pushing the door open an inch or so, he squatted and felt along its bottom edge, finally releasing her hand to do so. This was her chance to run, Ainslie thought. She didn't move.

"Okay, we can go in." He straightened and opened the door completely. "I guess this is the last time I'll have to reset it. This place is blown now."

"'Blown'?" she repeated, moving like an automaton ahead of him into the room. The wavering beam of his flashlight seemed to be growing fainter, and she felt a sudden sharp panic overlay the nebulous fear gripping her. His solid bulk brushed against her in the dark, and her panic eased a notch.

Which was stupid, she admitted to herself. He was the reason she was creeping around in the dark in the first place, jumping at the slightest sound. That flashing light over the door was a perfect illustration of just how unbalanced the man was—and how off balance he'd made her feel, since for a moment there, watching the red pinprick, she'd actually believed it meant something.

"Blown. Finished." His elaboration was perfunctory. "I won't be able to come back here again."

At his last words Ainslie heard a small clicking sound, and the next moment she was squinting her eyes against the harsh brightness that suddenly illuminated the room. Still blinking, she peered at him suspiciously.

"How did you do that? Is that another gadget you rigged up?"

He looked at her as if she were crazy. "Yeah. It's called a light switch."

"But...but the power to this place must have been cut off years ago."

She looked around her. The hotel room that this must have originally been was no longer recognizable as such. It was obvious that he'd been living here long enough to put his own stamp on the place. His own wacky stamp, Ainslie thought, not knowing whether to laugh or to be appalled.

Whatever the booby trap was that he'd jury-rigged at the entrance, it was hardly necessary. On either side of them were towering walls of bundled newspapers, and even as she turned she felt the wall nearest her sway ominously. He grabbed her arm.

"Watch out, they're balanced pretty delicately. Walk

behind me and try not to touch the sides. It opens out just past the curve.'' Setting off down his insane hallway, he kept talking, no longer making an effort to keep his voice low. ''I ran a line in. What the power company doesn't know won't hurt them. I needed the electricity to make the modifications, anyway.''

''What modifications?'' she asked faintly, following him. They reached the curve in the newspapers, and he stopped so suddenly that she almost ran into him.

''The door, for one. I replaced it with a steel one, and then painted it to match the rest of them again. And of course all the interior walls had to be sheeted with quarter-inch steel, in case they tried to get in from one of the adjoining rooms.''

''Good thinking.'' Ainslie pressed her fingers to her forehead, hardly able to absorb what she was hearing—and seeing. The man was a full-blown paranoiac. That was a given. But there was no denying he was also quite a handy renovator, in his own unique way.

Somewhere in the real world Sullivan would be attempting to apologize for her actions to an incredulous Pearson, she supposed. Somewhere in the real world the man whose wife she should have been by now would be wondering how he'd managed to read her character so inaccurately.

In that real world was a man she'd behaved unforgivably toward, Ainslie thought. She owed it to him to deliver her apology in person, and as soon as possible. Except that she first had to find a way out of this fantasy world she'd stumbled into.

She had no idea what the Rube Goldberg-esque contraptions around her were supposed to do. In one corner of the room was what looked to be the back half of a bicycle. Attached to it was a circular leather strap, and nearby were neatly lined-up rows of car batteries, each with alligator clips and wires snaking from each terminal. Out of the corner of her eye she could see similarly strange juxtapositions of junk, but she purposely didn't look at them. Instead she looked at their creator. Even as she did, though, he turned from her and headed toward the truncated bicycle.

"Thank God, I finished this yesterday," he said with a touch of satisfaction. "I figure the first thing they'll do is get the outside team to cut the power."

"The outside team? I thought you said they were coming up the stairs." She kept her tone carefully neutral. "Shouldn't they have been here by now?"

Hunched over his invention, he didn't look up, but she could hear the amusement in his voice. "That was the first wave. I've already taken care of them. If everything went the way I planned it, the four of them are in the basement right now, probably with a broken bone or two among them. Trap door on the first landing," he added, toggling a switch on one of the batteries. "I activated it at the same time I turned the lights on."

This time she couldn't hide her horrified reaction. "A trap door? For God's sake, it was probably a group of street kids on those stairs! Are you out of your *mind?*"

"The mechanism is weight sensitive. It can't even be tripped by a good-size teenager, only by a full-grown male who's packing a lot of muscle—and equipment." Setting a lever at the side of the bicycle wheel, he stood, turning to face her. "And no, I'm not crazy. But you're just going to have to trust me on that for a few more—"

The room was suddenly plunged into darkness once more, and Ainslie heard him draw in a sharp breath. "Tell me you did that," she said, fighting her sudden desire to reach out and touch him. "Another one of your gadgets, right?"

"No, that was them. They're moving faster than I thought." She heard him bend down again. "Here, put this on."

Something was pressed into her hands, and she started. Whatever it was it felt clammy and rubbery. Even as she opened her mouth to ask him what it was, a low humming sound started, gaining in volume and speed. A moment later the room was dimly illuminated with the weak yellow glow of a bare bulb in the ceiling. In front of her the bicycle wheel was spinning madly, the leather strap attaching it to the smaller flywheel near the batteries a brown blur.

"It's a gas mask. They used gas the last time, and I almost didn't get away. I wasn't expecting to need two of these, but I thought I'd better keep a spare handy." In the half light she saw him smile lopsidedly at her. "This must be our lucky day."

Malone's grin had been one-sided, she thought distractedly, fumbling at the rubber-and-metal mask with no real idea of what she was supposed to do with it. He put his on, the cylindrical snout of the mask giving him a distinctly alien appearance. Taking hers, he slipped it into place over her face and adjusted it at the back of her head.

Ainslie forced back the bubble of inappropriate laughter that suddenly threatened to escape her. The Bride Wore Army Surplus, she imagined the headline, feeling dangerously near hysteria.

She had no doubt that someone had attempted to enter the abandoned building a few minutes ago. She even accepted his assurance that whoever it was must have been big enough and heavy enough to set the trap door into action. But that was as far as she was prepared to go. He'd said himself that he had run an illegal electrical line here—why hadn't it occurred to him the power company might have sent someone out to investigate? Her theory made a whole lot more sense than his assumption that he was under siege.

He was gesturing for her to follow him, and when she didn't he took her by the arm as he'd done earlier. It was the final straw. Wrenching away, Ainslie started to take the gas mask off, her fingers clumsy and trembling. She heard a dull, explosive *thump* from where the newspaper wall led to the door, saw him look past her and then lunge for her, his eyes wide in alarm behind the protective lenses. She felt him jam the mask back onto her face. Instinctively she looked back over her shoulder. In the split second it took for her to comprehend what she was seeing, she became a believer.

He wasn't paranoid. He'd been right all along—they were after him, and they meant business.

Even in the dim light she could discern the thick yellow fog surging toward them from the open metal canister on the floor. The newspaper wall no longer existed, and incredibly, the metal door to the third-floor hallway now had a gaping hole punched through it. She thought she could see movement in the hall beyond, and her limbs turned suddenly to water.

This time when he grabbed her wrist, she needed no urging to go with him.

The bicycle contraption didn't appear to have been affected by the explosion. It spun at top speed, the lightbulb still glowing dimly above them, although in the spreading fog it was harder to see. Releasing her wrist and shrugging out of his heavy coat, the dark-haired man kicked at the solid wall in front of him.

It broke easily, and for a moment she didn't understand. Surely he'd told her he'd lined the room with—

She saw him pull the thin wood away, revealing a neat

opening about half the size of a door. Around the edges of the square she could see the thick steel that comprised the rest of the wall.

Was it a way into the adjoining hotel room? As he gestured for her to duck into the opening, she crouched swiftly and crawled forward. A moment later she felt him at her heels; she kept moving until the filter of her gas mask bumped solidly against something.

A faint red glow—enough to see by—came from somewhere above her and, looking around, Ainslie saw her companion push a button on what seemed to be some kind of primitive control panel. Just beyond she could see the yellow tendrils of gas drifting across the floor of the room they'd exited; she looked apprehensively at him.

He gave her a thumbs-up sign. Relief flooded through her, and a heartbeat later she realized that she trusted him totally.

An hour ago she hadn't known him. Half an hour ago she'd been convinced he was crazy, and maybe he was, a little. But he'd been right about everything so far, and his off-beat inventions, as unconventional as they were, had all worked.

She remembered the time she and Malone had taken a drive out into the country and her car had broken down. He'd twisted a piece of barbed wire off a nearby fence, asked her for a copper penny and had fished a stick of chewing gum out of his pocket. Then, whistling "Danny Boy" between his teeth, he'd stuck his head under the hood for a minute or so. When he'd called out to her to try to start the car, she'd turned the key and the engine had purred to life—

She felt a jarring jolt. From beside her, he put his hand reassuringly on her arm as she realized they were moving upward.

He'd built a homemade *elevator* in the air shaft between the walls. Already the opening to the room had slid out of sight below them. In the dim red glow she saw him reach up and pull off his gas mask, and then motion for her to do the same.

At this point if he'd told her it would be safe to jump off a roof she would have followed his lead, Ainslie thought wryly.

"This goes right up to the roof." As she gratefully stripped the rubber-and-metal mask from her face he leaned close, his mouth only inches from her ear. Despite his appearance, she realized disconcertedly, she could discern the clean scent of soap on his skin. "I've got a cable running over to the next building's fire escape. All we have to do is slide down it and we're home free."

They *were* going to jump off the roof. She flinched as the sound of a muffled explosion boomed hollowly up the shaft from below. Under the tangle of hair that obscured his brow she saw him frown.

"They just blew the door open. Any second now they'll find the generator and turn it off, but they've left it too late." He shrugged, and leaned back against the wall. "They'll get me one of these days, I guess. But today I survived."

With the heavy growth of beard it was hard to tell his expression, but as he closed his eyes Ainslie thought she saw a corner of his mouth lift briefly. As the echo of the explosion faded, another less ominous sound filled the small elevator. For a minute she didn't know what it was.

Then she realized what she was hearing. Oblivious to the mayhem, the man beside her was whistling, so quietly that at first it was hard to make out the tune. He couldn't be comfortable in such a small space, she thought. His knees were drawn up awkwardly in front of him, his battered work boots braced against the opposite wall. But for the first time since she'd first laid eyes on him, some of his tenseness had dissipated. Without the woolen coat, the heavily defined sheath of muscle on his arms was apparent. His wrists, large-boned and tanned, rested easily on his propped-up knees, and he seemed, for the moment at least, to be at peace.

His eyes still closed, he continued whistling softly between his teeth, and now she recognized the song.

The tune was "Danny Boy." And the elevator was filled with the scent of red roses.

Chapter Four

He'd gotten away from them again. He'd had a few bad moments on the roof, when he'd thought there was a chance the cable might not hold the weight of the woman and himself combined, but they'd safely made it to the metal fire escape of the building across the street. From there he'd followed the escape route he'd laid out over the past few weeks. They were now a good five blocks away, holed up in the basement of a parking garage and hidden from view thanks to a massive concrete pillar.

The woman was sitting a few feet away from him, her back against the wall. He'd loaned her his coat, but the dress she was wearing was already soiled and torn. He knew she was staring at him—he could practically feel that violet gaze of hers burn into him—but he kept his eyes averted.

The woman was obviously unbalanced.

When she'd first shown up, for a second he'd wondered if she was working with *them,* but almost immediately he'd realized she had her own unfathomable agenda. She'd kept insisting he was someone called Malone, and when he'd denied it that last time in the elevator—his headache had been building all day, and maybe the pain had made him a little curt with her—she'd refused to believe him. As if she was presenting him with clinching proof, she'd said something about the perfume she'd been wearing, a heavy rose scent that had permeated the enclosed space.

Funny. He didn't know much about women's taste in perfume, but he would have pegged her as the type to wear something lighter. With that chin-grazing blue-black hair and those eyes, she made him think of violets—wild violets.

Pain suddenly screamed through his head like an express train, and he squeezed his eyes shut, riding with it. He could feel sweat popping out on his temples, and a wave of nausea washed over him.

It hadn't been this bad for a long time, but for the past week it had been getting steadily worse. He could pinpoint the exact moment it had started escalating. He'd been going through a discarded *Boston Globe* page by page—wherever he was living, he made it a point to scan a major newspaper every single day. He'd never been sure what he was looking for, but he had the feeling that if he found it he'd know—and out of the blue it had suddenly felt as if his brain was exploding.

The nausea passed. Hoping she hadn't noticed anything, he opened his eyes and found himself staring into hers, only a few inches away.

"You're hurt, aren't you? What's the matter, did a piece of the door hit you when they shot in the gas canister, Malone?" Her voice was edged with worry, but at it his headache intensified.

She had to stop calling him Malone.

"That's not my name. Why can't you understand that?" It cost him to speak, but he continued. "In...in the pocket of my coat are some papers. Get them out."

Ignoring him, she leaned closer. The heavy perfume she'd been wearing seemed to have dissipated, and he was grateful for that. ''We have to get you to a doctor, for God's sake. There's a pay phone by the stairs over there. I'm going to call an ambulance.''

''No! No hospitals, no doctors.'' He gritted his teeth. ''Just...just give me the papers. I want to show you something.''

She hesitated for a moment and then reached inside the coat pocket, her gaze never leaving his face.

Her delusion was powerful. He'd hadn't wanted to force the truth on her, but obviously nothing else would jolt her back to reality. Briefly he wondered what kind of man the mysterious Malone was and just how he'd disappeared from her life.

He hadn't deserved her. The thought flashed into his mind with cold certainty. Whoever he was, he hadn't deserved a woman like this, and her actions today, as crazily impulsive as they'd been, proved that.

In the alleyway she'd said something about believing he was dead. The son of a bitch hadn't even had the guts to say goodbye to her.

But if Malone hadn't deserved her, the man she'd been about to marry today didn't, either. If he had, she wouldn't have had to look to the past to find the love of her life.

''Here.''

She thrust the papers into his hand, and for the first time he noticed the slight callousing on her knuckles. When he'd held her by the arm earlier, under the overblown frills of her sleeve he'd felt incongruously hard muscle. Even though it was a wedding dress, like the perfume, it was all wrong for her, he thought. She wasn't flounces and fussiness. She had the kind of beauty that could stand alone.

He pulled the rubber band off the small package of papers and cards, and shuffled through them, the left side of his head throbbing. That was where the scar was, hidden somewhere under his hair. It always hurt more in that area.

"My driver's license." He handed it to her. "A letter of reference from a garage owner I worked for in Idaho last year." He unfolded it and passed it over. "My photo ID and dock pass. I was a deckhand on a salvage vessel in Florida a couple of winters ago. Check out the name on all of them."

Watching her carefully as she looked at each item, he continued. "I've hit a run of bad luck lately, but I haven't always lived on the streets, lady. I've got a history. I've got an identity. I'm not the man you're looking for."

"John Smith?" There was a thread of incredulity in her tone. Holding up the license again, she peered at it almost fearfully. Her glance darted to him and then back to the ID, as if she suspected some trick. "John *Smith?* What kind of a name is that? That could be anyone's name!"

Time was running out. His usual practice after such a close call was to put as much distance between himself and them as possible, and he knew he had to get moving. But he couldn't leave—not yet.

With every minute that passed, the danger was lessening for her. They knew he traveled alone, and they knew he would never reveal his destination to anyone, so any interest they had in her would fade within hours. Still, he'd feel easier knowing that she was—how had she put it?—back in her own world, before he left.

And he needed to break through the barrier of denial she was putting up. This Malone bastard had run out on her once before. He wasn't going to leave her believing that the man she loved had abandoned her a second time.

"It's not anyone's name, it's my name." He tried to smooth out the hoarseness in his voice, suddenly wanting only to make the glaze of her tears disappear, to erase the shadow of grief that haunted her features.

"Maybe I look a little like him. It's been so long since I've seen myself without this—" he gestured toward his moustache and beard "—that I hardly remember what I look like clean-shaven. But a chance resemblance is all it is. I'm not him. You've got to believe me."

"But your *eyes*—they're exactly the same!" She sounded desperate, as if she was holding on to something that was slipping away. "And...and you were whistling 'Danny Boy,' just the way he used to!"

"I don't know much about my background, but I think there's more than a touch of Irish in it." The pain flared behind his eyes, sharper than before. "From his name, I'd guess your Malone and I have that in common. But that doesn't mean much."

"You called me Lee." Her gaze was brilliantly intense. She knew, he thought. She knew now, but her heart hadn't caught up to her head. "How did you know my name?"

"I didn't. I think you heard what you wanted to hear," he said heavily. "I'm not him, and he's not worth it, Lee. If he ran out on you, you're better off without him."

"John Smith."

She glanced down at the papers in her hand once more. He saw her shoulders slump, and the small movement of defeat came close to tearing him apart. She wasn't a tall woman. In the grease-smeared white gown and the now-filthy satin slippers she was wearing, she looked like a little girl at her own birthday party, watching the guests leave early.

Except she wasn't a little girl, he told himself as he saw her shoulders straighten. She was a woman. She had courage, she had the strength of her convictions, as misplaced as those convictions might be, and her only vulnerability was that she'd loved too well. Again a flicker of anger at the mysterious Malone flared in him. At her next words, it was snuffed out completely.

"I went to his funeral. I put red roses on his casket. You really aren't him, are you?"

The express train inside his skull screamed down the tracks, its rushing metal wheels throwing off sparks of unbearable pain. The nausea had come back in full force. She'd gone to his *funeral.* She'd stood by his grave and watched him being lowered into the ground. The man was dead. He hadn't run out on her, he'd *died.*

Instead of anger, the emotion now flickering just beneath the blanket of pain in his head was envy.

What would it be like to be loved so completely? The man was dead, yes—but even in death he had the love of the woman sitting here in front of him, her cheeks now wet with tears, her slight figure held ramrod-straight.

"No, I'm not him." Unsteadily he got to his feet, one arm braced against the concrete pillar for support. He reached down to help her up, but she stood unaided, her face averted from his. Slowly she slipped her arms out of his coat. She looked up at him with a shaky smile.

"I thought you were crazy. Now you must think I am."

"Not crazy." He shook his head. Thankfully, the pain seemed to be receding. "But you're going to have to let him go one day. This is no way for you to live."

"This is no way for you to live, either." Her smile faltered. "You really don't know who they are or why they're trying to kill you?"

"All I know is that they'll never give up until they do." He shrugged. "All I know is that the one time I went to the authorities, I nearly didn't get away alive."

"My brother runs an investigation and security firm.

Sully might be able to help you," she began, but he cut her off.

"Trust me, it wouldn't work." Pain flared again in the area of his scar. "But contacting your brother is probably a good idea, Ainslie. I can't stay here much longer, but I won't leave until I know you're safe."

"Why doesn't that surprise me?"

She took the quarter he held out to her, and handed him his coat with a wry smile. He watched her cover the hundred feet or so to the phone cubicle, watched her punch in a number, saw the strained expression on her face as she briefly spoke into the receiver. Then she hung up and came back to him, a slight upward tilt to her chin.

"I got him on his cell phone. He's only a couple of minutes away, and I got the distinct impression he intended to break every speed limit getting here." She took a deep breath. "The hotel. Apparently the fire department's there right now, trying to bring the blaze under control. It was fire-bombed, Sully said. He saw the motorcycle I borrowed in the alley beside it, and he…he thought I was still in there."

Her chin dipped to her chest, and then lifted again. "I would have been killed if it hadn't been for you. I wish there was some way I could repay you."

There was one more reason to envy the man she'd mistaken him for. When Malone had walked away from her that last time, he'd probably had no idea it was the last time he'd see her. He shrugged into his coat, carefully replacing the package of ID in an inner pocket. He had only a few seconds more with her. She would remember him for a while, but one day her memory of these hours they'd spent together would fade, and that was how it should be.

He would remember her for the rest of his life, however

much time was left to him. He would remember those eyes, remember the way her hair looked like midnight silk, remember the way she'd smiled even when she'd been forced to face the truth about him.

He wanted one more thing to remember.

"There is. You can let me do this."

Holding her gaze, he took a step toward her, obliterating the distance between them. She had to tip her head to keep her eyes on his, and slowly he slipped his hand around the back of her neck, feeling that silky hair slide coolly against his skin. He lowered his mouth to hers.

Her lips were soft, and slightly parted under his. He could taste a faint saltiness from the tears she'd shed earlier, but beneath that was sweetness—a sweetness so intense that for a moment he felt his heart turn over in pure ecstasy. He'd never tasted crystallized flowers, but this had to be what they would be like, he told himself dizzily. Sweet. So *sweet...*

From somewhere on another level of the parking garage came the squeal of tires taking a corner too fast. He lifted his mouth from hers, but for a moment his hand remained cupped around the back of her neck.

"That's got to be the brother."

She nodded, her eyes wide. "That sounds like Sully, all right." Her voice was uneven.

"I'd better leave." Reluctantly he let his hand slip away, and even more reluctantly he turned toward the nearby stairwell. He took half a dozen steps away from her and then turned. "I wish you'd been right."

She hadn't moved. She was still staring at him with that dark violet-blue gaze. He knew what he must look like to her—too big, too unshaven, a derelict dressed in ragged cast-offs. She was right. They did belong to different worlds.

But if they hadn't…

"I wish I could have been the man you hoped I was, sweetheart," he said softly. "Because if I'd been Malone, I would have come back to you. Not even death would have been enough to stop me."

He drank in the sight of her for one last time. Then he melted into the shadows as the green Jaguar came peeling around the corner.

HER HAIR WAS STILL WET from the shower she'd taken, but she hadn't wanted to waste time in blow-drying it. Instead she'd simply slicked it back off her forehead and secured it in a stumpy ponytail. She'd pulled an ancient black turtleneck over her head, dislodging the ponytail in the process, had found a passably clean pair of black jeans, and had shoved her bare feet into sneakers.

The ruined wedding dress, wadded up in a corner of her bedroom, had been a mutely reproachful reminder of what lay ahead of her. Sully, as he'd driven her back to her apartment, had been anything but mute.

"You could have been killed, goddammit! I thought you *had* been!" He'd still been wearing the dove-gray morning suit he'd donned for the ceremony, and under his tan his skin had been nearly the same color. "What the hell were you *thinking?*"

"You know what I was thinking, Sully." Her reply had been toneless. "I know it doesn't make any sense."

"Damn right it doesn't make sense. Neither does that insane yarn he spun you." Sully had taken his eyes from the road and glared at her. "The man was *involved,* Lee! Surely you must have realized that? Only drug wars get that violent and use the kind of weaponry you described!"

"He saved my life. A scumbag dealer wouldn't have bothered, Sullivan." She'd folded her arms and stared out of the window of the Jag. "He's a man in terrible trouble, and I'll never know how it turns out for him."

"Well, you've got Bailey to thank for the fact that your trouble isn't any more terrible than it is," Sully had grunted. "She saved your reputation today. When Tara told us what you'd done, Bailey went into labor. Not really," he added quickly at Ainslie's gasp. "But as far as the wedding guests know, that's why the ceremony was postponed. Pearson went along with it."

"Was he very angry, Sully?" Her question had been barely audible, and Sully had raised an eyebrow at her.

"If it was me, I'd be furious, but with McNeil, who can tell? He did seem a little more chilly than usual when I broke the news to him."

That would be Pearson's way, Ainslie thought now as she raised the burnished brass knocker on the front door of her fiancé's—ex-fiancé's? she wondered hollowly, jilted fiancé's?—carefully preserved Beacon Hill home. It was opened immediately, and by the last person besides Pearson that she wanted to see.

"I don't believe your nerve."

Brian, Pearson's brother, was still attired for a wedding, as Sully had been, but he'd stripped off his jacket. In one well-manicured hand was a squat crystal tumbler of some amber liquid.

"Believe me, Brian, my nerve is hanging on by a thread," she said tightly, stepping past him and dropping her shoulder bag on a nearby table. "Is Pearson available?"

"Pearson's in the library getting ready to leave. He's going to Greystones for a few days."

Younger than his brother and more raffishly good-looking, Ainslie knew Brian had never really warmed to the notion of acquiring her as a sister-in-law. But up until now he'd always hid his slight antagonism behind the charm he seemed to be able to switch on and off at will. It was a talent that would be useful to him when he ran for office, but it was obvious he no longer felt the need to trot it out for her benefit.

"Then I'm glad I caught him before he goes."

Of course Pearson would want to get out of the city for a while, she thought, averting her gaze as she passed the open French doors of the dining room. The antique dining table, a massive mahogany piece that could seat a dozen guests, was piled high with exquisitely wrapped wedding gifts. The McNeil's country house would have no such reminders.

"How the hell could you have humiliated him so publicly?" Brian had followed her down the hallway, and his voice at her shoulder was low with suppressed anger. "Whatever excuse you came here to give, it's not going to—"

"I wasn't humiliated, Brian. And if Ainslie feels she owes anyone an explanation, I don't believe it would be to you."

Pearson McNeil, his tall, spare figure seemingly relaxed, appeared in the open doorway of the library at the end of the hall. He was wearing what he would call casual clothes, although Ainslie had teased him in the past that he didn't know the meaning of the word. Charcoal flannel trousers were belted at the waist with a dark tan leather belt. His shirt, open just one button at the neck, was plain white cotton—but it was Egyptian cotton, Ainslie guessed.

"Ainslie, my dear." Crossing swiftly to her, he took one of her hands in both of his. "I'm glad you came."

Drawing her closer, he pressed a brief kiss onto her forehead and then steered her courteously toward the library, but not before she caught the flash of emotion that crossed Brian's handsome features as he turned on his heel and headed back down the hall. But Brian's feelings in this matter weren't her priority, Ainslie thought, turning her attention to Pearson.

"I was choosing some reading material to take with me to Greystones." Looking vaguely around the room, he frowned. Then he smiled ruefully, reaching for the pair of reading glasses on the top of his head. "I'm a little distracted today," he said, folding the glasses up carefully and putting them on top of the small pile of books sitting on the oak table beside Ainslie.

"It's been a distracting day," Ainslie said, not looking at him. She ran her fingers over the buttery-soft calfskin binding of one of the books, and then lifted her head to meet his gaze. "I came to apologize to you, Pearson. Now that I'm here I realize just how inadequate that sounds. What I did today was...was unforgivable."

"Oh, surely not that." He lifted an eyebrow. "Let's save that word for the really horrific deeds the human race commits every day. You simply changed your mind. That was always your prerogative, I believe—although I must admit I wish you'd exercised it a week or two earlier."

One of the books in this room was his own *History of Twentieth-Century Conflict,* Ainslie thought. But even though he was attempting to take a scholar's view of today's events, she knew he couldn't be as detached as he was pretending to be.

"But that's just it, Pearson. I didn't change my mind," she said unhappily.

Sully had told her that he'd said nothing to Pearson about her real reason for tearing out of the church, but she owed the man in front of her the truth. She should have told him about Malone a long time ago, she thought regretfully. Maybe if she had, her confession now would have been easier.

"In the crowd outside the church today I thought I saw a man...a man I was very much in love with once," she said softly, holding his gaze as steadily as she could. "Except I knew it couldn't be him, because he—"

"Because he was dead." Pearson finished her sentence for her in the same quiet tone. "You thought you saw Seamus Malone, Ainslie? Is that who the man in the crowd reminded you of?"

Taken aback, Ainslie could only stare at him in confusion. Bridging the distance between them, he put his hands lightly on her shoulders.

"I was talking with Father Flynn in his office when you arrived. I couldn't help hearing the name you called out."

"But...but how did you know he was dead? How did you know I'd once been involved with him?" She stared up at him uncomprehendingly.

"I've known for a long time—almost from the first, in fact." He sighed. "I wasn't prying, Ainslie. But beneath that toughly competent exterior you show to the world, I saw a deep sadness. I think I already knew I cared for you more than I'd ever cared for anyone. I wanted to know if there was anything I could do to lessen that sadness for you. So I made some inquiries, and when I learned about Malone I realized just how truly strong you were. A tragedy like that might have destroyed another woman."

"It almost did, Pearson." She closed her eyes, remembering. "I'm not as strong as you think I am. Today must have proved that to you."

Touching only on the essentials, she haltingly described her encounter with John Smith, saying nothing about his hunted lifestyle or the fact that his pursuers had nearly caught up with him while she'd been with him. That wasn't her story to tell, she thought uneasily. True, she'd shared some of it with Sullivan, but Sully's life hadn't always been as conventional as it was now. She'd hoped for more understanding from her ex-mercenary half brother, she admitted to herself.

Of course, even to Sully she'd said nothing about the kiss.

If she'd needed one last scrap of proof to convince herself that the man she'd been with today wasn't Malone, that kiss in the parking garage would have been it. Malone's lovemaking had always held a touch of teasing wickedness. Even during their most passionate moments, it had never been hard to detect the bad-boy glint in his eye, the delinquent one-sided smile he wore as they urged each other on to more dizzying heights together.

The man who'd kissed her today had done nothing more than touch his lips to hers, linger there for a moment, and then pull away. Instead of playfulness, there had been an almost hopeless desperation in his kiss.

It had felt as if he'd given her his soul, and left before she'd had a chance to give it back.

And from the second his mouth had come down on hers, the unshaven roughness of his skin chafing against the sensitive corners of her lips, she'd felt a dark flame flare into immediate life deep inside her…

"I'm going to have to agree with Sullivan on this one, Ainslie."

Pearson had listened to her without interruption. When she had fallen silent he had said nothing for a few minutes, but now he held her slightly away from him, his expression troubled.

"I think I can understand the anguish you felt when you saw him. It's important to you that you never had a chance to say goodbye to Malone, isn't it?"

He seemed about to say more, but at that moment the phone on the desk buzzed discreetly. With a glance of apology at her, he walked over to answer it. Ainslie found herself feeling obscurely grateful for the interruption. Turning away, she stared sightlessly at the rows of books in front of her.

Pearson McNeil might appear stuffy, but his stuffiness stemmed from a determination to do the right thing, whatever the circumstances. That wasn't stuffiness, that was integrity. Her actions today must have hurt him deeply, but his feelings for her hadn't wavered.

You can't go on running the rest of your life, she told herself somberly. Unbidden, the vision of a man who had been forced to do just that came into her mind. He was another one she would have to forget, she thought. She would never see him again, never even know if he had survived past today. Unconsciously, her hand went to her lips, her fingertips tracing the heat that she imagined she still could feel there.

"That was Sullivan."

Pearson's dry voice broke into her thoughts and she turned to him almost guiltily.

"It seems we didn't lie to Father Flynn after all," he smiled, his head tipped quizzically to one side. "Bailey went into labor half an hour ago. Sullivan says if you want to see your newest niece being born, you'd better get over to Mass General right away."

Reaching out for her hands, he clasped them loosely in his, his eyes on hers. "You said a few minutes ago that you hadn't changed your mind about going through with our marriage. I haven't either, Ainslie. But I want to give you time to come to terms with any lingering conflicts you might have. When I return from Greystones we'll have dinner together, just the two of us, and you can tell me if

Malone is really dead and not still alive in your heart. If he is, and if your feelings for me still include marriage, then we'll arrange a quiet ceremony as soon as possible.''

''And if he isn't?'' she asked softly.

Pearson released her hands. His smile was wry. ''If he isn't, then I went up against a ghost, and lost.''

Chapter Five

Megan Angelique Sullivan's name had been well chosen. The tiny, exquisite scrap of humanity she'd seen Bailey holding in her arms with tired joy a few moments ago *was* an angel, Ainslie thought. Her ex-mercenary, ex-playboy of a brother had been beaming down on his wife and daughter as if nothing else in the universe existed for him. With such a legacy of love, her newly born niece already had the most valuable gift her parents could ever give her.

Would any child that she and Pearson might have together grow up with that same sense of total security? Ainslie stood stock-still in the brightly lit hospital hallway as the answer came unhesitatingly to her. She cared for Pearson. She respected Pearson. And after his compassion and understanding today, she wished more than anything else that she did love him.

But she didn't. She'd handled things badly, and for reasons that now seemed foolish, but her instincts hadn't been wrong. She had no business marrying him. She had no business contemplating having a child with a man she couldn't love forever, and with all her heart.

Which means you're never going to have what Bailey's experiencing right now. You're never going to hold a Megan Angelique of your own, never going to create a new and perfect little being with the man you love. Because that man was Malone.

Slowly she resumed walking to the bank of elevators at the far end of the hall. By now Pearson would have already left for Greystones, and this time she was determined to do it right. A phone call wouldn't suffice. Punching the call button for the elevator, she tiredly massaged the troubled crease between her eyebrows.

The rest of the O'Connell females, including Tara and her aunts, had been allowed a two-second peek into Bailey's hospital room before being ushered firmly out by a sergeant major of a ward nurse. Tara had already announced she would be staying overnight with Aunt Kate—more, Ainslie suspected, because her adopted daughter had wanted to give her some time alone, than because the notion of getting up at five and accompanying Kate to the gym to watch the more dedicated of the boxers go through an early-morning workout was appealing to the teen.

Despite herself, she smiled faintly. Whatever the reason, Tara would be under the eagle eye of "Kiss Me Katie" for the next day or so, and for that matter, so would be the gym. After informing Pearson of her decision regarding their marriage—*and that's not anything I'm looking forward to,* she thought heavily—devoting the rest of the week to some solitary and serious soul-searching might be a good idea.

The elevator doors started to slide open. From the far end of the long hall behind her she heard footsteps, and, looking around, she saw a pair of orderlies approaching at a restrained trot, the gurney between them the obvious reason for their discreet haste.

"Hold the elevator!"

The orderly at the head of the gurney called out the command in an unpleasantly grating voice, and from a nearby room came the immediate and lusty bellow of a just-awakened baby. Giving a nod of acknowledgment to the approaching pair, Ainslie felt a twinge of sympathy for the unknown mother and a spurt of impatience toward the orderly. They were in a hospital, for God's sake. Didn't the man know any better than to shout—

"Ainslie! Get in!"

Startled, she whirled around, and met the same impossibly green eyes she'd seen from the steps of St. Margaret's. Dressed in hospital scrubs, with an operating mask covering the bottom half of his face and a surgeon's cap pulled low over his brows, he was standing in the elevator, his expression shadowed with urgency.

And despite what she'd just been telling herself, again she felt the impact of that gaze slam into her.

"John—what's happened? What are you doing here?" Finding her voice, she stared in concern at the man in front of her. "Surely it can't be safe for you to be seen in public like this!"

"It's not. And stop calling me that, Lee." His reply was muffled by the mask, but there was no mistaking the sharp edge in his tone. "Get in—*now!* They're probably already on their way up here."

"Who? The men who were after you?"

None of this made any sense, she thought in confusion. The events of the afternoon had been bizarre enough, but this was verging on insanity. He'd told her he couldn't risk staying in Boston, now that he'd been traced here. He'd told her he intended to disappear.

So why had he come back to her?

Suddenly, Sully's skepticism, so unpalatable only a few hours ago, seemed reasonable. In fact, she thought shakily, Sully might not have taken it far enough. Had there *ever* been anyone pursuing them? Right from the start, had it all been the smoke and mirrors of an unbalanced mind—smoke and mirrors that, in her own agitated state, she'd fallen for too easily? Had everything she'd accepted as coming from his mysterious enemies been just a few more examples of his crazed contraptions? Had he arranged the fire in his building himself?

"Yeah. I was careful, but I wasn't expecting them to have the hospital staked out. I think they spotted me." His tenseness was almost tangible. "Come *on,* Lee!"

Humor him, Ainslie thought with dreadful clarity. *This has gone far enough. You can't let him drag you into another of his insane nightmares.* She was suddenly grateful for the approaching hospital employees and their gurneyed passenger, now passing by the nursing station about a third of the hall length away, and coming closer.

"Okay, John." She stepped closer to the elevator opening, her tone conciliatory. "But keep the door open. Those orderlies have a patient on a gurney with them, and we can't just—"

"Orderlies?"

Under the loose-fitting scrubs his whole body froze into stillness. Whether or not there was any basis at all for his paranoia, Ainslie thought with a flash of compassion, the man's fear was real enough. Above the mask his eyes flickered briefly, as if he was making an instantaneous decision.

The next moment his hand had shot out, grasping her just below the elbow. With a jerk, he pulled her toward him, even as he punched repeatedly at one of the numbers on the bank of buttons just inside the elevator door. Reflexively she tried to pull away from him, but his grip held her like an iron clamp.

"Dammit, John—let *go* of me!"

"I told you, Lee—stop calling me that." The short sleeves of the scrubs barely fit over his biceps. As he kept his thumb firmly pressed against the elevator button, she saw the rigidity in his muscles. "Their being here can only mean one thing—for some reason, they're after you now as well as me. I'll bet good money that gurney's empty. *You're* the patient they intend to transport."

Had the approaching footsteps coming down the hall increased their pace? The metal ratcheting of the gurney sounded off-kilter, as if it were being pushed faster than it had been designed for.

The elevator doors began to slide closed. She didn't know who she was more annoyed with, Ainslie thought in frustration, him or herself. But she knew one thing. She wasn't going to allow him to drag her into two cat-and-mouse chases in one day, especially when she was beginning to suspect that there wasn't a cat at all.

She heard the swish of the doors coming together, heard the footsteps break into a run, heard the grating voice shouting angrily from only a few feet away. She relaxed her knees slightly, bounced up on the balls of her feet, and made a fist.

Not allowing his grip on her left arm to hinder her, with her right hand she let fly with a roundhouse punch, aimed at the point of his chin concealed under the medical mask.

For such a big man, his reflexes were incredibly fast. His head jerked back and his free hand caught her wrist just inches away from his face.

The doors slid firmly closed behind her, cutting off the angry shouts. Smoothly the elevator began to descend.

"I stashed a wheelchair behind a planter in the lobby. I hope to hell it's still there."

Releasing both her arms, he took off the surgeon's cap, stuffed it into a back pocket of the scrubs, and raked an unsteady hand through his hair. It had been tied back in an unkempt ponytail. He went on, seemingly unfazed by her attempted attack on him of only seconds ago.

"We'll leave by the emergency entrance, and try to get to my car without alerting them. I figure in this getup, and with you in a chair, we might not draw their attention so easily."

What little composure she still had shattered at his words. She glared at him, not bothering to conceal her outrage. "How about if I'm screaming blue murder while you're trying to sneak me out in my wheelchair, John? Do you think we might draw their attention then? Do you think they might notice if I hop out of the damn chair and throw a few more punches at you, John? Because that's exactly what I feel like—"

He pulled down the mask that had been covering his face. The beard was still there, but it had been inexpertly cropped to heavy stubble. He gazed at her, a spark of anger in his own expression.

"So help me, honey, if you call me that one more time I swear I'll go crazy all over again. I planned to tell you when we'd gotten safely away from here, but—"

He glanced at the floor indicator. They were on five, and still descending. He turned back to her, a tight and humorless smile lifting one corner of his mouth.

"The night we met we went back to your place and made love, three times before dawn. You made me coffee the next morning. It was undrinkable, because your coffee always is, but I didn't care. We let it get cold and we made love again."

He went on. "I bought you a pair of silver earrings shaped like crescent moons the second day. We sat in a park and held hands for an hour, not saying a word, just looking at each other. You gave me a bath once. I've got a scar on my left shoulder blade, and you kissed it. When

I looked at you, I saw that you were crying. Should I go on?''

He took her silence for acquiescence, and continued. ''You've got a tiny birthmark on your upper thigh. You used to go out of your mind when I kissed the back of your knee. The night I disappeared I asked you to marry me. As I was walking out the door you pulled me back in and whispered something in my ear.''

''What did I whisper?'' The blood was pounding in her head so loudly that she hardly heard her own question. Her lips felt so numb that she wasn't even sure she'd asked it until his answer came, prompt and unhesitating.

''You told me what you were going to do with me when I got back that evening. You said it included massage oil. I was so weak with desire when you finished describing what you had planned I could barely stand.'' He shrugged, the gesture no more than a controlled lifting of his shoulders. ''I didn't want to tell you like this, Lee. But you knew this afternoon anyway, didn't you? I'm Malone. I've come back.''

''No.'' She shook her head. ''No, Malone's dead. You're someone called John Smith, and right from the start you've come up with one crazy story after the other. You're not Malone. I buried Malone.''

She heard the soft *ping* that meant the elevator had passed another floor. He flicked his gaze to the indicator and a muscle in his jaw tightened.

''Ask me anything.'' His voice was edged. ''Ask me anything about our time together. I remember it all.''

Why was he doing this to her? Ainslie thought distantly. This was too surreal. She felt as if she was surrounded by a thick fog, a fog that was pressing in on her, making it hard for her to breathe.

''He made me a promise.'' Her voice sounded as if it

came from a long way away, through the enveloping layers of pain. "You can't know about that, because you're not Malone. I put roses on his grave."

"I promised you I'd never leave you the way you'd been left before." His eyes were dark. "You'd had a nightmare, and I heard you crying out in your sleep. I held you and you told me you'd been dreaming about your father and how he'd walked out of your life, taking your half brother with him. You said in your dream there were birds—great birds, with wingspans longer than a man's arm—and that they'd taken him away. I promised you I would never leave you. I promised you I would always come back."

"*Malone* promised me that!"

All at once the fog surrounding her was blown away, as if by some powerful wind. She could practically *hear* it, Ainslie thought in cold desperation—a howling crescendo of hurricane-like proportions that rapidly blotted out everything else in her head. She raised her voice to be heard above it, found her vision blurring from the tears it had brought to her eyes.

"*Malone* made that promise—and he didn't keep it! He *did* leave me! He *didn't* come back!" Hardly knowing what she was doing, she raised her fists and slammed them against the immobile chest of the man in front of her, the tears streaming down her face, her gaze fixed and brilliant on his. "Maybe it wasn't his fault, but he broke his promise. He *died*—don't you get it? He died, and not even Malone can come back from the dead!"

"But I did." The husky voice was shot through with pain. This time when he grabbed her wrists he didn't let go. "Don't *you* get it, Lee? I *was* dead—I've been dead for two long years. But I didn't break my promise to you. I've come back. I've come *back*, dammit!"

At his last words, the thundering in her head came to a shockingly sudden stop. In the abrupt silence she heard him suck in a ragged breath, as if he'd been running for too long and had used up the last of his strength. The elevator came to a jolting stop.

The doors slid open. He flicked a quick look out at the lobby, and then focused once more on her.

"Okay, say I'm lying about who I am." He spoke quickly, his tone so low it was almost inaudible. "That doesn't change the fact that right now we're only seconds away from being killed. Will you trust me that far?"

"No." She was trembling, Ainslie realized, but from the outside it wasn't visible. The tremors were on the inside, and they were almost shaking her apart. She stepped out of the elevator. "I don't trust you at all. Everything you've said is a lie."

Without looking back, she started to walk away. She had to get out of here. She had to get away.

She was almost at the doors when she heard him call out to her.

"Lee."

There was no urgency in his tone. She took another step forward and then, almost against her will, found herself hesitating. She stopped. She didn't look around.

"I get it now, Lee." The huskiness was more pronounced. "You wanted Malone to stay dead. He left you, like your father and your brother did, and some part of you never forgave him for that. You need him to be dead, Lee. That way he'll always be a perfect memory, and he'll never be able to leave you again."

Ainslie remained rigidly still. He was wrong, she thought numbly. She'd never wanted Malone to stay dead. She'd wanted him alive so desperately that she hadn't been able to accept his death. She'd prayed every night for him to come back to her. Now he had.

And he was nothing like the memory she'd held in her heart for so long.

The realization of what had just gone through her mind didn't register for a second. Then her eyes widened painfully, and her fingers flew to her mouth. She pressed them tightly against her lips, as if by sealing off her very breath she could delay the full impact of what she'd just acknowledged to herself.

About to turn to meet his gaze, she saw two men scramble swiftly out of an ambulance that had just pulled to a stop outside. They were both wearing suits, and one of them was speaking into a hand-held radio. As they strode purposefully toward the entrance, the glass doors slid open with a quiet hiss. The walkie-talkie emitted a burst of static, plainly audible as the two men were now less than ten feet from the open doors. Ainslie saw the man wince, say something into the radio and listen intently.

From over the radio came a grating voice. At Ainslie's distance the words were unintelligible but clearly urgent. The man with the radio looked up and caught her watching him.

"*Malone*—they're here!"

Unsteady, her voice carried across the crowded seating area, and as she swung her gaze Malone's way she saw a brief flash of some undefinable emotion cross his features. His eyes locked on hers, and for just a second it seemed as if they were the only two people in the lobby.

Then the moment passed. Three strides brought him to her side and she felt his hand on the small of her back, propelling her quickly around the corner and down a small corridor she hadn't noticed before. The corridor ended in a blank wall.

"Malone, it's a dead end! They'll trap—" She broke off abruptly.

"I scouted this out earlier. It's only used by the hospital staff."

The same utilitarian shade as the walls, the gray-painted metal door he impatiently pushed open was barely noticeable. Ainslie stepped out into near-blackness, and Malone bent to pick something up from the ground.

"This won't stop them for long, but it'll do." Grunting with the effort, he shoved what looked like an iron bar through the vertical metal handle of the door. "Take my hand, Lee—we've got to move fast."

He'd been expecting this, or something similar, Ainslie absently realized as his hand wrapped around hers and he pulled her into a run. She could hear angry pounding on the door behind them. And he'd not only had one plan of escape—he'd mentioned something about a wheelchair, she remembered—he'd also scouted out a contingency route. That iron bar hadn't been a handy coincidence.

"There's the car."

Beyond the short stretch of grass they were speeding across was a deserted but adequately lit street. The only car at the curb didn't look like anyone's idea of a getaway vehicle, she thought as he released her hand and sprinted around to the driver's side.

But it was a car. Three hours ago he'd let her believe he was a vagrant, his only possessions an assortment of junk in a shopping cart. Three hours ago he'd told her he'd never seen her before in his life. Three hours ago he'd denied his very identity to her.

He leaned over and opened the passenger side door for her. Even before she was fully in, the car's engine roared to life and the headlights flicked on, and while she was still fastening her seat belt Malone shot away from the curb.

Ainslie's hands had twisted together in her lap, her nails digging cruelly into the skin of her interlaced fingers. The damned trembling had started up again, she thought dispassionately. She didn't look over at him as she spoke, her voice sounding too loud in the silence.

"So I was right, this afternoon when I ran out on my wedding."

Out of the corner of her eye she saw him glance at her, but he said nothing. Still not looking at him, she persisted, her tone slightly lower.

"I thought I was seeing a ghost—a dead man—but deep inside I knew it was really you, and that somehow you were alive. And I was right all along."

"You were right," he said evenly. "But what you don't know is—"

"Then why did you lie to me?"

Now she did face him, turning toward him so swiftly that her hair swung in blunt spears against her cheeks. Her hands were no longer in her lap, but clenched into fists by her thighs.

"Why did you lie to me? Why did you walk away, letting me believe I'd made a terrible *mistake*—a mistake that no sane person would make? Why did you walk away from me, letting me think you were a complete stranger, a stranger I'd never see again?"

It was funny, she thought with a detached part of her mind. For most of this day her tears had been either threatening, spilling over or being held back. Now it seemed they'd completely dried up. She'd cried a damn river over Seamus Malone the past two years.

She didn't feel like crying over him anymore.

Slowly she unclenched her fists, and let out the breath

she'd been unconsciously holding. Her tone almost conversational, she asked him the two most important questions of all.

"Why did you let me think you were dead, Malone? And just where the hell have you been since I buried you?"

Chapter Six

He was in the bathroom. He'd been in there since they'd arrived, and that had been ten minutes ago. She could hear water running in the sink, and an occasional clinking noise, as if something metallic was being tapped against the porcelain rim of the basin. He was shaving off the last of that disreputable beard, Ainslie supposed.

Except what he was really doing was stalling.

He hadn't answered any of her questions in the car. In fact, he'd gone on to plant new ones in her mind by bringing her here. This apartment was his, obviously. The building itself was small and slightly run-down, and although the apartment was scrupulously neat, there was little in it but the bare necessities—some ugly furniture, a lamp or two, a kettle sitting on the stove in the galley-style kitchen. But it was his. He kept personal possessions here, because before disappearing into the bathroom he'd changed out of the hospital scrubs and into jeans and a sweatshirt. He'd seen her raised eyebrows at his attire, but he'd remained silent.

She could wait, Ainslie thought coldly. The man couldn't hide away from her forever.

But of course, that was exactly what he'd been doing for the past two years.

She heard the water being turned off in the bathroom and felt herself tense.

While she'd been grieving, he'd apparently been creating a new life for himself, right here in Boston. She had no idea how he'd obtained the ID and references he'd shown her earlier, but his stories of crewing on a salvage ship in Florida and working in a garage in Idaho had to be part of his inexhaustible supply of lies.

But just how inexhaustible were those lies? And had they started today, or when she'd known him? His reticence about himself hadn't seemed evasive while they'd been together, but in the bleak months that had followed she'd realized just how little she'd actually known about him.

Sully had been no help. He and Malone had been casual acquaintances only, she'd learned, with some business connections in common. Despite his obvious sympathy when she'd come to him with her questions a month or so after the funeral, her half brother had seemed uneasy about the subject, but that had been understandable. Any business contacts that might have existed between Sullivan Investigations and a man who worked for a government agency had probably been highly confidential.

That hadn't been the kind of information she'd wanted anyway. She'd wanted to know who his friends had been, how he'd gotten into his line of work. Malone had told her that he'd been raised in an orphanage, yet she'd wondered if he had any family, however far-flung, still living.

Like Sully, Malone's partner, when she'd asked him questions, had been bound by a code of silence. But as with Sully, she'd had the impression that there was little Paul Cosgrove could have told her about Malone even if he had been free to talk. She'd known at the time that the two of them had only recently been partnered.

Of course, Paul had lied to her, too, she thought stonily. He'd told her he'd been there when Malone had been killed. He'd told her he'd seen his partner's dead body. He'd stood beside her at that farce of a funeral. All the while he'd known that the man she'd been grieving over was walking around alive and well somewhere.

There was a certain irony to the situation. The man she'd thought she'd known had turned out never to have existed. He hadn't needed to fake his own death to turn into a ghost. He'd always been one.

Even as the notion crossed her mind he walked into the room, looking solidly real. Real, and disconcertingly like the man she'd fallen in love with so long ago, she thought with an unwilling ache. The beard was gone. The hair that had fallen past the shoulders of the derelict's tattered coat this afternoon now brushed the nape of his neck. It was still too shaggy, and even as she watched he wiped impatiently at a stray strand that had fallen into his eyes, but he was recognizably Malone again.

Whoever Malone was.

"So tell me, Lee—who was the man you came so close to marrying today?"

Crossing to the window, he stood to one side of the drapes, parting them slightly and glancing cautiously out onto the street. He let the drapes close and turned to face her. Ainslie gazed calmly at him.

"No, Malone, that's not the way we're going to play this game. I get to ask the questions. You get to try to lie your way out of them." Her smile was humorless. "You know, this isn't the way I used to imagine this miraculous reunion. Is this how you used to think it would be, coming back to me?"

"I never thought about it." His reply was clipped to the

point of harshness, and at it she felt as if she'd been sucker-punched.

A moment ago she'd been thinking of him as a ghost, she thought numbly. But she'd been wrong. A ghost would at least hold some echo of the man he had once been. She never *had* known the real Seamus Malone.

"So nothing was ever true." Her words were edged with pain, but behind the pain anger flickered and grew. "Tell me, Malone, have you ever been even a *little* bit honest with me?"

"I've been as honest with you as I know how to be." His tone was still devoid of any emotion, but as he spoke she saw a muscle twitch at the side of his jaw.

"Have you?" Her coolness was becoming harder to sustain. "Let's look at that, shall we? We'll skip the really big stuff for now—you know, like setting up a damn funeral for yourself and disappearing off the face of the earth. How about just concentrating on what you told me today? How *is* the salvage business down in Florida, anyway? Or the garage business in Idaho?" She saw him blink, but his expression remained grimly remote. "Or what about the phony ID you shoved at me, with the name John Smith plastered all over it. Was that being *honest?* Was that your conception of being *up front* with me?"

"Back off, Lee." The hard light in his eyes intensified, and his warning came out in a hoarse mutter. "It was all true. John Smith *was* my name, as far as—"

"*Stop* it, Malone! Just stop the *lying!*"

Jumping to her feet, she covered the distance between them in two swift strides, all attempts at detachment abandoned. Grabbing the front of his sweatshirt in both of her fists, she brought her face close to his.

"Sully thinks you're involved in drug dealing. Is that what this was all about? Is that why you had to disappear, why you've got identification in another name, why you're running for your *life?*"

With every unanswered question, her tight grip on his shirt jerked him closer.

"Did the Agency you worked for find out you were dirty, and go along with that faked funeral rather than letting it get out that one of their people had betrayed them? Am I getting close to the truth, Malone? Am I even *warm?*"

Her voice rose and cracked on the last few words. She still had a few tears left out of that river, she realized with quick chagrin, feeling them wet her cheeks but not bothering to dash them away.

His mouth was only inches from hers, so close that she could see a tiny scar on his bottom lip, so close that she found herself taking in the very scent of his skin. Beneath her clenched fists she felt the beat of his heart against the solid wall of his chest, felt the rise and fall of his breathing. As their gazes locked and held—hers spilling over with frustration, his dark with something that looked like anger—she could see every single shade of green in those unreadable eyes, could practically feel the spiky sweep of those thick, black lashes.

His jaw tightened. He inhaled sharply.

"I'll tell you everything, dammit."

His voice was so low it was little more than a harsh whisper. Under the hoarseness was the barest spark of emotion, but it flowed to her and back to him again like an arcing, uncontrolled current. The light behind those brilliant eyes caught, was instantly banked, and then flared fully into heat.

"I'll tell you it all in a second, Lee. But this has to come first."

His hands came up and cupped the sides of her face, his

thumbs slicking tightly over the wetness of her tears. His lashes flicked to the high ridge of his cheekbones, a small sound of impatient defeat rasped from the back of his throat, and he brought his mouth down hard onto hers.

Immediate desire slammed through her with the force of a body blow.

This wasn't how she'd imagined it would be, Ainslie thought with white-hot clarity as she felt her lips part under his, felt him move farther into her with no warning at all. She'd dreamed of this a thousand times, and he had always come to her slowly. *Tenderly.* He'd touched her face, touched her hair, traced the line of her lips with the softest of kisses, and then gradually taken his kiss deeper, his tempo perfectly attuned to hers.

Whether or not that considerate dream lover had any existence in reality, she didn't know. But he wasn't in this room with her right now. This Malone was someone she'd never dreamed of at all, or if she had, she'd buried those feverish dreams somewhere deep in her subconscious, rather than admit to herself that her desires could be so dark.

This wasn't how she'd imagined it in the past. But this was how she needed it to be now.

She felt his mouth move greedily against hers, felt him impatiently taste the soft underside of her lips, felt his hands spread wide and tighten against the back of her head. He pulled her to him even closer, his mouth opened wider, and against her cheek she felt the sharp spikiness of those dense, fanned lashes.

And she moved into him.

Immediately her need escalated past desire, past hunger, past want, and into a pitch-black realm of elemental sensation. Images flew across the unlit expanse of her consciousness—dark images, unidentifiable images, images that came and disappeared so quickly that she was left with only shockingly fragmented impressions.

Her palms slid damply down the well-worn softness of his sweatshirt to his jeans, and then slipped up and under, her fingertips splaying against the coarse arrow of hair on his stomach. She spread them farther, slid them higher, pushing his shirt up until she could feel the moist heat of his bare skin against her.

She wanted to *take* him. The thought spilled through her mind with a raw bluntness that was utterly unlike her, but its very crudity was apt. She wanted to take him, wanted to bring them both to their knees right here and now, wanted to urge him over the far edge of need. She didn't want to sink onto a bed with him, didn't want cool sheets and soft pillows beneath them, didn't want to make love to him.

She wanted to overwhelm him. She wanted to blot out everything else in his mind until all that existed for him was the way she tasted, the way she felt, her mouth on his body.

She pulled back slightly from his kiss, and flicked her tongue lightly at the edge of his bottom lip, licking it slowly and then moving past it to the still slightly stubbled line of his jaw. She heard him catch his breath and hold it. Beneath her outspread hands the muscles in his chest tensed. She ran her tongue back up to his mouth, gently took the fullness of his lower lip between her teeth, and lightly bit down.

The breath he'd been holding came out in a harsh gasp. A convulsive tremor ran through him, as if whatever remaining bonds of self-control that had bound him had suddenly frayed and snapped. Ainslie felt that same tremor race through her. Whatever he needed, she thought faintly, closing her eyes and pressing a kiss to the corner of the lip she'd just nipped. Whatever he needed of her he could have. Whatever he needed, she needed, too.

"Aw, hell," he whispered hoarsely against her mouth. "I wanted to be smart about this, but I'd rather be stupid right now."

"I don't want smart, either," she murmured dazedly, finding it almost impossible to string the words together coherently.

A moment later all coherent thought fled for good as he shifted slightly and she felt him, hard and more than ready, against her thigh. Liquid desire rushed through her and for a second it seemed that his hold on her was all that was keeping her upright.

And then he pulled back, drawing in a short, shallow breath.

"Good, honey," he said raggedly. "Because with me smart obviously isn't what you get. We've got to talk. I'm in bad trouble, and it looks like I've dragged you into it, too. I have to figure out some way to get you to safety."

Her eyes flew open in disbelief. Staring up at him, she saw dull color ridge the lines of his cheeks. The pulse at the side of his throat was still rapid, and his lips, the bottom one slightly swollen, were still parted, as if his body hadn't yet completely disengaged from their kiss. But even as she watched, the hard color faded and his mouth tightened to a grim line.

Letting her hands fall to her sides, she stepped abruptly away from him, feeling as though the heat inside her had just been doused with a bucket of freezing water.

"I think you're pretty smart, Malone. You know how to avoid giving me any straight answers, at least, but I'm not going anywhere until I get them." She folded her arms across her chest, willing herself not to tremble. "So am I close? *Did* the Agency find out you'd become involved in something dirty, and wash their hands of you?''

''Close enough,'' he said stonily, his eyes on hers. ''I think you've got to be pretty damn near to the truth, actually.''

Bile rose swiftly in her throat, and she fought to keep it down. She didn't believe it, she thought. She *wouldn't* have believed it—if it had come from anyone else. But why would the man damn himself in such a terrible way if it wasn't true?

''Sully was right, then. This was about drugs.'' Her voice sounded rusty and strange to her ears. ''That's why they're after you.''

She turned, not wanting to look at him for one second longer. When she felt his hand grip her shoulder she stiffened.

''I don't know *what* they want me for, dammit!'' His grip was painful enough that she was forced to face him. His gaze, as it met hers, was dark with anger. ''But it isn't drugs, for God's sake. If I thought I had that kind of blood on my hands, I'd give myself over to them willingly.''

Relief flooded through her; close on its heels came confusion. ''Then I don't understand.'' She searched his features, her expression anguished. ''Who's trying to kill you? And after all we were to each other—after what I *thought* we were to each other—why couldn't you let me know you were alive?''

Her voice faltered, and pain flashed across his face.

''I said I'd tell you everything,'' he said softly. ''And I will, starting with the night I left. But I want you to know right from the start that I didn't put you through this deliberately, Lee. What I told you earlier was true—Seamus Malone died the night he walked out of your arms.''

She felt the anger spark inside of her again, and this

time she didn't try to hide it. "I'm from the same background as you are, Malone, so cut the cryptic Irish crap. Dead man walking—is that what you're trying to tell me? Because a couple of minutes ago I could have sworn I felt a pulse."

A corner of his mouth lifted wryly. "You felt more than a pulse, honey." His grin faded. "Lee, I'm beating around the freakin' bush because I know you're not going to buy this. But from that night to just after I left you today, my memory's been a complete blank. I didn't know my name, where I'd lived, why I was being hunted. And all I knew about you was that when I saw your face in my dreams, it felt as if I was being torn in two."

"You're right, Malone. I don't buy it," she said in flat disbelief. "This isn't a soap opera. People don't just get amnesia for no reason at—"

"I was shot that night. It was a head wound." His voice was tense. "I don't know what you were told, but Paul and I walked into an ambush that night. We were supposed to meet an informant, and instead we found ourselves pinned in an alley, being shot at by a sniper on a roof. Cosgrove probably didn't make it, and I only survived through sheer luck and the skill of the surgeon who operated on me."

"Paul made it." Her knees suddenly weak, Ainslie sank down onto the sofa behind her, her gaze not leaving his face. "Paul didn't get a scratch. He went to your funeral. He told me he saw you die."

"I see."

His voice was carefully toneless, his expression blankly unreadable. Then Ainslie saw him suddenly flinch. He pressed the heel of his left hand to his eye, as if to block some terrible pain, as she remembered him doing earlier.

She half rose, intending to go to him, but he shook his head at her.

"That wasn't a bad one." He took his hand away and sighed. Walking over to a small table on the far side of the room, he picked up the wooden chair that was shoved carelessly against it. Bringing it back to where she was, he plunked it down in front of her and straddled it backward, his forearms resting along the chipped wood of the rail, his wrists hanging loosely.

"For about six months after the shooting, the pain was so bad I thought I'd go crazy. It's been building again lately, but today it came back in full force."

"Do you have any medication for it?"

"Yeah. But I won't take it unless I have to." His eyes darkened in memory. "Like I said, I was rushed into surgery. From what you just told me, Paul had to be responsible for getting me there. I came to in a private hospital room—or, at least, that's where I figured I was. There was an intravenous drip beside the bed, and my head was bandaged up. About three seconds after I opened my eyes I realized I had no idea who I was."

From the street outside came sudden shouts, and Ainslie saw him tense and grip the chair back. A girl's high, teasing laughter mingled with the other voices, and a moment later there was the sound of a car driving away. Malone relaxed.

"Nothing else that's happened since came anywhere close to terrifying me as much as I was at that moment. The door to the room was open just enough so I could hear two men talking out in the hall. I was about to call out to them—I knew I'd been in an accident of some sort, and I guess I was hoping that someone could fill in the blanks for me—when I caught what they were saying." His smile was tight. "I was wrong just now. *That* was the worst moment. They were arguing over the best way to kill me and dispose of my body.''

Ainslie's hands flew to her mouth. ''Dear God! Are you sure you heard them right?'' She shook her head immediately. ''But of course, you must have.''

''I heard them right. And besides, their agenda's still the same.'' He shrugged. ''Anyway, through some miracle I got away from them that night. The details are pretty hazy, but I remember cold-cocking a male nurse and taking his clothes, and then something about a laundry chute. I got a couple of blocks away from the hospital—not the same one as tonight, by the way—and then I must have collapsed. I didn't regain consciousness that second time for nearly a week, and when I did I found myself looking up into the face of the most beautiful woman I'd ever seen.''

Ainslie blinked. Then she managed a smile. ''You must have thought you were in heaven,'' she said with a touch of stiffness. Watching her, Malone gave her his first real grin of the evening.

''Honey, she was about sixty-five, more than plump, with a face like one of those dried-apple dolls. And she was still gorgeous to me.'' He sobered. ''Her name was Anna—Anna Nguyen. She was from Vietnam. She told me she knew a man on the run when she saw one. She'd found me on the street outside her grocery business, and somehow she'd hauled me inside to the little apartment she lived in at the back of the store. She said the police had come around a day later, asking if anyone had seen someone going by my description. She'd lied and said no. When I asked her why she'd taken such a risk for a stranger, she told me that forty years ago men in uniform had taken away her father and her brother, and she'd never seen them alive again. She didn't trust uniforms, she said.''

''She saved your life.'' It was hard to speak past the

sudden lump in her throat. "I'd like to meet her one day. You're right—she must be a beautiful woman."

"She was." His glance had fallen to his hands, still resting along the edge of the chair back. He looked up and met her gaze. "When I came back to Boston several weeks ago I went to see her. Her grandson told me she died last year."

He was silent for a minute, lost in his thoughts.

Silent herself, Ainslie studied him. Even discounting the beard and the hair and the clothes he had been wearing when she'd first seen him, it wasn't so impossible to understand her earlier confusion as to his identity. His ordeals had left their mark on him. His face was leaner, its angles harder. He'd always been tautly muscled, but now that muscle was even bulkier. The sleeves of his sweatshirt were pushed up, revealing the weight and broadness of his forearms and wrists, and the seams of the shirt pulled tautly across his shoulders.

But most noticeable of all was the air of strained alertness about him—the same air of tense desperation that an animal forced to flee for its life might have, she thought, like a timber wolf or a cougar or any other predator with a bounty on its hide.

He'd been a hunter. Now he was the hunted.

She caught herself. Malone was being hunted now, yes, but he hadn't been the one doing the hunting before. She'd never known much about his work for the Agency, but he'd stressed to her that it consisted mainly of tedious routine. Sullivan had been a hunter. Her father, who'd also been a mercenary and who'd died in battle, had been a hunter. Their lifestyles of war and death and violence had been repellent and incomprehensible to her, which was why Malone's reassurances about what he did for a living had so relieved her, and why she'd had no inkling, the night he'd left her, that he might be going to his death.

But there was still too much he hadn't explained.

"Even today you insisted you were someone called John Smith." She frowned. "You seemed convinced of that."

"I was." He lifted his shoulders in an absently weary gesture. "Anna Nguyen said that was the name of the man the police were searching for. They left a copy of the artist's sketch with her to put up in her store, and it was me, all right, so I assumed that was my name. I got the ID later, through unofficial channels, and John Smith was ordinary enough so that I didn't feel I had to change it."

"You worked under that name down in Florida and out in Idaho?" His litany of jobs had been a minor part of his story, but for some reason, finding out that they really had existed was important.

"And in about ten other states." He took a ragged breath. "Sometimes only for a week or so, sometimes long enough so that I'd start to feel safe. But however long it took, each time the day would come when something would alert me to the fact that they were closing in on me. A waitress at a coffee shop would tell me that some old friends of mine had been in, asking about me, or I'd answer the phone at work and get a dial tone after I said hello."

"That's why you had the hotel rigged up the way you did," Ainslie said flatly. "The lights, the signals, the booby traps."

His eyes remained shadowed. "Yeah, but today it almost wasn't enough, or maybe my reflexes weren't working the way they should. Like I said, the pain had come back so bad I wasn't thinking straight. By the time I left you in the parking garage, I barely had time to make it to another hideout before I passed out."

His tone was so matter of fact, he could have been talking about the weather, but Ainslie wasn't fooled. How much sheer strength and dogged determination had it taken for him to get her to safety today? she wondered. Would any other man have been capable of managing that hair-raising, split-second escape while coping with the twin burdens of excruciating pain and an unforeseen, unwilling companion?

"I must have been unconscious for an hour or so." He still sounded detached, but the edginess had returned to his voice. "When I came to, the pain was almost completely gone. On top of that, a big chunk of my memory had returned. I knew who I was, who you were, and why I'd felt compelled to come back to Boston. I knew about the existence of this apartment, where I'd hidden the key to it, and that both the rent on it and on the garage where I kept a vehicle would have been automatically taken out of an account for the past two years, although I couldn't remember setting the arrangements up and I had no idea why I would have done such a thing. I even knew why it had been so important to me to search the newspapers every day while I'd been on the run."

"The newspapers? Why? What were you looking for?" Ainslie stared at him. Everything he was telling her was confusing, but this last made no sense at all.

"News of you, Lee." His expression was grim. "Any news of you I could find, although I didn't know it at the time. But that must have been how I knew to be at the church today—I had to have seen an announcement of the wedding."

"But why?" She heard the tremor in her voice, and controlled it. "You didn't even remember who I was at that point. Why would you be looking for any mention of a woman whose name would have meant nothing to you?"

"I don't know." He raked back his hair in a suddenly frustrated gesture. "Dammit, there's still too much I don't know, and I'm not even sure where to look for the answers. But I think I came back to Boston for the same reason I had to show up at your wedding today, Lee." He met her eyes, and the gaze he turned on her held the same anguish she'd seen from the steps of St. Margaret's that afternoon.

"They've been hunting me all this time, and they couldn't catch me. I think they've given up. I think they're after you now."

Chapter Seven

Ainslie rose swiftly from the sofa, pressing her palms against her jeans. Needing suddenly to do something—anything—to dispel the irrational dread spreading through her, she strode toward the window. Out there was the normal world, she told herself forcefully—*her* world. Malone's world might include mysterious enemies who were hunting him down for no reason at all, but her world didn't.

"Don't open the drapes."

His warning was so harsh that she jumped. Then she spun around, her nerves strained past the breaking point, but as she looked at him her retort died in her throat.

His features were etched with sharp fear—fear for *her*. He'd been able to live with the knowledge that he himself was in danger, she thought slowly. It was tearing him apart that now she could be, too. For no reason at all, she remembered the way he'd kissed her this afternoon, when he'd still thought he was John Smith, and that he would never see her again.

That kiss had had his soul in it. And whether he'd known it or not at the time, it had been Malone's soul he'd been handing her. A few minutes ago she'd told herself that this wasn't the way she'd imagined him coming back to her, and it wasn't...but the circumstances weren't important.

He *was* back—back from the dead, back from the grave, back in her life again. Nothing else mattered. And whatever his world included was part of her world, too.

Except now they were fighting his enemies together—and she was pretty sure she knew who at least one of those enemies was. She walked back to the sofa.

"Paul lied about your death. That means he has to be part of this—that the damn *Agency* has to be part of this, and that it's you they want, not me." A note of anger crept into her voice. "You had to have stumbled upon something that you weren't supposed to know, Malone. They're not targeting you because they found out you were dirty, they're targeting you because you found out *they* were. What the hell did you learn that made you so dangerous to them?"

Green eyes clouded, and then his gaze slid away from her. Abruptly he stood, pushing the chair aside and jamming his hands into his back pockets.

"I don't know." His words were clipped. "Look, Lee—there's a good possibility I'll never get everything back. Yeah, I remember our time together, every minute of it. I remember bits and pieces of my last couple of weeks at the Agency, but most of that's foggy. Anything prior to meeting you is still almost a complete blank, like what it was about my lifestyle that made it seem natural to me to have set up a safe house like this for myself. At best it's like a collection of snapshots that don't mean a thing to me—quick pictures of places I don't recall visiting, faces of people I must have once known."

Briefly he closed his eyes, as if by sheer will he could force his past to resurface. Or as if he was trying desperately to keep it submerged, Ainslie thought suddenly.

She thrust the foolish notion aside. "Then we'll start with Paul," she said firmly. "We'll go see him tonight."

He looked up at her quickly. "No. I don't want you any more involved than you already are. I brought this on you—this, and everything else. I never should have come into your life." His eyes searched hers. "You said you put roses on my grave. You shouldn't have had to go through that."

"Red roses," she agreed steadily. "Red roses for true love, Malone. Even if you'd never come back to me, I wouldn't have regretted a single moment of loving you."

She saw him start to take a step toward her, and then check himself. He shook his head. "Maybe not. But today you had a chance to make a new life for yourself, and instead I dragged you into my nightmare again. At the very least they want to use you as a way of drawing me out. It was you they followed to the hospital this evening."

"You don't know that, Malone—" she began, but he interrupted her.

"I looked up your brother's number in the phone book and called his house, saying I was an old friend of Sully's who'd blown into town. The woman who answered said his wife had just gone into labor and he'd rushed her to the hospital. I figured you'd show up sooner or later, so I was waiting for you and I saw you arrive, but before your taxi had a chance to drive away, two men pulled up behind it. One of them got out and talked to your cabbie for a minute. They must have been the orderlies you saw on the maternity ward."

"So two men drove up behind my cab," Ainslie said shortly. "Maybe it was a coincidence, for God's sake."

"It's never a coincidence." Finally crossing the space between them, he took her hands in his and pulled her from her perch on the arm of the sofa. "I've answered your questions. Now I want an answer to the one I asked you. The man you were supposed to marry today—who is he? Does he know why you ran out on the wedding?''

''His name's Pearson McNeil.'' Ainslie tried to pull her hands away, but he held them tight. ''And yes, I talked to him afterward. He said until I finally laid you to rest, I wouldn't be able to start over with someone else. He was...he was very sweet about it.'' She looked down at her feet, the memory of her meeting with Pearson still an unhappy one.

''He sounds like a good man.'' Transferring both her hands to one of his, he tipped her face up, forcing her to meet his gaze. ''I think you should take his advice, Lee. I've been dead for two years. Bury me again. Build a life with your Pearson, and forget that I ever came back.''

She stared at him in disbelief. ''But you did.''

''And maybe I shouldn't have.'' Finally releasing her, he swept an encompassing glance around the sparsely furnished room, the tightly closed drapes at the window. ''If you're married to someone else, they'll leave you alone, Lee. They'll know whatever connection there once was between us no longer exists.''

''And they'll be wrong. *You're* wrong, if you think that.''

There was no heat in her tone, but her chin lifted. ''I'd already decided to tell Pearson our marriage was off for good before I met you at the hospital tonight. Even death hadn't been able to destroy what I felt for you, and I knew that however long I lived, and whoever else came into my life, nothing ever could.'' At her sides, her hands curled into fists. ''The connection *exists,* dammit. It'll *always* exist, on your part as well as mine. They took away your memories, but they couldn't completely erase me from your mind, could they?''

"No, they couldn't do that." His smile didn't reach his eyes. "Whatever else they do to me, they'll never be able to do that. But maybe one day you'll want to sever that connection yourself, Lee. Maybe one day you'll realize that even though it existed, the man it bound you to never really did."

"Because you can't remember your past?" She took in his tensely watchful stance and the tight set of his mouth, and her voice softened. "It has to be hell for you, Malone. But I *knew* the man I fell in love with—knew him right down to the depths of his soul. And even if your memory never comes completely back, I'm not worried that there's something hidden there that would turn me against you."

His gaze held hers. "Still a fighter, aren't you, Lee? I should have known you wouldn't give up on me."

"Once a boxer, always a boxer," she agreed evenly. "It takes a knockout punch to put me down for good, Malone. Nothing less ever took me out."

"You're a tough one, O'Connell." He reached out and gently tucked a blunt section of hair behind her ear. "You know, when I saw you in that alleyway today, for a minute I thought you weren't real. You looked like a princess."

"Come off it, Seamus." She felt a sudden prickling behind her eyelids. "The dress was awful."

"The dress was awful," he agreed, his smile one-sided. "But you were beautiful. I was almost afraid to touch you."

"John Smith did more than touch me," she said softly. "What was going through his mind when he kissed me, Malone?"

"Oh, I don't know." His gaze was pensive, and his hand still rested on her hair. She could feel him idly twining a strand around one finger. "That you were proof the world wasn't all violence and fear. That your eyes were as blue as a summer evening. That he wished he was the man you thought he was."

He let her hair untwine from his finger. "That he knew he wasn't."

For a long moment the two of them stood, a hand span apart, their eyes on each other, and neither of them saying anything.

They didn't need words, Ainslie thought, drinking in the sight of him. Words were for other people, not for them. They'd always known what was in each other's heart.

She shifted slightly, and slowly he let his hand drop to her shoulder. His gaze, which only a moment ago had been so open she'd felt she could see through it to his innermost thoughts, became once more opaquely unreadable. A muscle in his jaw moved.

"You're right, of course," he said expressionlessly. "Paul was my partner. If anyone can give us some answers, he can."

He walked over to the small table, and picked up the set of keys he'd thrown on its surface when they'd arrived. He tossed them in his hand, once, and then she saw the broad shoulders under the dark sweatshirt stiffen in resolution. He shot her a tight smile.

"So let's go ask the man some questions," he said shortly, turning to the door. He opened it for her.

"And let's pray we can live with the answers," he added in an undertone as she preceded him out into the hall.

SHE HADN'T SAID MUCH since they'd left the apartment, but once or twice Seamus had felt her glance his way. He'd returned her glances, and in the dark interior of the car had seen the gleam of passing lights pick out an answering light in her eyes, had seen the slow curve of her smile. He'd forced himself to return her smiles.

He didn't feel like smiling. He didn't want to be doing this. He had the feeling that pretty soon everything was going to go down, and go down bad. He turned off the main thoroughfare, slowing a few minutes later to make a second turn.

Paul had joked once about being the complete suburbanite, with the gas barbecue, the split-level, ranch-style house, the ruler-straight landscaping that was indistinguishable from every other house on his block. His joke had been self-deprecating, but his smile had been that of a man who was completely content with his life. At the time, Malone had envied him. He didn't now.

He was about to blast Paul Cosgrove's safe and ordinary little world into so many pieces that all that would be left after tonight would be a smoking ruin. If his ex-partner was lucky, tomorrow morning he might be left standing in the middle of it.

Nausea rose in his throat. The scar on the side of his head throbbed. He took his foot off the gas and let the nondescript Ford coast past neat lawns, most of them raked clear of fallen leaves. This was the American dream, he thought bleakly, or at least one facet of it. He was the nightmare.

"We're probably going to wake him up, Malone." Beside him Ainslie was peering doubtfully at the passing houses.

"Yeah, it looks like we will." She was obviously trying to keep her tone conversational, but he'd heard the unsteadiness in her voice. He forced his own to remain unconcerned, wondering if this would be the final time anything he might do would be capable of allaying her fears. "Folks go to bed at a decent hour around here, city girl."

He heard her quick laugh, and despite the circumstances, his heart did a foolish little flip-flop in his chest. His right hand tightened on the steering wheel, and with his left he felt surreptitiously for the automatic he kept beside the driver's side door.

What he'd told her had been the truth—he *did* remember every single moment of their time together. It had been the closest to heaven he supposed he was ever going to get.

And it had all been built upon a lie, because if she'd known the truth about him at the start, she would have shown him the barest of social courtesies.

Sullivan had known, of course. Since then he apparently hadn't found it necessary to reveal to his sister that the man she grieved over hadn't been what she'd thought he was. Malone didn't know whether he was grateful for Sully's reticence or not, but he knew one thing for sure.

If Terrence Sullivan had ever even suspected the real truth about his sometime buddy and possible future brother-in-law, he would have taken Malone out, or died trying.

You don't know for sure, he told himself bleakly, easing off on the gas as he saw Paul's house just ahead. *You don't know anything for sure, dammit, because you can't remember.*

Except that, too, was a lie. He had one startling clear and horrific memory, and it was enough to tip the balance between faint hope and cold certainty. And if it wasn't, Paul would soon fill in the blanks.

"There's a light on inside, Seamus. I hope Celeste isn't still up."

As he pulled over to the curb, Ainslie fumbled with her seat belt. Her hands were shaking, he noted.

"Sorry." Her voice was curt, but he knew her curtness

wasn't directed at him. "I'm nervous. This...this isn't going to be pleasant."

"No." He hoped his own edginess wasn't showing. "But I didn't see any suspicious traffic in the area, so I think we're safe enough."

"That's not the part that's bothering me. After your funeral, Paul was the only one I felt understood what I was going through. He held me in his arms and let me cry until I couldn't cry any more. I didn't stay in contact with him, but I never forgot the kindness and compassion he'd shown me." Her voice hardened. "He knew all the time. He knew at the *funeral,* damn him."

If Paul's betrayal could pierce her so deeply, how would she survive the next few minutes? Malone thought in sudden despair. He couldn't *do* this to her. It would be better to not know for sure, to turn away from this quiet, ordinary house on this shadowed street, to get her to safety and then to get as far away from her as he could, never to see her again. He didn't need the confirmation he'd come here for. He knew what he was. He just didn't want to see that knowledge reflected in her eyes.

And that was the real reason he wanted to turn tail and run. Sick self-loathing washed over him. She needed to know. She needed to have her image of him destroyed so completely that the next time he was buried, not even the smallest fragment of her heart would be placed in the grave with him. The truth was going to set her free.

And it was going to condemn him.

"Paul knew," he agreed harshly. "But maybe he thought his silence would shield you, Lee."

"From what?"

He'd spoken too carelessly, he saw. His Lee—*I can think of her as mine for the next few seconds, at least,* he thought stubbornly—had a fighter's instincts. Her head had jerked up, her expression, as she looked sharply at him, held the faintest glimmer of alert suspicion. She could sense the blow coming, Malone thought. She just didn't realize yet that it was the knockout punch she'd spoken of earlier.

The one that'll take you out of my life for good, sweetheart, he told her silently. He shrugged, suddenly wanting to get this over with.

"That's what we're here to find out. Let's go."

There was a dim bulb shedding feeble yellow light at the side entrance of the house, located just before the set-back garage. Making a quick decision, Malone nodded at Ainslie.

"Not the front door. It's too exposed. We'll be out of sight from the street here."

Accepting his whispered command, she fell into step beside him, and almost immediately stumbled over a crack in the paved walk that paralleled the drive. He caught her arm, and she glanced gratefully at him.

"He's the only one who hasn't raked his leaves," she said in an undertone. She frowned. "Watch those poles."

He'd seen them already, carelessly heaped at the side of the house, some of them partially obstructing the driveway. They were long metal tubes, and even in the poor light it was possible to see that they were painted in bright shades of orange and green. Tangled in a heap across them were lengths of steel chain.

Ainslie paused. She nudged one of the chains with her sneaker-clad toe, and then looked up at him, her brow clearing.

"It's just a swing set," she said softly, a hint of rueful amusement in her voice. "It must belong to..." The slight smile disappeared from her lips and her expression became stricken. "They've got a little boy, Malone. I'd forgotten."

He could feel the solid weight of the gun in the small of his back, where he'd snugged it in the waistband of his jeans. He looked away from the swing set.

"It's too late for him to be up, Lee. All we're going to do is talk to his father, and then leave."

"And Celeste's a teacher. She's probably asleep, too, by now." She sounded as if she were trying to reassure herself, but she moved past the pile of metal without further comment.

Either Paul wasn't the complete suburbanite he'd claimed to be, or he'd let things slide lately, Malone thought cynically, avoiding a dislodged chunk of ornamental edging. He raised his hand to knock on the paint-peeling side door.

"No." Ainslie touched his arm. "He might panic if he sees you. Stay out of sight until he opens the door."

She was right—probably more right than she knew. If what he feared proved to be true—*and it will,* he told himself coldly, *you know damn well it will*—then Paul's reaction would be far past panic. He would know immediately, and with hopeless, doomed certainty, that Malone was there for one reason only.

Melting into the shadows a foot or so away, he reached around behind him and unobtrusively slid the gun from the waistband of his jeans. He snapped off the safety just as Ainslie's knuckles rapped firmly on the door.

"I can hear someone coming." She didn't turn to him as she spoke, but kept her eyes ahead and her voice low. "It sounds too heavy to be Celeste."

"As soon as I step forward, get out of the way."

This was it, Malone thought. This was the last moment that she would be his. This was the last moment of the love she'd told him would never die.

And then my soul, if I have one, will have lost the only

home it ever knew, he told her silently. *Your brother once told me he believed in myths, Lee. He thought that when a mercenary died, the wild geese that the Irish legends warn of would come down and take him with them, searching for all eternity to find redemption. But I don't believe in fairy tales. I just believe in hell.*

"My God—Ainslie?"

Through the aluminum screened door came Paul's voice, instantly recognizable even after all this time. But the sharpness of surprise in it was overlaid with a slight slur. His grip tightening on his weapon, Malone frowned.

"I know it's late, Paul." He saw Ainslie clasp her hands nervously in front of her, and knew the gesture wasn't an act. "It's unforgivable for me to show up here out of the blue like this after all this time, but I have to talk to you. It's...it's about Malone."

"Malone?" The slurred tone was gone. "Maybe you'd better come in." From his vantage point Malone saw the screened door swing open, saw Paul's arm, incongruously clad in a baggy plaid sleeve, holding it there. "What about Malone? Has someone been asking questions about him?"

Swiftly Malone stepped forward out of the shadows. "You could say that, Cosgrove." His voice sounded harsh, even to his own ears. The effect on the man in front of him was electric.

Paul's face was instantly ashen. His eyes widened in what looked like horror, and the skin over the dark cheekbones seemed suddenly stretched taut. He opened his mouth, but no words came out.

Beside him Malone heard Ainslie's quickly indrawn breath. She had been expecting some sort of reaction from Paul, but not this, he knew. He felt her confused gaze turn his way, but he kept his eyes on the man in the doorway.

Even as he watched, the dark eyes closed briefly, as if in acceptance, and the shoulders under the plaid robe sagged.

"You've come to kill me. I guessed you would someday." Paul's voice was flat. He opened his eyes and met Malone's gaze. "She knows nothing about it, I swear. I know you have no reputation for mercy, but she must have meant something to you once. Let her live. Kill me, but let her live."

"What's he *talking* about, Malone?" Ainslie's voice was tremulous with outrage. "'No reputation for mercy'? What's that supposed to mean?" She turned to Paul, still standing motionlessly in the doorway. "It's Malone, for God's sake! Who did you think it was? We just came to ask you some questions, Paul—you owe us that much, dammit!"

"She doesn't know?" Paul looked suddenly sick. His gaze searched Malone's.

"She doesn't know. And let's pretend I don't, either." Without warning, the pain stabbed once, cruelly, through his head, and Malone fought to keep his tone even. He made a small gesture with the gun. "So answer the lady's question, Cosgrove. Just who *do* you think I am?"

"I won't spend the last seconds of my life playing some stupid game with you." Paul's jaw tightened. "All the reports say that at least your kills are quick and clean. You can give me that, damn you."

"Who do you think I am? *What* do you think I am, Cosgrove?"

Malone felt rather than saw Ainslie take a small step away from him. She was half way gone, he thought dully. She proved him wrong immediately.

"He's stalling, Malone." Her words tumbled over one another. "Don't you see? He's using your amnesia against you, just like they've done from the start!"

"Amnesia? Dear God—so you really *don't* know." Paul's eyes widened again, this time with comprehension.

"I really don't know," Malone agreed evenly. "I'm pretty sure of what you're going to tell me, but I need to hear it. Who am I?"

There was no reply from his ex-partner, and suddenly he felt something inside him snap. In a blur of movement, he grabbed the lapels of the plaid robe, jerking the other man out of the doorway and bringing the gun up and under his chin.

"Who *am* I, goddammit?" he whispered hoarsely, his face only inches from Paul's. *"What the hell do you know about me?"*

"They...they call you the Executioner, you bastard. And every civilized government has a price on your head."

Paul's voice came out in a strangled, hate-filled croak. "You're a mercenary *assassin,* Malone—one of the most feared and loathed killers the world has ever known."

Chapter Eight

The man was crazy, Ainslie thought coldly, either that or he was following some twisted agenda of his own. And he was good. At his insane pronouncement, she'd stared at Malone in shock, seen the revulsion in his own face and had immediately known he was as sickened as she was by Cosgrove's lie.

She would *never* forgive Paul, she thought angrily.

As the three of them, herself bringing up the rear, walked down the basement stairs to what had to be the room Paul kept for his own personal use, she found it hard to reconcile the grimness of the situation with the mundane setting around them. A computer with a plastic dustcover pulled over it sat on a desk in the corner, and on the other side of the room were a sofa and a couple of easy chairs. Malone nodded at the sofa and, without protest, Paul dropped heavily down onto it.

"There's no chance we'll disturb Celeste or your son?" Malone asked, frowning.

Paul looked down at his hands, now clasped loosely between his knees. "No chance," he said tonelessly.

"Good. No matter what you choose to believe, Cosgrove, I'm not here to kill you. I just need information."

As Malone sat on the edge of the chair nearest to Paul,

Ainslie took the other one, first removing a crocheted afghan that was balled up on the seat. As she pulled it away she heard a clinking sound and looked down to see a bottle of vodka and a single tumbler.

Wordlessly she set them on the low table in front of the sofa. Paul's eyes met hers, and for a second she was taken aback by the deadness in his expression. Then her own hardened.

"Were you always a secret drinker, Paul?" She sat, her gaze flinty. "Or did you just start after the funeral, when your conscience started bothering you?"

"I started after the funeral, Ainslie."

His use of her name touched a reluctant chord in her. Had it all been an act? she wondered with a sudden, aching sadness. This man had been there to help her through that first terrible period of denial and grief. Was there any way he, too, had been duped by the same people who had turned Malone's life upside down?

She wished desperately that she could convince herself of that. But she couldn't.

He'd told her there had been a reason Malone's casket had been closed. He'd planted that horrifying image in her mind to bolster his assertion that he'd seen the lifeless body of the man she'd loved.

"You lied to me." Her voice shook with the intensity of her anger. "Why bother? Why did you go to such trouble to convince me beyond a doubt that you'd seen him dead? You had to attend the funeral, to keep up the Agency's pretence that he'd died in the line of duty, but there was no need for you to strike up a personal relationship with me. I was *nothing* to the Agency! Nothing I could have said would have raised any official doubts about his death, so why go to such lengths to convince me?"

"I wanted to destroy any hopes you might have had that there'd been a mistake. I never wanted you to think there was a possibility he had survived." Paul looked up from his clasped hands, his face carved in deep lines. "He'd already torn your life apart. There was nothing I could do about that—just like there was nothing I could do about the other innocent victims he'd destroyed. But I thought I could make sure that eventually you could pick up the pieces and start over."

"I see. You're still sticking with your cover story." Ainslie looked at him in frustration. "Maybe one day you'll know how I felt, watching the earth fall into the grave of the one I loved. Maybe one day *you'll* realize what that's like, Paul."

"Maybe, Ainslie." His eyes, slightly bloodshot from the alcohol, held hers and then slid away. "But you had the strength to get through it."

"If you wanted me dead so badly, why bother getting me to the hospital the night I was shot?" Malone's question broke into the brief silence that had fallen. "You could have had a real corpse on your hands easily enough, but instead you saved my life."

"I saved the life of my *partner.*" Paul's tone was harsh. "I saved the life of the man who'd been working the Executioner file with me, the man who'd been brought in because of his special knowledge of the killer. The Agency had only put the last pieces of the puzzle together earlier that day. The decision was made not to tell me that the man I was working with—the man I'd come to *like,* for God's sake—was the same murdering scum we'd been hunting for so long. They thought I might not be able to carry it off, and somehow you'd guess that your cover had been blown." He swallowed thickly. "They were right. If I'd known the truth about you, I wouldn't have been able to hide what I felt. I'd seen the photos. I'd read the reports."

He turned to Ainslie. "Do you know even yet what he is? What crimes he's committed?" A muscle bulged under the dark skin of his jaw. "He doesn't kill for money, he kills for the sport of it. And his kills are always carefully calculated to lead to more deaths—in some cases, genocide. He sees the world as his own private anthill, and he loves to watch what happens after he gives it one good kick."

Whatever he believed, it was the Executioner he was talking about, not the man she loved, Ainslie reminded herself forcefully. It seemed that Malone was content to let him go on, as long as they got the information they had come here for. She would follow his lead.

"You make him sound like the bogeyman," she said evenly. "Genocide? How could a lone assassin, no matter how inhuman, kill thousands?"

"Because he studies the anthill," Paul said with grim conviction. "He knows just where to place that single kick. A few years ago rumors began trickling out of an isolated jungle region in South America—rumors of a terrible tribal war that had flared out of control. When government troops were finally sent in, what they saw sickened even the toughest soldiers. Two complete cultures had been wiped out—right down to the children."

His gaze flicked to Malone. "And how many bullets did you have to expend to bring that about? Two, wasn't it? One for the young wife of one tribal leader, the other for the second tribe's most revered elder—because right at that moment, the political situation there only needed a spark to set it blazing out of control. You knew that, and you struck the match. Just like you struck it in the Balkans five years ago. Just like you struck it when you assassinated

Mocamba in Africa. Just like you struck it at least seven other times that we know of over the last ten years.''

He took a deep breath. With a detached part of her mind, Ainslie saw that his hands were trembling. ''You *are* the bogeyman,'' he said softly. ''I only wish the Agency sniper had aimed better that night in the alleyway.''

''So the Agency did sanction the hit. And when it went wrong, it went wrong all the way down the line.'' Malone shrugged tightly. ''The wound wasn't immediately fatal, and they'd made the mistake of keeping you out of the loop, so you got me to a hospital before they learned I was still alive. By the time they got their act together it was too late.''

''When the surgeon told me you were going to make it I was so relieved I could hardly get the words out to thank him. Then Watkins, our team leader, arrived. It was Noah who finally briefed me—told me how you'd infiltrated the Agency by coming to us and offering your expertise. All the while, you were monitoring the progress of the case against you.'' Paul's gaze darkened. ''After the alarm went out that you'd somehow escaped, I was one of the dozens combing the streets of Boston for you. You must have had the devil on your side that night.''

''Did you really expect me to lie helplessly in a hospital bed, waiting for a second bullet?'' For the first time Malone's tone held an edge of anger. ''Who was he, anyway? Someone I'd shaken hands with? Someone I'd *worked* with, dammit?''

''The sniper? If I knew I wouldn't tell you.'' Sinking back into the sofa, the agent looked at the gun in Malone's hand without interest. ''I hope they've made your life hell, Malone. They'll never rest until they stop you, and if it comes to a shootout, Ainslie stands a good chance of becoming the first casualty. Is that how you want it to end for her?"

"It's not going to end that way. But if it did, I'd rather go down fighting by the side of a man I believe in than turn my back on him and spend the rest of my life trying to dull my conscience any way I could." Unable to sit a moment longer, Ainslie stood, unsteady with outrage.

"You worked with Malone, Paul. You don't believe any of the lies you've just told us—you *can't!* Is it blind loyalty to the Agency that forces you to go along with this? Are you afraid you'll lose everything—your job, your pension, this house—if you stand up for the truth? Is *that* it?"

He smiled crookedly up at her. "The Agency can't take anything I care about away from me. I don't work for them anymore, Ainslie."

Leaning suddenly forward, he sunk his face into his hands, his shoulders bowed. His almost inaudible words were directed at the floor in front of him, as if nothing in the room held any interest for him anymore.

"He lied to you from the start, and God help me, I kept up the lie after the funeral. I didn't see any point in hurting you more than you'd been already. He was a mercenary, Ainslie—a mercenary who'd found that legitimate battle wasn't enough. His assignment with the Agency was only temporary. He didn't tell you that, did he?"

"No, I didn't tell her that, Cosgrove." Malone's voice was flat. "You're right, I lied to her. I guess I lied to her about nearly everything."

Ainslie glanced sharply over at him, disconcerted without knowing why. He was still attempting to play the other man along, she thought. That had to be what he was doing. His gaze met hers for the briefest of seconds, and then wavered.

He looked away.

"You're incredible, Cosgrove!" Her outburst was immediate, her tone halfway between a gasp and an angry little laugh. She didn't look again at Malone, but she directed her next words to him. "Whether Paul works for the Agency or not, they've obviously still got some kind of hold over him, Seamus, and he's never going to tell us the truth. Coming here was a waste of our time."

She turned stiffly, the need to leave suddenly urgent, and behind her she heard quick movement. She felt a hand on her arm, and broke her stride.

Malone was still sitting on the edge of the chair, his shoulders bowed. The hand on her arm belonged to Paul, and as she tried to wrench away from him his grip tightened.

"They don't have a hold over me. There's nothing left in my life that anyone could threaten to take away from me, Ainslie." He was wearing a worn T-shirt under the robe, and from its frayed collar his neck muscles stood out like cords. He looked suddenly much older than she'd thought he was.

"I don't care about the Agency. I don't care if I live or die. I'm the one person you can trust to tell you the truth, because I'm a man with no motivation to lie."

"How did they die, Paul?" As Malone met his expartner's gaze, his own was shadowed with sharp sadness. "What happened?"

Shocked, Ainslie stared at the man standing beside her, and suddenly everything fell tragically into place—the dismantled swing set, the general air of neglect about the home, even the solitary drinking.

She'd told him that one day he would feel what she'd felt. She wished with all her heart that she could take those words back.

"It was just before Thanksgiving last year." He could

have been talking to himself, his voice was so low. "They'd gone to visit her folks in New Hampshire. I couldn't get away from the office, but I told Celeste to take Robbie and to have a good time. They hit what the state police said was a patch of black ice on the way back, and the car slid right into an oncoming tractor-trailer. One of the cops from the highway patrol told me they wouldn't have even had time to realize what was happening."

"Oh, Paul, I'm so *sorry.*" Ainslie laid her hand on his. "I wish there was something I could do or say to help. But there isn't, is there?"

"No." Gently he released her. "Just like there's nothing I can say that can help you. But I think in your heart you know I've been telling you the truth."

"Whether she does or not, I do." A few feet away from them, Malone stood. "I wasn't sure before, and I guess I was hoping that you'd hand me a miracle, Cosgrove. But I wasn't really expecting one."

"You came back from the dead, and if what you're telling me is true, with your past erased." Paul's glance was quizzical. "Count that as your miracle, Malone. Who knows? Maybe you and Ainslie *will* disappear and make a new life somewhere where the Agency never finds you."

"I'll be turning myself in to the Agency tomorrow morning." Faint surprise colored Malone's answer. "Now that I know what I'm wanted for, I can't keep running. It's time to end this."

"You didn't do those things. Whatever Paul believes, he's wrong. The *Agency's* wrong." Ainslie stared at him in disbelief. "They've made a mistake, or someone's deliberately framed you. I know you, Malone—there's no *way* you could have done what they're accusing you of!"

"You don't know me at all, Lee. All you know is what I told you, and Paul's right." Malone's face was grim. "I was a soldier of fortune, just like Sully used to be. That's how I knew him. I'd only been attached to the Agency for a few weeks when we met."

"You're wrong. You don't know that, for God's sake—you *couldn't* know that for sure," she said automatically. "The amnesia—"

"I told you I remembered every minute of the time I had with you. I remember deliberately lying to you about what I did. I remember Sullivan telling me that you hated everything about the mercenary trade, and two seconds after you walked into my life, I knew I wasn't going to let you know that I was part of what you hated so much." Malone dragged in a shallow breath. "I told myself I couldn't risk losing you before I'd even had a chance with you. I'd probably do the same thing all over again, Lee."

"You...you *lied* to me? You were a mercenary, like Sullivan was? Like my *father* was?"

She fought for composure, but her limbs felt paralyzed with shock and all of a sudden the floor beneath her feet seemed dangerously uneven. Clutching the back of the nearest chair for balance, she grasped at the one truth she felt she could be certain of.

"So you weren't up front about being a mercenary," she said, her voice flat. "I don't think I'll ever forgive you for that, Malone, but it still doesn't change the fact that you're not the Executioner. Whoever he is, he's pure evil. A man like that can't hide what he is from the people around him—not for long, anyway."

"I think I got so good at hiding what I was that in the end I concealed it from myself," he said, so softly that she had to strain to hear him. His gaze was clouded and faraway, as if he were trying to see through a thick fog. "Except you're right—I couldn't bury it completely. I *know* I'm the Executioner, Lee."

He closed his eyes for a second, and as she saw his jaw tighten she knew he was riding out another wave of pain. Even so, when his gaze finally met hers again she was horrified by the expression in his eyes.

He looked like a dead man, she thought unwillingly—or a man who wished he was dead. And when he spoke, she knew why.

"I told you that I had flashes of memories of my life before I met you," he said harshly. "And one of the clearest is of killing Joseph Mocamba, the leader whose death unleashed so much violence and bloodshed that it almost destroyed a country."

AINSLIE WALKED into the apartment ahead of Malone, took a few more steps and then just stood in the middle of the living room floor, as if she could go no farther. From the radio on the nearby table came low but discordant late-night jazz, the music an unconscious echo of her own jumbled thoughts.

He'd warned her himself, earlier this evening, she thought numbly. He'd told her that the day might come when she would want to sever the connection between them because the man she'd thought she loved had never existed.

He'd been a mercenary like Sullivan, like her father, like other men she'd seen occasionally in the company of her brother—big men, men tanned by foreign suns, men who laughed and joked with Sully, but whose eyes always seemed to be seeing ghosts and shadows. She'd told Sullivan once that being with men like that made her feel as if *she* was the one fading away, and the surrounding shades becoming more real than she was.

She spared a brief flicker of anger for her half brother. Sullivan had known, dammit. He'd known and he'd kept quiet about Malone's soldiering past, probably out of some misplaced and romantically foolish reluctance to derail their affair before it had had a chance.

"I don't think you should stay here tonight."

His quiet words split the silence between them as explosively as if they'd been shouted out. After leaving Cosgrove, they'd driven back here without speaking to each other—without even looking at each other. Now Ainslie did look at him.

"It's after midnight, and as I understand it, the Agency now thinks I'm on your side. I can't go home, Malone, and I'm certainly not going to dump myself on my brother so he can baby-sit me for the next few hours, especially since he just became a father today." She jerked her chin at the sofa in front of her. "If I have to, I'll sleep on that. But I don't plan on sleeping much."

"Then you keep the gun." He reached around to the small of his back and held it out to her. She stared at it without taking it.

"What the hell for, Malone? I hate guns, you know that."

"Yeah, I know that." He shrugged. "But it might make you feel safer."

She frowned in confusion. Then his meaning became clear, and she exhaled sharply. "Because I'm spending the night with an international assassin? If you were the Executioner, I'm sure you'd have bigger fish to fry than me, Malone. As it happens, I still don't buy that ridiculous theory. For God's sake, you're basing it on a single fragment of memory, dredged up from a brain that suffered such extreme trauma that for a while you couldn't remember anything. You saw a news clip of Mocamba's death or read about it in a newspaper five years ago when it happened. Then when your amnesia was so total that you were searching for any memory you could to fill the void, you incorporated that recollection as one that you'd really experienced.''

''I don't think it works like that,'' he said softly.

''You don't know *how* it works!'' Her retort was instantaneous. She took a step toward him. ''*I* don't know how it works. But there has to be some innocent explanation for that memory, Malone, because if there isn't then *nothing* makes sense in this world—and I'm having enough trouble trying to make sense of what I thought we had.''

She took a shaky breath. ''How could you have kept it from me about being a mercenary, of all things? When your time with the Agency was up, were you planning to go back to your real profession, dammit?''

Instead of answering her, he turned away, walking over to the drapes at the window. Still with his back to her, his attention apparently focused on the street below, he spoke, his tone as flat as if he were talking about the weather prospects for the coming week.

''Soldiering was all I knew, Lee. That *world* was all I knew. And then I met you, and I felt as if I'd been given a second chance—a chance I hadn't deserved and hadn't expected, even in my most fever-ridden dreams. You brought me to life again. And I was terrified of losing you.''

He let the drapes fall closed. Still he didn't face her. ''When Sully introduced me to you as someone who worked for the government, I didn't see the need to elaborate. The next day it was already too late. I'd fallen in love with you, and I knew if you learned I was no different from your father and your brother, you'd walk away from me as fast as you could—and I couldn't blame you for that. Remember how we talked, that first night?''

"I remember." Pain washed through her and unconsciously she closed her eyes, trying to block the image that had come to her at his words—Malone in bed beside her after they'd made love for the second time, one elbow propped up on a pillow, his eyes gleaming faintly in the darkness as he listened to her tell him about her family. "I remember, Malone," she said again, unsteadily. "I poured out my soul to you."

"I know. And the first thing I'd told you about myself had been a lie," he said, turning from the window and facing her. The light from the one lamp in the room cast deep shadows on his features, making his expression hard to read, but even total darkness wouldn't have been able to conceal the stark self-condemnation in his voice.

"I *wanted* to be the man I'd told you I was, Lee. Obviously, I wanted it so badly that even now I won't let myself remember the full enormity of my deception—including the fact that my past included much more than just the soldiering. But the night I asked you to marry me, I finally realized I couldn't let it go on any longer. I'd made up my mind to lay all my cards on the table when I got back and just pray that you could forgive me."

He passed a hand over his face, and in the gesture there seemed to be a world of lost chances, missed opportunities, and hopeless regret. "But I never returned that night. It took me two long years to find my way back to you. When I did, I knew I would just have to turn around and walk away again—this time forever."

"Because you think you're the—"

Ainslie broke off in midsentence, freezing to attention. Malone had heard the same name that had caught her attention, she realized, because even as she turned an inquiring glance on him he was striding across the room to the radio on the small table by the wall, turning the volume higher with an abruptly tense flick of his wrist. The name was repeated in the unemotional tones of a late-night newscaster.

"...tentatively identified as that of a government employee, Paul Malone. Although authorities are still not releasing details of the gruesome shooting, they are alerting the public to be on the lookout for an older-model sedan, black or dark blue in color, and with a crumpled front right fender. The driver is presumed to be armed and extremely dangerous, and may be accompanied by a female companion. Anyone who sights this vehicle is urged to call the following hotline..."

"They got Paul." Malone snapped the radio off and turned to her, his expression grim. "They got *Paul,* goddammit—and I signed his death warrant by going to see him. They must have arrived just after we left, and found out that he'd talked. I *killed* him, Lee. I killed him as surely as if I fired the bullet that took him down myself."

"But you *didn't* fire that bullet." Before she even knew what she was doing, Ainslie was standing in front of him, meeting his anguished gaze. "Paul didn't deserve to die, Malone, and I feel as badly about this as you do, but the fact is that you *didn't* fire that bullet. You and I both know you're innocent, no matter what story the Agency is putting out."

She saw his eyes darken in belated comprehension, but she said it anyway.

"You didn't kill Paul, Malone. The *Executioner* killed him."

Chapter Nine

He'd insisted she take the bed. She'd insisted that after the day she'd just gone through—a day that had started with a wedding that hadn't taken place and had ended with a murder—not even the lumps in the sofa would keep her awake. He'd disappeared into the bedroom just long enough to change into a worn and faded pair of jeans to sleep in, folded his six-foot-plus frame awkwardly on the couch and refused to argue with her any longer.

Despite what she'd told him, there was no way she was going to fall asleep. Staring up at the ceiling in the dark, Ainslie knew her wakefulness had little to do with Pearson or Paul Cosgrove, as wrenching as thinking about them was. Today had also been the day that the only man she'd ever loved had come back into her life.

Or had he?

He'd changed, she told herself unwillingly. The Malone she'd once known would have been in this bed with her. And perhaps she'd changed, too, because two years ago she would have insisted on falling asleep with his arms around her.

I felt closer to him when I believed he was dead, she thought. *It's as if there's a wall between us, and it seems to be getting higher all the time.*

But at least he was no longer convinced that he was responsible for the crimes the man called the Executioner had committed. And although she still found it hard to accept that he hadn't been completely honest with her before, at least she now knew why he'd lied to her about being a mercenary.

He'd been afraid of losing her. Some part of her could understand that, because she'd always been afraid of losing him. The only difference was that she'd never gone away—and, whether it had been his fault or not, he had.

"I got to thinking about it, Lee."

His low voice came out of the darkness. Her heart thumping, swiftly she sat up in the bed, barely able to make out his silhouette framed in the doorway of the room.

"Thinking about what?" she countered, her tone an effort to mask her sudden nervousness.

"About how unfair it was that you should get this bed all to yourself." She saw him make a slight movement that might have been a shrug. "About how I wanted to be in here with you. Were you thinking anything along those lines?"

In spite of the deliberate lightness of his words, there was an edge of uncertainty in his voice. She heard an echo of it in her own as she answered him.

"Maybe. But I wasn't just wondering why we'd ended up in separate rooms, Malone. I was wondering why we seemed to be in separate universes, when once upon a time we'd been so close that I'd felt we were two halves of the same whole. Have you thought about that?"

"Yeah, honey, I have."

He sighed, and pushed himself away from the door frame. Walking over to the bed, he sat, and she realized as he did that he was wearing nothing under his jeans. She was suddenly conscious that her own attire consisted of no more than a heather-gray cotton sports bra with matching high-cut briefs.

Her outfit wasn't much skimpier than something she might wear in the ring, but for some reason she felt ridiculously exposed. She felt even more so a moment later.

She felt rather than saw him bend and reach over near the wall. A faint glowing light suddenly softened the blackness surrounding them, and Malone straightened, his eyes not meeting hers. Ainslie looked down at the source of the light, and then back at him.

"A night-light?" she said in disbelief. "A night-light in the shape of a— What exactly *is* that, Malone? A duck?"

"I think it's an owl," he muttered. "I picked it up earlier today at a gas station convenience store when I was getting the car filled." He looked over at her, his expression slightly testy. "It's no big deal, Lee. Turn it off again if you want. I don't have to have it on."

Ainslie sank back against the pillows, still watching him. "I don't mind," she said carefully. "I'm not that crazy about the dark, either, Seamus."

What had they done to him? she thought with a quick flash of anger that she was careful not to let show on her face. The physical changes that two years on the run had wrought in him she'd noticed earlier—the wary watchfulness, the lean and even more heavily muscled build, the coiled-wire tautness of his body. But what had living like a hunted animal done to the man inside?

She felt tears suddenly spring to her eyes, and held them back.

Some of the tenseness in his posture had eased. Leaning back, he looked over at her in the soft light, one corner of his mouth lifting wryly.

"I let you down, Lee," he said, his tone quiet. "I did the one thing I told you I'd never do—I walked out on you. That's why we're circling around each other like strangers, you wondering if you can ever trust me again, me wondering if you'll ever forgive me for what I did to you. In the end I turned out to be just another man who'd left you."

"But it wasn't your fault, Malone." She shook her head in denial. "I know that now."

"It *was* my fault." His jaw tightened. "If you'd known I was in the one profession you hated above all others, you never would have become involved with me in the first place. And some part of you had to know even then that I was hiding something from you, Lee."

"I think you're right about that, at least," Ainslie said slowly. "While we were together, and then after I'd been told that you'd been killed, I wouldn't let myself examine our relationship too closely. I needed to remember it as perfect."

She frowned, trying to clarify her thoughts not only to him, but to herself. "Anything else would have seemed like a betrayal, somehow—a betrayal of you and of everything we'd been to each other. But even though you didn't tell me the truth about what you did, you weren't shot as a soldier of fortune, Malone. What happened to you happened while you were working temporarily for the Agency."

"Because of my mercenary connections," he said shortly. "Either I went to the Agency or it came to me because there was a chance I could help them catch the Executioner, according to what Paul said tonight. Somewhere in the past our paths must have crossed, and that would have been in my life as a mercenary. When I met you, I thought there was a chance I could escape what I was. But all I did was pull you into a world you had never wanted to enter, Lee."

"It was the world I was born into, whether I liked it or not," she said flatly. "I became a fighter, after all. Perhaps Thomas Sullivan didn't walk out of my life without leaving me something to remember him by."

"But I did." He took a deep breath. "I left you with nothing at all, not even hope. They made you believe I was dead."

He raked a tense hand through the spill of dark hair that had fallen across his forehead. "This wasn't a good idea." His smile was halfhearted. "I'd better take my night-light and get on back to my sofa."

At his small joke, the last cold vestige of the ball of ice that had lodged inside her a few hours ago when she'd first learned that he'd deceived her suddenly melted away completely. As he started to stand, she levelled a wide-eyed gaze on him.

"I told you, Malone—I don't like being alone in the dark, either."

For a moment even his breathing seemed to stop. Then he gave her a strained smile, exhaling sharply as he did so.

"It's been two years for me, honey. I'd better wait until I can manage slow and romantic, because that's what I want to give you when we finally do make love. But right now I'm pretty sure that's beyond me."

Without another word he turned and walked out, the corded muscles of his back gleaming in the dim light as he left the room.

Ainslie heard the creak of protesting springs from the other room. She narrowed her eyes in the direction of the door, and waited.

But not for long. Almost immediately the springs creaked a second time, and then he was leaning up against the door frame again, his posture deceptively casual.

''I got to thinking about it, Lee,'' he said unevenly.

''Yeah, Malone.'' She flipped back the covers from her legs. ''Sometimes I think you do too damn much thinking. What makes you so sure I can manage slow and romantic tonight, either? If you keep sashaying around with your jeans half unzipped like that, I might not even let you get them all the way off.''

She saw the quick flash of his grin in the shadows, and then he was pushing himself away from the door frame. ''That's pretty down and dirty, all right,'' he said, walking toward her. ''I probably can do a little better than that.''

She began to move over, expecting him to get in beside her, but before she could wriggle herself into position he was on the bed, one jeans-clad leg on either side of her hips. With the same swift economy of movement, he firmly grasped her two wrists and pulled her gently up. She found herself rising smoothly back into a sitting position.

''Hey,'' she protested in a suddenly breathy voice, unable to take her gaze from the shift of heavy muscle in his arms. ''Illegal hold, Malone.''

''You wanted down and dirty.'' He looked at her, his eyes as green as a cat's, his hands still trapping her wrists. ''That means no holds barred, O'Connell.''

He turned one of her palms slightly outward, and in the shadows she saw him bend his head to her hands. The next moment she felt his tongue trace a slow, wet circle in the hollow of her palm, and she stifled a gasp. He didn't raise his head, but continued licking his circular way down her palm to her inner wrist, adjusting his hold on her minutely.

She felt his lips warm on her pulse. Then he did lift his mouth slightly, but instead of giving her a chance to recover her scrambled senses, he blew lightly on her still-moist wrist.

Ainslie's eyes had been half closed. Now they flew open

wide as a thousand tiny feathers of sensation swirled into life inside her like snowflakes trapped in a glass ball. She felt one of those feathers uncurl against her spine, and an involuntary tremor ran through her.

He was watching her, she saw, his own gaze brilliant.

"I want to do things to you, Lee," he said softly. "I want you to do whatever you want to me. It's been so damn long since I felt you beneath me."

"There's been no one else for me since you," she said unsteadily. "I just thought you should know, Malone. It was always you, even in my dreams. But I don't expect you to have remained—"

"My memory was gone," he said, firmly cutting off what she'd been about to say. "But some part of me knew it wouldn't be any good with anyone else. I never even looked at another woman, Lee." He pressed his lips to the inside of her elbow. "I just thought you ought to know, too," he murmured against her skin.

He let his mouth trail slowly along her arm, always keeping to the soft and vulnerable underside. When he reached her shoulder, she felt his hair brush against the side of her cheek, and it seemed as if he was caressing her with every part of his body.

Gently he released her wrists. Hooking one finger under the fabric of her bra strap, he slipped it off her shoulder. In the soft light she saw him smile.

"One of these days I'm going to get you something decadent, Lee," he said, a hint of laughter in his voice. "Like a thong and a lace push-up bra. Maybe garters."

"I'm not a femme fatale, Seamus." She glanced down at the boy-cut briefs, the workout-wear top. "Besides, push-up bras need something to push up."

"You really don't have a clue, do you, O'Connell?" He traced the swell of a breast, his touch light. "These are perfect. The way your waist curves in is perfect, and the way your hips flare out again is perfect. And don't get me wrong about your tough-girl panties.'' His smile was rueful. ''You used to have a pair of jeans that rode low on your hips, and a T-shirt that didn't quite cover your belly button. When you wore them together with your juvenile delinquent underwear, all day long I would keep catching glimpses of white waistband. It drove me crazy.''

''I knew that.'' Ainslie looked through her lashes at him. ''Why do you think I always wore my Calvin briefs with the lowest-cut jeans I owned, Malone? But I just don't see me in a lace thong.'' She shook her head slightly, and the ends of her hair swung against her cheeks. ''My sister-in-law, Bailey—she's beautiful. Tara's going to be a stunner. I'm just a grown-up tomboy.''

''You're crazy, honey.'' His tone was mild. ''Gorgeous, but crazy. With that blue-black hair and those blue-purple eyes and that creamy skin, you're definitely a femme fatale. Sorry to disillusion you, champ. Even in the ring, there was never any doubt.''

''You never saw me fight,'' Ainslie retorted, idly running a finger down the side of his neck, and pausing at his collarbone. She bit her lip regretfully. ''I wish you had, Malone. It wasn't long after that I hung up my gloves professionally. I still practice with my girls at the gym, but real competition is different. I was good.''

''I know.'' To her surprise, he winced slightly. ''The night after we met you had a match. I'd played hooky from the Agency all day, and I told you I had to catch up on some paperwork, but really I snuck off and bought a seat about twenty rows back. When you put on those gloves and that head protector, and your handler shoved that mouth guard between your teeth, I didn't know if I could stand to watch the actual fight. But I made myself stay, even though I was a nervous wreck all through the thing. You were up against a Latina boxer, and she connected once—a wicked punch right over your eye. The guy beside me began rooting for her, and I nearly started my own personal fight right then and there. But in the fifth round you put her down, and she stayed down. The crowd went crazy, and I went crazy with them."

"I remember that fight. Marlena and I still get together for sparring practice once in a while." She frowned suspiciously. "And I remember what happened afterward, when I came home to you. I don't think we got to sleep at all that night." Her eyes widened in belated comprehension, and a gurgle of shocked laughter escaped her. "You're *bad,* Malone! You got all hot and bothered watching me, didn't you?"

"There's something very sexy about a woman who can kick ass, honey," he admitted with a grin. "And believe me, I wasn't thinking tomboy while I was watching you. I was thinking babe."

"So instead of a thong and garters, you'd really like me to wear headgear and a mouth guard in bed with you. You're so twisted, Malone," Ainslie murmured. "Besides, if I did I wouldn't be able to do this."

He was still astride her, and she slid down a little on the bed. Flicking her tongue against the vee of dark hair arrowing from his chest to his stomach, she watched with interest as he tensed.

"Or even this," she added thoughtfully. She placed her lips against the smooth expanse of tanned skin, and brought her teeth together in a gentle nip. She felt a tremor run through him.

"That's true." His voice sounded strained. "But I could still do this."

So adroitly that she wouldn't have been able to prevent

him if she'd tried, he pushed the stretchy bottom edge of the workout top up and over her breasts. Not stopping there, he tugged it over her shoulders and her head, pulling it completely off and tossing it aside casually. His gaze met hers innocently.

"And this."

As he spoke, his hands wrapped around her waist, and he lifted her effortlessly out from under him. Ainslie found herself in the same kneeling position as he was, their bodies almost touching as they faced each other. She placed her palms on his bare chest and felt the heavy beat of his heart against his ribs.

"You're right." There was a husky edge to his words. "You don't need lace. Your skin is pure satin, all by itself."

She felt her breath catch in her throat, and she blinked, her vision suddenly blurred. "You lied, Malone," she said unsteadily. "You said romantic was beyond you tonight."

"I thought it was. But romantic is how you make me feel, Lee."

The diffused glow from the light near the floor softened the hard angles of one side of his face, leaving the other in shadow. His hands slid up the length of her arms and stopped at her shoulders, his grip suddenly almost desperate, as if she might slip from his grasp.

"I look at you and I wish I was a poet. I wish I could tell you to pick any star you wanted out of the sky, and give it to you. I wish I could make the world perfect for you." His lashes dipped briefly. He shook his head. "Hell, Lee, I never knew what you saw in me. I was just damned glad you seemed to be blind, where I was concerned."

"I'm not blind, Seamus." Leaning forward slightly, she brushed her lips against the corner of his mouth. "I see a man who's gone through hell, and survived. I see a man who never took the easy way out. I always saw the real Seamus Malone, even if I didn't know exactly what his profession was. I fell in love with him."

She met his gaze. "But you can still give me stars and poetry," she said softly. "You've given them to me before."

They were so close that she could feel the warmth of his breath stirring the strands of hair at the side of her face, so close that she saw his eyes shade to deep emerald, and then even darker.

"When we reach heaven, honey, just tell me which one you want and I'll bring it back for you," he said huskily.

This time it was his mouth that lightly brushed hers, but even as their lips touched his grip on her shoulders tightened and he pulled her to him. From somewhere in the back of his throat she heard him give a small sound, half sigh, half purring growl, and then his mouth was open on hers in an urgently seeking kiss. His hands spread wide, slid past her shoulder blades, met at her spine, locking her in his embrace.

Ainslie felt her head tip back on her neck, and her own hands moved up to frame his face. She felt the rough prickle of stubble under her palms, and then her open fingers moved into the coarse silk of his hair. Holding him to her, she returned his kiss with hungry desperation.

She remembered the way he tasted, she thought dazedly, feeling his tongue flick against hers. He still tasted like that—brandy and sugar, hot and sweet. She could get drunk on him, she told herself, searching deeper and feeling him going deeper in her—no, she already *was* drunk on him, because nothing else could explain this dizzy, soaring sensation.

"I want more of you."

His words were almost inaudible, murmured against her

parted lips, but when she tried to answer him she found that she was incapable even of that much. She nodded instead, her eyes still closed, her hands still framing his face. She felt his mouth, open and wet, moving unhurriedly past the curve of her chin, down the line of her neck and then to the hollow at its base, felt his tongue lapping at her as if she were cream. Her fingers tightened in his hair as he reached her breasts, and her back arched as she felt him take one nipple into his mouth and slowly trace a tantalizingly lazy circle with his thumb around the other.

It felt as if depth charges were being set off inside her, she thought, biting her lip to keep from crying out, each one plunging further down into the very depths of her being before exploding; each tiny explosion sending shock waves radiating through her.

"All of me, Seamus." It was all she could do to whisper the unsteady command. "Take all of me into you. I—I want to feel you *surrounding* me."

He'd always made her feel like a wanton, she remembered with a thrill of erotic satisfaction as she felt his mouth gently cover the tight, hard peak of her nipple and the soft swell above and below it. He'd always led her further than she thought she dared go, had always brought her most secret desires to urgently heated reality. Sometimes they had made slow, languorous love, and sometimes he seemed to know instinctively that what she wanted was rawer, more immediate, more elemental.

She'd known earlier today that slow and languorous wasn't what she needed from him this time. She'd had two years of making dream love with Seamus Malone, two years of fantasy kisses and couplings so fragile that they disappeared with the dawn and her tears. But he was back with her now.

He was real. He wasn't a dream, he was solidly male,

solidly real. Now she wanted everything to be as hard and as urgent and as basic as they both could stand it—because only that could totally reassure her that he wasn't the ghost that had visited her when she'd thought the man had left her for good.

His mouth moved to her other breast, the blunt ends of his hair flicking against the sensitive tip of her nipple, and she felt his palms flat against the tautness of her stomach, slipping easily on her suddenly slick skin. His thumbs hooked under the waistband of her briefs, and then pushed them down and over her hips. As he cupped the twin curves of her rear she felt one hand slip between her legs, and immediately she was suffused with heat. Hardly aware of what she was doing, she shifted slightly, parting them a fraction wider.

He pulled her close enough to him that the denim of his jeans was barely a barrier. She felt him press hard against her thigh, felt his biceps automatically tightening around her, and she knew neither of them wanted to wait any longer.

Her fingers trembling, she felt blindly for the zipper on his jeans, found it, and attempted to slide it all the way down. She felt it jam.

And then his hands were on hers, helping her release him, his fingers fumbling with impatience, too.

"Aw, hell, Lee." His voice was an unsteady rasp. "Are you sure? Is this going to be right for you, honey?"

As he spoke the zipper suddenly eased downward. Malone's breath caught harshly, as if he was trying to impose some semblance of control over himself. Still guided by the hands covering hers, Ainslie felt the rigidity of him move slowly into her grasp, felt her fingers slide into the dense thicket of coarser hair as she gently gripped him.

A stiff shudder ran through him. Looking up at him in

the shadowy half light, she saw the cautious rise and fall of that broad expanse of chest, saw the thick bulge of muscle tightly delineated in those strong arms, saw those dark lashes brushing his cheekbones. He dragged in a shallow breath. He opened his eyes just enough to meet her gaze.

"Maybe they buried me, Lee," he whispered hoarsely. "But they buried you, too—buried you so deep in my memory that I thought you had to be just another of my illusions. Is this how we both come back to life?"

"Make this as real as you know how, Malone." He felt the same way, Ainslie thought hazily. He needed this, too. "No one walks away from this thinking it was a dream or an illusion—*no* one."

There was a sudden note of desperation in her voice, and at it, he nodded tightly. His smile was little more than a momentary flash of white.

"I'm not your dream lover, sweetheart. But you want me to prove it, don't you?"

Before she could reply, his hands were on her waist, lifting her out of her kneeling position and laying her back against the pillows, her legs slightly bent. His hair falling into his eyes, his own legs still braced as he knelt in front of her, he leaned over her and one-handedly scooped her derriere a few inches off the bed. With his other hand he maneuvered her briefs past her hips, one corner of his mouth lifting briefly as he did.

"Sexy as hell, babe," he said tersely. "But they've gotta go."

Stray strands of her hair had fallen across her face. Ainslie didn't bother to push them away. She stared up at him through it, seeing the sheen of moisture on his hard torso, the indisputable evidence of his readiness for her no longer confined by his unzipped jeans. This was the Malone she'd believed she'd lost forever, she thought, liquid heat running through her like a tidal wave. The briefs she'd been wearing slipped down her calves, past her ankles, and then he was looking at her, his hands at his jeans, his eyes glazed with desire.

She reached up to him and tugged at a belt loop. Even that small movement seemed to make the room swim dizzily around her in a swirl of shadow and light.

"Sexy as hell, babe." Her voice was softly slurred. She was amazed that she could speak at all. "But they gotta go."

"I was hoping you'd change your mind and let me get them off," he murmured, moving to the edge of the bed and sliding the worn denim down the lean muscles of his legs. He turned back to her. "Everything else can go exactly how you planned, honey."

"Then this is how I planned it, Seamus," she breathed.

She pulled him onto her, and as his mouth found hers she let her eyes close completely. This wasn't the dream, she thought hazily, lifting herself slightly to meet him. This couldn't be the dream she'd had so often, the dream that always ended with her arms empty, her heart crying out in anguish. This was Malone's rough cheek grazing hers, these were Malone's arms, corded with muscle and sheened with moisture, on either side of her, and this was the man she loved—first, last, and always—entering her.

She gave an involuntary little gasp, and he slowed immediately. She caught her bottom lip in her teeth and with difficulty moved her head from left to right on the pillow.

"No, don't...don't stop." Her voice was low with urgency. "I want you in me, Seamus. We've waited too long for this."

She looked up at him through her lashes, and saw him nod, once, his jaw tight.

"Way too long, Lee," he rasped. "But never again, I promise."

He thrust gently forward again, and she felt herself opening to him, taking him in. Her teeth sunk deeper into her bottom lip, her hands on his shoulders tightened, and then she felt him deep inside her and the pain had disappeared. She exhaled softly.

All at once everything was right, everything was perfect, everything was *real.*

He'd come back to her. He'd walked away from her, but that didn't matter anymore, because he'd finally come back to her. He was here with her now. He was here with her now, and she would never, ever let him go again.

He was withdrawing and moving into her, with slow, steady thrusts, going deeper each time. She found herself moving with him, matching his tempo effortlessly, as if even the blood in her veins was surging in time with his.

This was basic. This was elemental. This was the pulse beat behind everything. It had been going on since the dawn of time and it would still be going on, long after Ainslie O'Connell and Seamus Malone were just a memory, she thought disjointedly. But for right now, they were part of it. She was the dark, wet shore that he poured into, and he was the wave that ebbed and flowed, covering her and retreating, only to surge farther into her each time.

A bubble of laughter burst silently inside of her like the pealing of an invisible bell—a silvery little laugh of pure joy, partly because of her fanciful notions, but mostly because she couldn't help herself. There had always been such an edge of sadness to her dreams, she thought, even when in them he'd been holding her desperately close. But all that was gone now, like the troubling but rapidly fading memory of some scrap of nightmare. She felt him enter her again, felt as if she was on a swing, rushing upward toward a blue, blue sky, and then she was arcing toward the ground again.

At some point the bonds that held them here would break totally free, Ainslie thought. Any moment now they would both fly higher into that blueness—higher than the trees, higher than any vee-shaped flight of birds, so high that it would be as he'd said. They would sweep upward through a field of stars, she would pick one out, and he would pluck it for her from the sparkling sky. Then the two of them, wrapped around each other, would slowly float down again to the soft brown earth far below.

...ashes to ashes, dust to dust...

She froze, her nails digging into him, her eyes suddenly wide open. Above her, his eyes were in shadow and for a moment she saw only blackness where there should have been brilliant green. A terrible coldness seemed to wrap itself around her—coldness, and something else.

Red roses for true love...

A heartbreakingly lovely scent, like wine and perfume and a lover's kiss all swirled together in one, drifted through the room, wafted closer to her and the man holding her, and began to fill her very being. She felt the muscles in Malone's arms tense, heard his breathing falter slightly, and all of a sudden icy fear gripped her. She held him tightly to her, squeezed her eyes shut to block out the shadows, and put her lips to his ear.

"Take me there now," she said, her voice thready with desperate urgency. "Take me with you. Take me with you *now,* Seamus."

As if he'd been waiting for her to say the words, his eyes opened, and that deep green gaze locked onto hers. His lips were parted, and he dragged in a rasping breath, his body rigid with effort.

"I love you, Lee." His voice was barely audible.

"Whatever else you believe of me, you have to believe that. I've loved you from the first moment I saw you. I'll love you till the day I die, and beyond."

His gaze held hers steadily. Wide-eyed, she stared back at him, and slowly the fear disappeared, the sadness melted into the past, and the intoxicating scent of roses drifted away, leaving only a ghostly memory in the air.

"You only die once, Malone," she said softly. "I won't let you go into the darkness a second time. Whatever else *you* believe, believe that."

"Oh, I do, champ." Brief humor touched one corner of his mouth. "I think you'd fight the devil himself, and win."

Even as she spoke she saw the last of his control slip away, saw those green eyes close, saw that black hair fall across them in damp spikes...

...and then she was with him, and nothing was holding her back. A molten heat began spreading through her, heavy and dark, as if her blood was turning slowly to liquid gold, as if her whole body was becoming something less stable, more formless. She knew he was saying her name over and over again, and as if from a long way away she thought she could hear herself calling out his, but then everything shattered around her in a blinding explosion of heat and pure, brilliant light, and she was leaving her own body behind.

It was the *essence* of Ainslie O'Connell that was flying up with him, she thought dizzily—the essence of both of them. She understood now, she thought disjointedly. She'd been wrong before—real had nothing to do with the bodies of Seamus Malone and Ainslie O'Connell, somewhere far below them. Real was this. Real was the part of him that loved her, the part of her that loved him, and it could never be destroyed. She'd asked for poetry, but that truth was as eternal as any sonnet.

And here, too, were the stars he'd promised her. But they weren't around her, they were passing *through* her, dissolving in her like liquid diamonds, bursting into crystalline heat as they flared inside her. She was lost in them, showered in them; and later she would never really be sure for how long it had lasted, because time itself had no meaning during that exquisite bombardment of sensations...

But finally all but the last of them had disappeared. She felt it sparkling inside her, felt herself tumbling back down to earth, felt Malone's arms cradling her as the shadowy light of the bedroom appeared once again through her half-closed eyes. The final tiny starburst came as his hand stroked back her damp hair and she felt a last tremor run through him, too.

Through her lashes she saw him slowly open his own eyes and meet hers, his gaze still slightly unfocused. Lightly he traced the line of her parted lips with a gentle finger.

And then he reached over her, fumbling with something on the wall near the floor. She heard a small click and the room went black.

"I thought you didn't like the dark, Malone," she said cautiously as he settled back, snugging her head into the hollow of his shoulder.

"It's not dark in here."

She could hear the slight smile in his voice, and she knew he was looking at her.

"For the first time in two years, it's not dark at all, Lee," he said huskily, pulling her close to his heart.

Chapter Ten

"Moira practically runs Sullivan Investigations when my brother's not there. She said he's taken off the rest of the week to be with Bailey, so as long as I get the car back before he shows up at the office he won't even have to know I signed it out." Ainslie looked around the small diner. "It's a good thing this place serves a late breakfast. I was starving, for some reason."

"I don't know why." Malone drained his coffee. "Just because you kept me up all night with your insatiable demands—"

"Oh, I'm sorry, Gramps." She lifted an eyebrow at him, still unused to the gray rinse that dulled the sheen of his hair. "So when you woke me up at dawn this morning you just were trying to hobble off to the bathroom?"

"Of course. Us old coots sometimes have that problem, you know." He gave her an assessing look over the gold half-moon glasses he was wearing. "Although I might just give it another go tonight. You make a very sexy blonde, in a cool, hands-off kind of way."

"Down, boy, it's just a wig. But you're pretty sexy yourself, for an old guy. And I love the tweed jacket." She shot him a smile, and then sobered. "Are we fooling anyone in these getups, Malone? I feel so conspicuous."

"I've spent a couple of years trying to look as unlike myself as possible. What you've got to remember is that people will accept just about anything at face value."

He passed a hand over his steel-gray hair. "A tattered coat and a beard turned me into a street person believable enough to fool even you for a time. Thanks to Moira and the resources of Sullivan Investigations, we now look exactly like what we're trying to be—an absentminded professor type and a visiting guest lecturer on—" He paused. "What was your field again, Ms. O'Connell?"

"The mating habits of sea turtles. The Galapagos Islands are beautiful this time of year, Professor," Ainslie said promptly.

She looked down at herself. Malone might be used to slipping in and out of disguise, but she still hadn't gotten over the disconcerting feeling that she was playing dress-up. The tailored charcoal pantsuit was one that Moira, her brother's invaluable secretary, had brought with her when she'd met them earlier at Sullivan Investigations. The smoothly bobbed wig was part of an extensive collection of hairpieces, accessories and clothing that was kept at the office for the use of operatives.

Moira hadn't asked questions, and for that Ainslie had been grateful. All Sully's secretary knew was that yesterday's wedding hadn't gone as planned—and that today the renegade bride had shown up with another man in tow, seemingly intent on spending the next few days incognito.

Moira's imagination was probably running along the lines of an enraged Pearson, gunning for the man who'd stolen his bride from him at the eleventh hour, Ainslie thought, smiling sadly at the unlikely image. Her smile faded as another, more horrific picture entered her mind.

In the borrowed sedan—the police would be on the lookout for any vehicle matching the description of Malone's car, so alternate transportation had been their main priority—they had finally felt marginally less exposed. That illusion of safety had been shattered when Malone had switched on the car radio in time for them to catch the morning news.

The authorities were being closemouthed about Paul's murder, but some details had leaked out to the media. He'd been killed at the same side doorway to his house that they'd entered through. A single bullet had been fired through the back of his head in a manner the press was already characterizing as "execution-style."

Ainslie took a sip of her coffee, now tepid, but in the very act of swallowing a thought struck her and she almost choked. She set her cup down hastily.

"He knew his killer, Malone." She felt sick. "Whoever it was that carried out the hit, Paul knew him—and trusted him."

"Yeah, I figure it that way, too. And at that time of night, it's a safe bet that Paul could only have been expecting a visitor he himself had summoned." Malone's gaze hardened. "It wasn't the Executioner who killed him, Lee. It was someone Paul contacted at the Agency after we left."

"That doesn't make any sense." She shook her head firmly. "Maybe Paul didn't work for them anymore, but he was still on their side. He phoned the Agency to alert them that you'd returned from the dead. He was *helping* them, Malone."

"Put that in the past tense and I think you'll be closer to the truth," he said shortly. "Paul's usefulness to the Agency was over as soon as he informed them that I was back. Unless—"

He stopped, his gaze suddenly bleak.

"Unless what?"

"There was one final way he could be of use to them." Malone's jaw was tight. "But he had to be dead first."

"Dear God." All at once the diner's atmosphere seemed suffocatingly close. "You're saying he was killed just to reactivate the official hunt for you?"

"That convenient description of us and the car we were using didn't come from some suspicious citizen, dammit. That neighborhood was all tucked up in bed for the night, remember?" Even with the gray hair and the glasses, he looked suddenly formidable. "Paul told whoever arrived that I'd been with you, and had left in a beat-up Ford with a dented front fender. That was enough to give to the police—after committing the murder the Agency needed to pin on me to make catching me a priority."

"But it's a legitimate government organization." Her voice had risen enough so that a young couple sitting at a nearby table looked over with mild curiosity. Ainslie lowered her tone, but her eyes still sparked with outrage. "What kind of a mandate does it operate under, that even *murder* can be sanctioned?"

"I don't think the Agency does sanction murder—not officially, at least." Malone shrugged tightly. "I think there's a traitor working behind the scenes, and he's high enough up in the organization so that he's been able to pursue his own agenda with the Agency's resources."

Ainslie frowned. "But who's the mole, Seamus? Who infiltrated the Agency—and why?"

"Whoever he is, he's not the Executioner himself," he said flatly. "Look at it this way—assassination isn't a full-time business, Lee. The Executioner has a life that he disappears from occasionally in order to indulge his hobby of murder, and that alternative persona has been in place for at least ten years. From what Paul told us, the first killings that could be definitely attributed to him occurred around that time.''

''And if he'd been an Agency mole all that time, he would have derailed their investigation long before it got off the ground. Is that what you're saying?''

Before he could reply, their waitress, a hatchet-faced older woman whom Ainslie had heard barking out orders to the cook in a no-nonsense voice for the past half hour, bustled up efficiently with a full pot of coffee. She fixed an automatic smile on her face while the woman refilled their cups and dropped a handful of creamers on the table. Malone would be captivating the ladies when he was an old codger, she thought, watching him turn his charm on the grim-faced waitress.

Don't fight it, sister, she silently told the woman as she saw the pursed mouth curve into an almost girlish smile. *I'm a professional, and even I found myself on the ropes two minutes after I met him.*

Where would she and Malone have been today if their lives hadn't been ripped away from them that fateful night? she wondered, her gaze clouding. Would their relationship have withstood his eventual revelation about his mercenary past? And if they had married, would they have had a child of their own by now, a little girl or boy who could have been a cousin to Sullivan and Bailey's Megan?

The image that came into her mind of a black-haired, green-eyed little girl was suddenly so real that she felt a stab of grief when it faded. She blinked, squaring her shoulders tensely under the tailored jacket.

Daydreaming about what might have been was futile, she told herself flatly. The past two years *had* been stolen from them, and even now their lives weren't their own—not while there was a very real possibility that their deaths might come as unexpectedly and as brutally as Paul's, not while Malone was still being hunted down for crimes he hadn't committed. Even her hopes for a future with the man she loved would have to be shelved until she knew for sure that they *had* a future.

But not everything had been taken from them.

Last night they'd snatched a few precious hours for themselves—and a day ago she hadn't expected to know even that much happiness again. As the now-beaming waitress walked away and Malone looked absently down to stir his coffee, Ainslie gazed at him, her vision suddenly misty. Living without him had been like enduring a drought, she thought, like praying for rain every day, and going to bed every night with the landscape of her heart still cracked and parched.

But last night the rains had come, bringing her back to life again. She and Malone had made love three times before they'd finally fallen asleep, his arms cradling her tight to his chest, one long leg thrown over hers. They'd awakened shortly after eight this morning, and they'd made love again—this time with all the dreamlike slowness that they hadn't allowed themselves before.

It had been a physical confirmation of the bond that had never broken between them. But as sweet as remembering those hours in his arms was, last night had been an interlude that they would have to put behind them for now. Their lives depended on it.

"She gave me real cream. I see you only got skim milk," Malone said complacently. He handed her one of the small plastic containers in front of him. "Of course, yesterday I probably would have been booted out of here before I'd even sat down."

"Yesterday you were a bum." She unpeeled the lid from the creamer. "It's like you said, people take things at face value, and that's probably how the Agency mole's escaped detection so far."

"I think you're right. He's someone with a spotless record, someone whose authority isn't questioned." Malone touched the side of his head lightly, and Ainslie immediately frowned.

"Is the pain back again?" If it was, they wouldn't even be able to get him to a doctor, she thought with a spurt of helpless anger. The Agency would have covered that possibility, too.

"Not really. It was just a twinge." He pinched the bridge of his nose with a weary gesture. "It seems to happen when a memory comes close to the surface. I think that's why it got so bad yesterday, just before everything came flooding back, but whatever prompted it this time, it's gone."

"Maybe we're going at this from the wrong angle," she said slowly. "The mole could be anyone in the Agency. It's like trying to pick out the right needle in a haystack full of them. We've been overlooking the one element that we are sure of."

"And that is?" Behind the glasses his gaze sharpened.

"You, Malone." She sat back, meeting his eyes. "Why were you picked to be the fall guy? In fact, why were you brought in on the investigation in the first place? You were an outsider, for heaven's sake. I'm no expert on how an organization like the Agency works, but that must have been unusual in itself."

"I remember them questioning me several times about an incident that had happened at some airport a few years previously. I couldn't give them much. In fact, I personally thought they were barking up the wrong tree, but since I usually collected a paycheck by letting people shoot at me and shooting back at them, I looked at it as one of the cushier jobs I'd ever had."

A corner of his mouth lifted wryly. "They seemed to think I might actually have seen the Executioner in the process of changing from his Dr. Jekyll identity to his Mr. Hyde persona, and from what I know of him, that means I belong to a select club." He shrugged. "So select, apparently, that none of the other members are still alive."

"For once the Agency had to have gotten it right." Ainslie tried to control her excitement. "Don't you see—even if you didn't have much faith in their theory at the time, what's happened since bears it out."

"Yeah." His jaw tightened. "Unless I was right the first time, and that memory of seeing Joseph Mocamba between the crosshairs of my rifle is the real one."

"Which it can't be." Her tone was sharp. "Paul's death has to be part of this. As terrible as his murder was, at least it should have convinced you of your innocence, Malone. The Agency has been tracking you from state to state. The only justification for that has to be that your very existence is a threat that the Executioner can't overlook, and his puppet in the Agency is pulling out all the stops to find you. Even to the point of killing one of their own people." She paused, trying to put her ideas into some kind of order. "Did you come to them with this information about the airport incident, or did they come to you?"

"They came to me." His gaze clouded in thought. "I must have gone over my story dozens of times for them, which is why I remember it, I suppose. Like I told you before, the only period that I recall with any real clarity is the couple of weeks before I was shot, and that's when these debriefing sessions were going on."

His words came out slowly, as if he were dredging up the recollection with reluctance. "The incident they were questioning me on would have happened about three years earlier—five years ago, now. From what I can remember telling them, I'd just come off an assignment where I'd been fighting with a band of rebels in a region that had once been part of a dictatorship. A core of hard-liners were trying to turn the clock back to the bad old days, but eventually the rebels ousted them, and my job there was finished."

"So the good guys won that time?" Ainslie asked tightly.

This had been his life, she reminded herself. As much as she hated to acknowledge the violent business he'd been in, to pretend that part of his past had nothing to do with him now was foolish. He'd been a soldier for hire. Death and destruction were commonplace to him. But his answer surprised her.

"No one really wins any war." His tone was harsh. "It took me too long to learn that simple fact, and by the time I did, it was too late. I didn't know anything else but soldiering, so I kept taking on the next job, and the next. And in between jobs I tried real hard to blot everything out by getting drunk and staying drunk until they poured me onto whatever transport plane I'd been booked on."

He stopped and looked up at her, a bleak smile on his face. "I guess I finally made it. After all those years of trying to wipe out my memory by any means I could, in the end someone did it for me. Maybe I owe that shooter in the alley that night a vote of thanks."

"Except those memories are still inside you, no matter how deeply they're buried," Ainslie said evenly. "All that's changed is that you can't confront them anymore."

"Perhaps I don't want to confront them." His gaze flickered away from her. "Anyway, the plane I was on developed engine trouble. We barely made it to an airport, and when we did we were told that it would take at least twenty-four hours to arrange another flight out.'' He grimaced. ''An unscheduled stopover in Paris or Rome is one thing. But hell, I couldn't even pronounce the name of this place. It was one of those breakaway Balkan republics, not exactly a hot spot for nightlife by any means, and I was just telling myself I might as well buy a bottle of vodka, unroll my sleeping bag and camp out in the terminal instead of going into town, when I heard someone calling my name.''

He saw her raised eyebrows. ''Not that unusual, Lee. I'll bet if I walked into Logan Airport right now, within a couple of hours I'd see someone I once fought with—or against. I ran into Sully in downtown Boston, and I'd last seen him on the other side of the world.'' He shrugged. ''This time it was Chris Stewart, a guy I hadn't seen for years, but we greeted each other like long-lost friends. He told me he knew of a bar that had pretty decent booze, pretty decent music and a pretty accommodating hostess—'' His head jerked up, and Ainslie saw a flush of sudden color under his tan. She sighed.

''You told me you were a mercenary, Malone. I never thought you were a monk,'' she said dryly. ''Besides, I didn't even know you then. So you went out with your friend that night?''

''No. That's just it.'' His normal color returning, he frowned. ''We were supposed to. We talked for a few minutes and he gave me the name of the bar and suggested a time to meet there later on. Then he said something about not expecting to meet one old acquaintance in a godforsaken dump like this, let alone two, and that only minutes before seeing me he was sure he'd spotted someone he'd known years before at college.

''We went our separate ways at that point—Chris to see

if he could find his friend, me looking for a taxi to get me into the city. I finally got one, and as it was pulling out of the airport a Mercedes passed us. Chris was in the passenger seat, but his head was against the window and his eyes were closed. I got a vague impression of the driver, but he was wearing sunglasses, and the Mercedes streaked by the clapped-out Russian Zil I was in too fast to get a good look at him.''

''And then what?'' she prompted impatiently.

''And then when I saw Chris again, he was lying in a ditch beside that same road leading from the airport, with his throat cut from ear to ear. That was the next morning, when I was returning to catch my flight out,'' he said quietly.

Ainslie felt the blood drain from her face, but Malone seemed oblivious not only to her, but to the busy noise and activity of the diner around him.

He was seeing ghosts, she thought with a pang of unreasonable fear, those same shadows and ghosts that she'd seen in the eyes of her brother long ago, the same ones she'd seen in the eyes of Sully's other mercenary friends. And maybe it was just for the moment, but right now those ghosts were more real to him than she was. She found herself clenching her hands together under the table as he continued, his tone oddly detached.

''I'd waited for him the evening before. When he didn't show, I figured he'd found more interesting entertainment. He liked the ladies, Chris did. One of the rules of the mercenary world is that you don't ask personal questions, but I knew there'd been some trouble with a girl in his past. From things he'd let drop, I was sure he came from an old Boston family and that they'd cut all ties with him years before.

''Anyway, I drank a little too much, got up with a hangover the next day and thanked my lucky stars I'd had the foresight to bribe the Zil driver to pick me up and drive me to the airport. If I hadn't, I probably never would have made it out of the country."

One corner of his mouth quirked up in a humorless smile. Her gaze widened.

"Dear God...I know where you're talking about now. It's in the same area as Chechnia, isn't it?"

"Not bordering, but close. And it's even smaller than Chechnia, so the media's largely ignored it. Plus no one seems to know how to spell its name, since it seems to be all consonants." His voice hardened. "Not a sexy war, I guess. But people are still dying over there, and have been since the night their president was assassinated."

"The night you spent waiting for your friend," she said tensely.

"The night I spent getting so drunk I can't really remember what I did." Malone's grin was tight. His eyes were unreadable behind the glasses. "But I'm a soldier by trade. I wasn't drunk enough to sleep through the first sounds of gunfire the next morning. I grabbed up my equipment and raced outside just as my driver arrived. He knew it was bad, too, but he wasn't going to let a little thing like a civil war stop him from making a few more American dollars. Besides, people find it hard to accept that their lives have been turned inside out in a matter of hours. They stick to their routine for as long as they can, which was why the police were by the side of the highway investigating the murder of one man, when already dozens were being killed in the streets of the city. The traffic had slowed to a crawl by then, and I saw that the body they were standing over was Chris's. I made the driver pull over."

"Didn't the police try to detain you?" He *had* been

lucky he'd gotten out of the country unscathed, Ainslie thought faintly. Especially after presenting himself to the authorities as a convenient suspect—make that the only suspect, she corrected herself—in a murder investigation. He shook his head.

"They took statements from me and the cabbie right there. There were two of them, and the younger one might have been considering taking me in, but the older cop told me to go. I think he knew he'd be signing my death warrant if he kept me any longer. As it was, I got the last seat on the last plane out before the airport shut down completely. I suppose my statement must have been filed at some point. That had to be how the Agency learned of my involvement."

"And the man in the Mercedes—he's the one they thought might be the Executioner? He killed your friend because he'd been recognized?"

"That was the theory they handed me. At some point they obviously came up with a new one—that I was the Executioner myself. I don't know if I blame them."

Despite, or maybe because of, the emotionless way he'd told his story, Ainslie was numb with horror. Her nerves already stretched thin, at his last remark they snapped completely.

"*I* do. Even if the evidence against you—evidence that the real Executioner's man inside the Agency must have created—was overwhelming, why weren't you arrested? Why weren't you questioned? Why were you set up like a target in a shooting gallery, for God's sake? That's not the way things work in this country, Malone!"

"Not normally, no." His voice was even. "But even a decent man like Paul would have pulled the trigger on me with no hesitation after he'd been told who I was. Who they thought I was," he amended, holding her gaze. "It's like the old question, If you could go back in time and eliminate Hitler, would you? Monsters have been arrested and set free, only to pick up where they left off. They wanted to be sure I never had the chance to start another bloodbath in another corner of the world, Lee.''

''*Distance* yourself, dammit.'' Her tone was like ice, her eyes even colder. ''Distance yourself, Malone, or we're beaten before we start. Stop talking about him as if there's a possibility he's you. Stop seeing their side.'' She gave him the same tight smile that he'd given her a few moments ago. ''Understand one thing—if you're on their side, then I'm fighting against you. Because I intend to bring them down. I won't stop until I do.''

''It's not your fight—'' he began, but she cut him off before he could finish, leaning across the table to him.

''They stole you away from me!'' Her whisper was harsh. ''Don't ever tell me it's not my fight, Malone, because it is. What you've got to decide is whether it's yours, or whether you're willing to let them bury you all over again.''

Abruptly she shoved back her chair and stood, slinging her bag over her shoulder and praying that the trembling inside her wasn't visible. ''It's that one memory, isn't it? That memory of Joseph Mocamba in your sights. I don't accept that you had anything to do with his death, but it's obviously tearing you apart. I guess I can understand that. I've got a memory that still tears at me, too.''

She took a deep breath, and got herself under control. ''We haven't paid yet. I'll wait for you outside in the car.''

She turned to go, but he stopped her with a question.

''What's your memory, Lee?'' His voice was quiet. ''What is it that tears you apart?''

She looked back at him, and some part of her felt the need to rush to him, to touch his face, to feel his heartbeat.

She still didn't quite believe he'd come back to her, she thought shakily. She was so afraid of losing him again.

"They gave me a little silver shovel. I dug up some earth and tipped it onto your coffin. I don't think I'll ever forget that terrible sound, Seamus. I don't think I'll ever forget how that felt. I couldn't go through that a second time."

He'd risen and had thrown some money down on the table, but suddenly she needed to be out of the close atmosphere of the diner, and in the fresh air.

She strode a few paces ahead of him and had almost reached the curb where he'd parked the car when she felt him grip her arm roughly.

Startled, she spun around, only to find herself looking into the face of a complete stranger. Behind him was Malone, but even as he took a swift step toward them Ainslie felt something hard press into the small of her back under her jacket.

"I've got a .45 right against the lady's spine, Malone."

The stranger's words were calmly conversational. As a businessman hurried by, Ainslie realized that to anyone watching, the scene probably looked innocuous.

"It's Noah, right?" Malone's gaze was shuttered. "Let her go, Watkins. I'm the one the Agency's been looking for. She doesn't have to be part of it."

"Yeah, she does. She's my guarantee that you won't get away from me again." His smile was thin, but Ainslie could hear the thread of hatred in his voice.

"Like you did two years ago, Malone—the night I thought I'd killed you in that alleyway."

Chapter Eleven

"Tell me something, Watkins."

They were about an hour outside of Boston. In the driver's seat in front of them, Malone flicked a quick glance into the rearview mirror.

"When you killed Paul last night, was there an instant when he realized what you intended to do? Or did he die thinking you were his friend?"

"I don't know." The man seated beside Ainslie lifted his shoulders in a tensely dismissive movement, keeping his gaze fixed on Malone, the ugly weapon in his hand aimed at her. "That was something I thought of asking you. But I figured you'd lie about it, anyway."

Ainslie turned away. It was a perfect autumn day, she thought dully as the scenery blurred by. Drifts of gold and scarlet blanketed the landscape beyond the freeway and the sky was a hard, late-October blue, as if the sun had polished it to a high gleam in readiness to be put away for the winter.

Cutting across it she could see a wavering vee of geese traveling in the same direction as they were, and the sight rang a faint bell in her mind. Sully, she thought. Once he had told her that when mercenaries died, their souls took on the form of wild geese and they flew for eternity, searching for redemption.

No, they don't, Sully, she told him silently. *When mercenaries die, they're buried like anyone else. They're lowered six feet down into the cold, hard ground, and it's the ones they leave behind who search in vain to find some meaning in their deaths.*

She'd told Malone she wouldn't be able to stand going through that again, but she'd lied. She would have to go through it again. If everything went according to Watkins's plan, and he managed to finish the job he'd botched two years ago, she wouldn't be able to allow herself the luxury of accepting her own death. She had to survive, even if surviving Malone a second time meant living with unceasing pain for the rest of her life.

Tara had already lost one mother. *She* was the one who didn't deserve to suffer a second loss.

But if there was even the slightest opportunity of catching Watkins off guard and giving Malone a chance to take the man down, she would risk it, Ainslie thought coldly. Despite the gun he had aimed at her, Watkins's attention wasn't fully focused on her. That might be his undoing.

She shifted cautiously, studying him from the corner of her eye. He wasn't a man to command attention at first glance. His height was average, his hair a close-cropped sandy-brown and his features, nondescript. Only his eyes gave him away. They were pale blue, so light in hue that in the bright sunlight they seemed to be almost colorless. Sailor's eyes, Ainslie thought. Or marksman's eyes. Even if he hadn't already admitted it, she would have known instinctively that he'd been the one who had held Malone in the crosshairs of a nightscope, and who'd coolly pulled the trigger on him.

"Do you mind if I take this off?" She touched the smooth blond wing of hair skimming her jawline.

"Go ahead." For the first time, those pale eyes looked directly at her, and with a small shock she saw a flicker of emotion at the back of them. "Just don't make any sudden moves."

Slowly she pulled the wig backward from her forehead, feeling like herself again as her own hair fell forward. Folding her hands carefully in her lap, she turned back to the window.

If she'd seen that emotion in anyone else's eyes, she would have identified it as compassion, she told herself shakily. But Noah Watkins was a self-acknowledged killer for the Agency, who even now was taking a man to his death. Whatever he was feeling right now, it wasn't anything as human as pity.

"Take the next exit, and then the first road off it to the right, Malone." His voice was devoid of inflection. "I'm told you have a soft spot for your girlfriend here. Don't count on me counting on that. Seeing you die has been all I've dreamed about for two years now, and today it's finally going to happen."

"I wondered why we were heading out into the country." Malone slowed for the exit. "But now it makes sense, it being your dream, and all. I guess the setting has to be just right."

"Why didn't Paul get the same treatment?" Ainslie asked, tearing her suddenly burning gaze from the scenery and turning to meet those colorless eyes. "Why did he have to die at all? The Agency never intended for the police to be the first to find Malone, so what was the point of that murder?"

Instead of answering her, Watkins searched her face, the expression on his own almost curious. Then his glance flicked away. "I don't think that's something you need to know. If it is, then someone else can fill you in. I don't consider that part of the job."

"How about this one, then?" The road to the right that Watkins had referred to was unpaved and badly rutted. Malone maneuvered onto it cautiously. "How did you locate us, Noah?"

"I sent out doves," Watkins said curtly. "Just concentrate on the driving, Seamus. The road curves up ahead. Follow it around the lake."

As he spoke Ainslie saw a glimmer of blue through the feather tracery of the tamaracks lining the road. The car took the curve and the trees became sparser, the lake coming into full view.

She felt her breath catch in her throat. It was *beautiful,* she thought unwillingly. The shoreline was softened by massively old willow trees, and as they came nearer she saw a pair of mallards skim lightly down onto the mirror-like surface of the water. At the top of the gentle rise that overlooked the lake, a long-ago fire had destroyed all but the gray stones that had once made up the outer walls of a mansion.

The place had a kind of forgotten enchantment about it that would soon be shattered by the violence Watkins intended to carry out here. On a sudden impulse she reached over and touched Watkins's sleeve as Malone slowed the car.

"He'll kill you, too." Her voice cracked with urgency. "You know he will—you're the only one who can connect him to all—"

"He's not going to kill me. I intend to make sure that Paul was his last victim." Watkins studied her face even more intently than before. Slowly he shook his head. "You finally accept it, don't you? You didn't know for sure before, but Paul's death was the final straw for you, wasn't it?''

She stared at him, but he seemed to take her confusion for acquiescence and once again she saw a flash of something like pity in his gaze.

''I was at the funeral, too. I saw you there with Paul, and I heard that he watched over you for the next few days. You're right, he of all people didn't deserve to die.'' He reached past her for the door handle on her side and unlatched it. ''Get out slowly and stand away from the car. Malone, you do the same.''

After the close confines of the vehicle the air outside was instantly cool against her face. The slight breeze stirred a few strands of her hair as she did what Watkins had instructed her to do, and took a couple of steps away from the car, the autumn-dried grasses making a sound like rustling taffeta as she moved through them.

Her gaze sought Malone's, but he was looking away from her, squinting against the sunlight toward the sprawling stone outline of the house at the top of the rise. His profile was grim.

''Was it a setup in your dreams, too, Noah?'' he said harshly. ''Because that's what I think you just walked into. Lee, stay as far away from him as you can.''

Watkins had come up beside her, and with one part of her mind Ainslie realized that he was no longer aiming the gun at her. She started to distance herself from him, but he grasped her wrist.

''You know you don't trust him anymore. If he can use you, he will, and that's exactly what he's trying to do, Ainslie.'' In the bright sun his irises were silvery. ''Paul once thought of him as a friend, too, but in the end he'll destroy anyone who gets in his way. Like you said, if he could, he'd kill me, because I can tie him to all the other deaths—but letting you live would be an even greater risk to him. Malone *eliminates* risks like you and Paul.''

For a moment she just stared at him. His expression was implacable, but his words had been delivered with a kind of heavy reluctance, as if he found no pleasure in what he was telling her. A terrible suspicion began to take shape in her mind.

If you could go back in time and eliminate Hitler, would you? Malone's hypothetical question came back to her, and suddenly everything became shockingly clear.

''There was a chance in a million that you were fully aware of what he was, and were working with him,'' Watkins went on. ''I wasn't completely convinced of that, and now I know for sure. You just fell in love with the wrong man.'' He released her at the same time as his other hand lifted and aimed the gun at Malone. ''Get back in the car. There's no reason for you to have to see—''

''You really *believe* it!'' She felt as if the air had been slammed out of her. ''You weren't his puppet, you were his *dupe!* From the first you've seen this mission as some kind of noble crusade, haven't you?'' Her voice climbed. ''I was with Malone last night. He didn't leave my side, dammit—not even for a *second.* He didn't kill Paul, and he's not the Executioner!''

Too swiftly for Watkins to prevent her, she stepped in front of him. Behind her she heard Malone's quickly indrawn breath, heard the rustle of grass as he started to move toward them and then checked himself.

''Get the hell out of the way, Lee,'' he said in a strained voice. ''Noah, stay cool. I'm raising my hands where you can see them, okay? For the love of God, Lee, get out of his line of fire!''

''He went back.'' Ignoring Malone, Watkins addressed her, his tone forceful. ''After the two of you saw Paul,

Malone left you in the car and went back, didn't he? Maybe it was only for a few minutes, maybe he told you he had one last question for him, but he had to have left you and gone back to the house. That's when he did it. It had to have been something like that.''

''We left Paul alive. We both got in the car at the same time, and we drove away together,'' she said flatly. ''Up until a couple of minutes ago, I thought *you'd* killed Paul. But Malone was the only one you were willing to gun down in cold blood, wasn't he?—and then only because you'd been convinced he was a monster who couldn't be allowed to live.''

''He is. My source was unimpeachable, for God's sake! I was given hard *proof*—''

''Your source was the Executioner, no matter who he presented himself as.'' Her eyes held his. ''*He* killed Paul.''

''I'm willing to turn myself in to the authorities as long as you can guarantee Ainslie and I get there alive, Noah. If you don't trust me on that, go ahead and pull the trigger.'' Dropping his hands slightly, but still keeping them in sight, Malone stepped forward, coming between her and Watkins.

''But after you do, get Ainslie in the car and drive like hell. Throw yourself on the mercy of the FBI if you have to, but insist on protection for the two of you. This looks too much like a trap to me.''

''Don't come any closer, Malone.'' Watkins's jaw tightened. ''I can't *afford* to believe you, dammit! If any of what you're saying is true, then that night in the alleyway—''

Ainslie saw the pale eyes darken in denial.

''You gunned down an innocent man?'' Malone's smile was bleak. ''I don't think you have to worry about that. I don't remember much of my past, but these hands aren't totally clean. Blood has a habit of sticking to a man, no matter how hard he tries to scrub it off."

"You were a soldier. Whatever blood you spilled was spilled in the line of duty, for God's sake." Tension rang in Ainslie's voice like a steel cable stretched taut. "You were following *orders,* Malone. You can't blame yourself for—"

"Whose orders were you following, Noah?" Ignoring the gun in the other man's hand, Malone moved closer to him.

The bulky tweed jacket made his shoulders seem even broader than they were, Ainslie thought, and with the heavy streaking of gray dulling the black of his hair he looked like a stranger. She was suddenly filled with an obscure apprehension.

"You're putting it all together in your mind, aren't you?" Malone's voice was soft. "And one or two things just don't add up. Maybe at the time you wouldn't allow yourself to examine them too closely, because by then you were committed to hunting me down. But when he told you I'd killed Paul, you had to wonder how he knew about the crumpled fender on the car I was driving. Some part of you knew he could only have gotten that information from Cosgrove, just before he put a slug into the back of his head."

"There was a man taking his dog for a late-night walk," Watkins said slowly. "He told the police he'd seen a car with a couple in it, speeding away a few blocks from the scene."

"Go through the police reports yourself. I'm betting you won't find anything about a witness in them." A corner of Malone's mouth lifted ironically. "The dog's a nice detail, though."

From her vantage point, Ainslie saw the doubt grow in Watkins's eyes, saw the gun waver briefly in his hand. Then his expression closed again and she knew that he was through listening to them. He gave his head a quick, hard shake.

"No, Malone, I only got one thing wrong. The girl's in this with you. But it all ends here."

Even as he spoke, Ainslie saw Watkins's gun start to come up toward the man directly in front of him, and sharp terror tore through her.

"Get down, Lee!"

Even as Malone shouted the hoarse command he was moving swiftly, eliminating the last few inches between him and Noah Watkins, knocking him backward against the car. Ainslie saw his hand close powerfully over the other man's, saw Watkins struggling to regain control of his gun, his mouth opening in a rictus of pain as Malone slowly forced his wrist back.

Then she heard a nauseating snapping sound, and her own hands flew to her mouth in sick horror as Malone wrenched the gun from Watkins's suddenly useless grip. His broken wrist canted at an unnatural angle, with a desperate lunge, Watkins tried to get away. Malone's bulkier frame easily body-checked him, ramming him back against the car and momentarily blocking the Agency operative from her view.

The shot was explosively loud. Malone looked over his shoulder at her, his face etched with some strong emotion she couldn't identify, and past him she saw Watkins's pale gaze staring sightlessly up at the sky as his body slumped sideways.

She looked at Malone in shocked disbelief.

"But...but you'd *disarmed* him!" Her voice was a high,

unsteady thread. "Dear God, Malone, why did you *kill* him?"

He never answered her. Moving so fast she didn't even have time to react, he leaped at her, still holding the gun. A split second later his body smashed into hers with all the force of a battering ram. Ainslie felt the breath leaving her lungs, felt herself falling with him—and heard the second shot ring out from somewhere above them.

When he'd taken her down with him, Malone had tucked her head into his chest. Now he released her, and as he met her gaze she saw the blood running into his right eye from a gash on his forehead. He wiped the back of his hand across it, and stared grimly at her.

"He must have hit the headlight. We've got to get out of here, Lee." He flicked a quick glance toward the house on the rise. "He's got the high ground, and a hell of a lot more firepower than I do. We don't stand a chance if he disables the car."

"I—I thought it was you who—" She didn't finish her sentence.

"I know you did." There was no recrimination in his tone. "But that doesn't matter right now. We're going to crawl to the other side of the car and get in the passenger-side door. When we do, I want you to stay hunkered down on the floor until I tell you it's safe to get up, understand?"

Ainslie nodded, her eyes wide and stricken with guilt. She saw him gaze irresolutely at her for a second, and then his mouth came down on hers in a brief, hard kiss.

"Don't look like that, honey," he said softly. "I don't blame you for thinking what you did."

"It was only for a moment, Seamus," she said, her voice an anguished whisper. "Only for a *moment.*"

"Don't think about it anymore. Think about getting out of this alive, okay?" The blood trickled down near his eye again, but he ignored it. "The keys are still in the ignition. If anything happens to me, don't stick around. He's got a telescopic sight up there with him, and once he sees I'm down he'll come for you. Get to Sully if you can and tell him everything. He'll know what to do."

His face was bloody and streaked with dirt, and the tweed jacket was stained dark crimson—with Noah Watkins's blood, she realized sickly. But the eyes were the same as always. They would never change, she thought. They would never waver, never look at her with anything but love.

"Remember, stay low."

With one last urgent glance at her, Malone started crawling on his belly around the back of the car. Ainslie followed suit, copying his movements exactly. He'd done this before, she thought distractedly, feeling the tall stalks of grass that only minutes ago had looked feathery and delicate razoring her hands as she pushed her way through it. This had been a way of life for him—taking cover under fire, reacting instantly, facing death on a daily basis. No wonder he had survived the Agency's hunt for him.

The Executioner had picked the wrong man to frame, she thought as they neared the passenger-side door and she saw him reach up for the handle.

This time the explosive crack was coupled with the sound of shattering glass, and she instinctively buried her face in the ground. She could taste dirt, she thought faintly—dirt and something else, something warm and slightly salty.

"Lee!" Malone was beside her, his expression agonized as she lifted her head. "Were you hit? Dear God, Lee, *say* something!"

"It's just my cheek, I think," she managed. "A stone

must have ricocheted and hit me. I—I've gotten worse in the ring, Malone."

"Screw this. I'm getting you out of here, goddammit—*now.*"

His eyes dark with anger, he rose to his full height, wrenched open the car door, and slid across the seat and behind the wheel, not bothering to shield himself. Swiftly he turned the key in the ignition, and the car roared instantly to life. As she scrambled to her feet he leaned over and pulled her in. She only just managed to close the door behind her before he threw the vehicle into reverse.

"Stay low, honey," he muttered, slinging his arm across the seat back and looking over his shoulder as he trod down heavily on the gas pedal. Ainslie lurched forward as the car shot backward.

"Screw that, Malone." She looked up at the pile of gray stone, and thought she saw the wink of a reflection on the upper floor. She concentrated on it rather than Watkins's body sprawled on the dirt track in front of them. "He's got us on the ropes, and that's bad enough. I never huddled on the mat for any opponent, and I'm not about to start now."

"Then brace yourself, O'Connell." He gave her a reluctant grin. "This is where it gets interesting."

His foot jammed down on the brake and instantly the rear end of the sedan slewed sickeningly sideways. Through the windshield in front of her the landscape blurred with merry-go-round dizziness, as if it was revolving around them. She flinched instinctively as she heard the flat crack of another shot ring out, and saw tatters of white bark fly from the trunk of a birch tree.

It looked like a miniature flag of surrender, she thought distractedly. But no one was surrendering here.

The car rocked to a halt, and she was thrown against

the door, but before she had even caught her breath Malone released the clutch. Gravel sprayed up behind them as the sedan's tires fought for purchase, found it, and propelled them forward.

"If it's going to happen, it'll happen now," he said tightly, his eyes on the road ahead. "He can track his next shot now that we're following the road."

The slender birch that had been hit had been the only tree that could have afforded them some cover. Ainslie sat rigidly in her seat, waiting for the shot that would end either her life or Malone's, and feeling as if the sedan had a huge bull's-eye painted on the side of it. Ahead of them chips flew from a boulder as the Executioner's next bullet slammed into it.

The birch had been only five or six inches in diameter, at most, she thought numbly. It was one thing to hear of the assassin's skill, but seeing it in deadly action made it chillingly clear just how formidable their opponent was. The birch hadn't been a lucky shot, or a misfire—the man had deliberately chosen a target that he'd known they would see, as a demonstration to his quarry that he could pick them off anytime he chose.

So why hadn't he?

Even before the question had fully formed in her mind, she knew the answer. She turned to Malone, her gaze dark with dawning anger.

"It's not going to happen." Her pronouncement was flat with conviction. "He never had any intention of taking us out here. He's been playing cat and mouse with us, Seamus."

The glance he threw her was startled. Then she saw his grip on the steering wheel tighten. "Because if he'd wanted to kill us, he would have by now," he said harshly.

"Of course. The bastard's been jerking us around, dammit!"

He looked past her to the ruins of the stone mansion behind them just as one last shot lodged harmlessly in the massive trunk of an old oak they'd just passed, and then they were cresting the hill leading away from the lake, the woods around them thickening. Malone allowed the sedan's speed to ease off slightly.

"He meant to kill Noah, not you. That wasn't an accident, was it?" She heard the foolishly high note in her own voice, and realized she was trembling.

"It wasn't an accident. It was marksmanship." His jaw was rigid. "But why, for God's sake? Why not finish the job and take us out, too?"

"Paul said he likes kicking the anthill and watching what happens," she said slowly. "How much fun would he get by destroying the anthill all at once? He sees this as a game, Malone—a game where he makes up all the rules, and we have to figure them out as we go along."

They'd reached the intersection of the dirt track and the paved road that led back to the highway, and as they came to a stop in a cloud of dust he looked over at her.

"It's not a game, Lee. That's not how he sees it at all." He shook his head. "He wants to pick the time and place to kill us, and he wants us to be fully aware that we're going to die. No, he doesn't see this as a game."

His hands tightened on the steering wheel until his knuckles whitened. He stared at her grimly.

"He sees this as a sport. And today he officially opened hunting season."

Chapter Twelve

"This is going to sting a little."

Ainslie uncapped the bottle of antiseptic she'd bought on the way to the motel, wrinkling her nose at the sharp scent. While Malone had sat on the edge of the bath, she'd carefully tweezed out every sparkling sliver of glass she'd been able to see. Now he winced as she dabbed the pungent cotton pad at the cracked rivulet of dried blood nearest his eye.

"For crying out loud," he muttered. "That doesn't sting a little. It hurts like hell."

"If you don't want me to save your sight, just say so," she said. "I'm sure you'll look dashing with a patch over one eye."

Her sharpness was a mask for her worry. She threw the cotton square into the wastebasket by her feet and automatically pressed a new one to his temple, her lips tightening as she saw fresh crimson staining through.

"It's deep?" Malone's open eye glanced up at her.

"Very deep," she said shortly. "I know what you said about going to a doctor, Seamus, but it needs stitches."

"Then I hope you've got a needle and thread." His tone brooked no argument. "A hospital's completely out of the question."

He was right, she knew. And since their trail had been picked up either at Sullivan Investigations or at the apartment itself this morning, neither of those places was an option for them, either. It had been by the sheerest good fortune that she'd remembered the Galway Motel and its owner, Billy Dare, a retired trainer who'd carried a torch for Aunt Kate for years.

At the thought of her aunt's old friend, a solution came to her.

She grabbed Malone's wrist and placed his hand on the cotton square by his eye. "Keep that there and don't move," she commanded. "If we can't get a doctor for you, you'll have to settle for the next best thing."

"A veterinarian?" he asked suspiciously.

She gave him a quelling look. "No. But that's still a possibility, so don't knock it."

Before he could protest any further, she was out of the bathroom. A moment later she was ringing through to the motel's main office where she'd checked in only half an hour ago. As she hung up, she saw Malone walk unsteadily into the room.

"I'm still holding the damn gauze," he said, forestalling her. He sat heavily on the edge of the lumpy but scrupulously clean bed, his face paler than normal. "This Dare, Lee, can you trust him?"

"Billy could see me shoot a man in cold blood, and he wouldn't blow the whistle on me," she said, worry etching her expression as she took in his pallor. She saw his raised eyebrow and smiled reluctantly. "Well, maybe I'm exaggerating just a little," she conceded. "But yes, I trust him. He and Aunt Kate go back a long way."

"I'd like to meet your aunts." His gaze held hers. "Somehow we didn't do much socializing before, did we, Lee?"

"I think we came up for air a couple of times." Her own eyes darkened in remembrance and she smiled at him. "But we did seem to stay in bed an awful lot, Malone."

"And this time we seem to be getting shot at an awful lot." He looked away. "Maybe you should cut your losses while you still can, honey."

"And miss all this?" Gesturing expansively at the room around them, she kept her tone light. "No way."

Malone's jaw set stubbornly. "I mean it, Lee. Your brother could assign a bodyguard to you until all this blows over, and—"

To Ainslie's relief, a sharp rap on the unit's door cut off the rest of his sentence. Her movements suddenly jerky, she turned from him, feeling as if she'd just gotten a reprieve.

"Hey, doll."

Billy Dare—Big Bad Billy, as he'd been called when he'd been fighting—breezed into the room, his frame no longer as massive as it had once been, but still imposing for a man of his age.

"I thought you might be in trouble when you drove in. The Galway's a decent enough joint, but when a nice girl like you books a room, tries to euchre me about whether she's got a man with her and parks her car 'round the back where it can't be seen from the road, the bells go off. Holy liftin'!"

He stopped stock-still a few feet from Malone, his normally good-natured expression appalled.

"She won't let me look in a mirror. Now I think I know why." Malone tried to stand, but sank back on the bed. He held out his hand wryly. "Seamus Malone."

"Billy Dare. Jeez, man, what the hell have you gone and done to yourself?" Shaking Malone's hand perfunctorily, Dare grabbed a nearby chair and dragged it over to the bed, tossing down the paper sack he'd brought with him.

Ainslie came to stand beside the big ex-boxer. "Aunt Kate always said you should have been a surgeon, Billy. We need one right now," she said tensely.

"I chose the sweet science over medicine, baby girl."

He peered closely at the wound, not noticing the faint grin that Malone shot at Ainslie. Despite herself, she grinned back, amused at both the older man's choice of endearments and his use of the sportswriter's traditionally reverent phrase for boxing. He pulled back abruptly, and switched his attention to her.

"I think I can fix your boy up. I've done it often enough in a dressing room after a fight." He frowned. "But I won't get in Dutch with Kate over this, not even to help out the best little boxer I ever took to see her first fight. You gotta be straight with me, sweetie—is this good-looking lug bad news for you? Should I be sending him on his way and calling your brother to come pick you up?"

"If you call Sully, we'll both be gone before you hang up the phone," Ainslie said evenly. "It's true we can't let the authorities know about this, Billy, but that's not Malone's fault. We're in a jam, but if you don't feel easy helping us, we'll understand."

"I'm supposed to have killed a man." As Dare glanced swiftly at him, Malone went on, his tone flat. "Probably two, by now. You make that call to Sullivan, Dare. Just give me enough time to get out of here before the police arrive."

"Don't listen to him, Billy," Ainslie snapped. "If you check higher up under his hairline, you'll see a scar from an old head wound. Sometimes he talks crazy. I'm not letting you leave here without me, and that's final, Malone," she added tersely.

"Then that's that." Dare sighed and reached for the paper bag. He spared a briefly sympathetic glance for Malone. "The O'Connell women never change their minds once they decide on something. If Ainslie here says she's sticking by you, she's sticking by you and there's not a damn thing you or I can do about it. As for the other, well..."

His gaze hardened. "There was a fighter once, went by the name of Hurricane Carter. They hung a bum rap on him, too. It took twenty years behind bars before his name was cleared and he won his freedom back again. If you say you didn't do what they're saying you did, I'm inclined to take your side against the boys in blue."

"Thanks, Billy." Ainslie swallowed past the sudden lump in her throat. "I won't forget this."

"Neither will I, doll." Dare raised an eyebrow. "I'm counting on you to plead my case before your mule-headed aunt the next time I come courting her. But let's get your man stitched up first."

Aunt Kate had been right, Ainslie thought half an hour later, Big Bad Billy Dare had missed his calling. She watched in awe as he tied off the last stitch and clipped the thread close to the surface.

Despite the pain medication that he'd taken on the insistence of Dare, Malone's face was drained of all color by the time everything was finished. He mustered a lopsided smile as Dare stood back and surveyed his handiwork.

"If that even leaves a scar, I'll be surprised." The craggy face bore an almost smug satisfaction. "Now, what do you intend to do about that car out back? It looks like it caught a few rounds, too."

"Ditch it," Malone said regretfully. "Like you say, it's noticeable."

"I know a guy who knows a guy..." Dare tapped the side of his nose, and Ainslie wondered briefly how many times it had been broken. "Give me the keys. I can have it back to you tomorrow morning, good as new. I'll just have to make sure my buddy knows this one doesn't get loaded onto a freighter heading to parts unknown for a quick resale."

A more unlikely guardian angel would be hard to imagine, Ainslie thought a few minutes later as Dare crashed out of the unit, the sedan's keys dangling from one meaty finger. But Dare, despite his rough-hewn exterior and his dubious contacts, had come through for his old flame's niece. She *would* put in a good word for him with Aunt Kate when this was all over, she thought, closing the door behind him. And that reminded her...

"I have to call Tara," she said firmly, turning back to Malone. "I won't tell her where I am, but she and Aunt Kate will worry if—"

She broke off in midsentence. He was sprawled across the bed, his face a muddy gray under his tan, his breathing even enough. The loss of blood combined with the strong pills he'd taken had been too much for even his constitution, Ainslie thought. Sleep was probably the best thing for him right now. Crossing quietly to the bed, she covered his prone body with a light blanket, and then squared her shoulders as she sat at the desk. She would have to contact Pearson after calling Tara, she told herself somberly. It wasn't a conversation she felt ready for, but she had no right to put it off.

Two men had been killed in the past twenty-four hours. Malone had been right—the Executioner's latest hunt had begun, and so far the deaths were his way of flushing his real prey out into the open. Sooner or later even he would tire of the hunt and would want to bring it to a conclusion—and when he did, he might well decide to strike at them closer to home.

Malone knew that. Already he had tried to persuade her to leave. But she had hostages to fortune, too.

Tara was one of them. And as unlikely as it seemed, she couldn't afford to dismiss the possibility that as far as the Executioner was concerned, the other would be the quiet, considerate man who'd cared enough for her to want to make her his wife.

Twenty minutes later Ainslie shakily hung up the phone and took a deep, calming breath. If she'd had any idea that Sullivan would be at Aunt Kate's, of the two calls *that* would have been the one she would have dreaded more. As it was, she'd been totally unprepared when he'd answered the phone. After he'd reassured her that Bailey and Megan were both doing well and expected home the next day, the conversation had rapidly gone downhill.

At first he'd refused to believe her assertion that Malone was not only alive, but that she was with him. She couldn't really blame him for that, she thought wearily, since only yesterday she herself had conceded to him that the man she'd seen outside of St. Margaret's couldn't have been Seamus. But finally he'd had to accept that what she was telling him was true. Then the real fireworks had started.

Part of his anger at her masked his anger at himself, she guessed, anger that he'd kept silent about Malone's mercenary past when it might have made a difference. When she'd told him that she knew of Seamus's former career and still intended to stand by him, Sully'd switched tactics, asking her how she could be so certain that the Agency had gotten it wrong, asking her if she could be sure that the man she was with—the man, he reminded her forcefully, who'd already lied to her once—wasn't the killer the authorities believed him to be.

And for that, as well, she couldn't blame her brother, Ainslie told herself heavily. How could she, when for one split second today doubt had touched her, too?

In the end Sullivan had tersely informed her that he would assign round-the-clock security for Tara, without informing his teenage niece of the real reason why. He'd made one last attempt to get Ainslie to tell him where he could reach her, and when she'd refused he'd told her that he would expect another call from her by noon the next day or he would be going to the authorities. Ainslie wasn't sure which of them had managed to slam their respective receivers down on the other first, but their conversation had terminated abruptly.

She glanced over at Malone, her expression softening as she took in the regular rise and fall of his chest under the blanket she'd laid over him. Some of the color had returned to his face, and the lines of pain that had bracketed his mouth earlier were smoothed in sleep. Once again she felt a rush of gratitude for that other woman who had watched over him. Anna Nguyen had probably saved his life, she reflected somberly. If the grocery store owner's faith in him had wavered even once, he would have been doomed.

That thought cut too close to home. Her shoulder bag was gaping open beside her on the desk, and she pulled it toward her. Although she knew Pearson's Beacon Hill number, she'd seldom phoned him at Greystones, but she was sure she'd noted it in her address book. She extracted the slim volume from her purse and then frowned.

Instead of her address book, what she had in her hand was a collection of poetry—Yeats, she saw with faint surprise. But how—

She remembered the pile of books that Pearson had been going through not twenty-four hours ago, and a sudden pang of sadness shot through her. It wasn't the first time she'd come across some token of his affection for her tucked into a pocket or dropped unobtrusively into her purse, for her to find later. Yeats was one of his favorite poets. He'd obviously hoped his spur-of-the-moment gift would have some meaning for her.

Sitting back in the chair, she balanced the book on her palm. Yesterday she had been ready to marry the man who had given her this. Yesterday her life had been set to follow a predictable pattern that would never have included the numbing fear she'd experienced today when she'd seen Noah Watkins murdered...but that also would never have included the starry highs she and Malone had reached last night in each other's arms. If she'd taken the vows that she'd gone to St. Margaret's to pledge, she would have kept them, Ainslie thought. But eventually something inside her would have withered away forever, and Pearson, with his sensitivity where she was concerned, would have come to realize it.

She never would have made him happy. Leaving him at their wedding had been unforgivable, but marrying him would have caused him much more grief in the end. He deserved a woman who shared his interests, who was content, as he was, with experiencing life at one step removed from all its intensity. Even his dreams and ambitions weren't for himself, but for his brother.

She leafed through the small book in her hand unseeingly. Brian was Pearson's alter ego, the public figure who chaired committees, wielded growing influence, and who quite probably would one day achieve the position of ultimate power he sought. Other and better contenders might challenge him, but his golden-boy charm was a formidable asset.

It had bound his brother to him, Ainslie thought, often,

she knew, against Pearson's own better judgment. But despite Pearson's indulgence there was a moral line over which he would not and could not cross, not even for Brian. She had sometimes wondered if the younger man knew that line existed, and if he knew, how he would react if he stepped over it and found his brother had turned his back on him forever.

She shivered suddenly, and for no discernible reason. Her gaze focused on the open book in her hand, and she read the words she had been blankly gazing at for the last few minutes.

"September, 1913." It had to be one of Pearson's favorite poems, because in pencil he had lightly underscored portions of it, including the line whose reference to wild geese had its roots, Ainslie presumed, in the same legend that Sullivan had told her of so long ago. She closed the book, thoughtfully running her fingertips along the richly embossed calfskin binding. Pearson was a very private person, but in giving her this book he had allowed her a glimpse into his soul. Behind the outward facade of stuffy correctness was a man romantic enough to believe in the concepts of truth and honor reflected in the poem he'd marked, no matter how outmoded those concepts might be today.

He and Malone had that in common, she thought slowly and with a return of the fear that she'd earlier pushed aside. Those beliefs were what made both of them strong in their individual ways...but those beliefs could also prove to be their undoing at the hands of someone as ruthless as the Executioner.

Dropping the volume of Yeats into her purse, she pulled out her address book, quickly flipping to the entry for Greystones and dialling the number before her courage faltered. She had no idea what kind of message she would leave if he wasn't there, she realized suddenly, but almost immediately the phone was picked up.

"Hello?"

The calmly courteous voice belonged to Pearson himself, and at it Ainslie felt her foolish hesitation melt away. She wouldn't be able to tell him everything, she thought, but even if her warnings and hints struck him as puzzling she knew he would take her as seriously as he'd always done.

Wanting to ease into the reason for her call, she gave him the news about Megan Angelique, and promised to pass on his congratulations to Bailey and Sullivan. Then, taking a deep breath, she launched into the same vague explanation her brother had told her he would tell Tara—that Sullivan Investigations had received a threat against not only its owner, but anyone connected with his family, and that until the perpetrator of the threat was uncovered Sullivan was taking the matter seriously.

"I think you should, too, Pearson. Is anyone with you at Greystones?"

"Not at the moment, no, although Brian arrives tomorrow for a few days. But the estate's well secured, Ainslie. I'll certainly take every precaution, if you think it's necessary." He sounded dubious.

"I'm probably making a mountain out of a molehill," she admitted. "It's just that I..." She hesitated, and then went on, her voice soft. "I don't want any harm to come to you. I care for you very much, Pearson."

On the other end of the line he was silent for a moment. All at once she could see him in her mind's eye—his tall, spare figure immaculately if casually dressed, his reading glasses pushed up into the pale hair that he'd ruefully told her had been getting annoyingly thinner since he'd reached forty, his mobile and sensitive mouth turned down a little at the corners. She hadn't given him her decision in so many words, she thought heavily. But he knew.

"I know you do, my dear," he said quietly. His sigh was so light it was nearly inaudible, but almost immediately his voice lifted. "If I see any suspicious characters slouching around the property I'll call the police right away, I promise. Does that ease your mind?"

"It does, Pearson. Thank you—and not only for that."

Her throat threatened to close, and she gripped the receiver tightly, knowing that a display of emotion at this point would only make him uncomfortable.

"Thank you for everything," she ended inadequately, hoping he hadn't heard the quaver in her tone.

If he had, he gave no sign. "I'll make sure the alarms are set, although most likely Brian will forget the security code and set them all off when he comes." He gave a small laugh that she knew was for her benefit. "I'll tell you all about it when we meet for dinner later this week."

He probably would, she thought unhappily as she hung up the phone. They would sit across from each other amid shining cutlery and sparkling glassware, and he would attempt to smooth the awkwardness of their parting with casual conversation. Pearson would see that as simple good manners.

"Except I'd feel a whole lot less guilty if he reamed me out like I deserve," she muttered, abruptly standing and looking at her reflection in the nearby dresser mirror with sudden distaste.

Her appearance wasn't the real reason she found it hard to meet her own gaze in the mirror, she thought dully. She turned away and shrugged out of the ruined jacket.

She'd been given a miracle. The man she loved had been returned to her, and she'd told herself that nothing would ever shake her faith again. But at the first test of that faith she'd failed.

"You lied to Watkins."

Startled, she looked around, wondering just how long he'd been awake. As he removed the blanket and swung his legs off the bed, she went to him.

"You shouldn't be up, Malone." Ignoring what he'd just said, she sat beside him and peered worriedly at Dare's handiwork. "How are you feeling?"

His smile was wry. "It's just as well that I'm nearly at the end of those pills. I could get used to the buzz. You lied to Watkins, honey."

He wasn't going to let it go. Ainslie met his gaze.

"I shaded the truth a little, but so what? I know you didn't shoot Paul Cosgrove."

"Maybe I did." His smile was gone. "I went back to the house while you were getting into the car, like Watkins said."

"You were gone for half a minute, if that," she countered. "You wiped the door handle where I'd touched it, just like you'd wiped my prints from the bottle and the glass I'd handled while we were talking to him. If you hadn't done that, the police might trying to pin his murder on *me* by now."

"But if he was alive when we left, why would I have been worrying about leaving prints?" He didn't let her answer. "Oh, I know what I told you, Lee—that if Paul called in the Agency I didn't want them to have anything they could use against you. But maybe I went back and killed him."

She stared at him in confusion. "Except you know you didn't."

"I don't remember doing it. But somehow that doesn't reassure me a hell of a lot." He looked down at his hands, and when he spoke again he seemed to be talking to himself rather than to her. ''What if it's all true? What if I've done all the things they say I did, and I've learned how to block out the guilt by erasing all those memories? All except one,'' he added tightly.

''Fine. If you want me to play devil's advocate, I will.'' Ainslie forced a sharpness into her tone. ''If you did go back and kill Cosgrove, why didn't I hear the shot?''

''I used a silencer.'' His reply was automatic. ''I got rid of it later. Try again, Lee.''

''I suppose you'll say that what happened at the hotel yesterday could all have been rigged up by you to convince me that we were in danger, so I won't even bother with that,'' she said shortly. ''But what about Watkins? What about the sniper who was shooting at us today from that burned-out house? Dammit, Malone, you said yourself that *had* to be the Executioner.''

''And that's exactly what I would say. Especially if the person I was really trying to convince was myself, Lee.'' His eyes darkened. ''That shooter could have been there as Noah's backup, and when he saw that the situation had turned bad on his partner, he tried to take me out. But he missed, and got Watkins instead. It wouldn't be the first time a man was killed by friendly fire.''

''And the next five shots missed their target, too?'' Her voice rose. ''For God's sake, Malone, that doesn't make sense!''

''He panicked. He'd just killed his partner, and he knew it. And from what Watkins said earlier, the shooter probably wasn't convinced that you were part of this, so picking me off without taking out another innocent person wasn't that easy. It could have happened that way, Lee.''

''It didn't happen that way, because if it did that would mean that *you're* the Executioner, and you're not!'' Fear harshened her voice. "You *know* you're incapable of doing the things he's done!"

"How do I know that, Lee?" His gaze seemed suddenly brilliant. "Except for the fact that I chose the most violent profession of all, I don't know anything about the kind of man I am or what I've been capable of in the past. How do I know I *didn't* cross over the line from soldier for hire to assassin?"

"Because *I* know you couldn't cross that line, dammit!" Her eyes blazing, she brought her face close to his. "If you can't rely on your own memory of the man you used to be, rely on mine. I fell in love with you, Malone! I fell in love with you, and even if we only had two weeks together, I knew the kind of man you were. I knew you completely!"

"Yeah, honey, I think you did. Even if you can't admit it to yourself, I think you still do." His voice was hoarse, and the brilliance had faded from his gaze. A muscle at the side of his jaw moved.

"And that's why just for a moment today you thought I'd gunned down an unarmed man," he said softly. "Because some part of you has to know that I'm capable of *everything* they say I've done."

Malone stood. "No other explanation fits the facts, Lee. The best we've been able to come up with is that Watkins betrayed every oath he'd sworn to uphold as a government agent, and was taking orders from the Executioner himself without realizing it. I didn't know the man well, but I don't think he was that stupid. He'd been given hard proof that I was a killer who had to be taken out, no matter what."

"Hard proof from his unimpeachable source," Ainslie said tightly. "That's why my theory *does* fit. Whoever the Executioner is when he's in his Dr. Jekyll mode, he has to be someone whose word is accepted unquestioningly."

"So who do you propose we focus on?" There was an edge to his tone. "The director of the Agency? Or hell, maybe Watkins was getting information from the Oval Office itself. That would fit all our half-baked—"

"*Stop* it, Malone!" With no clear recollection of even having gotten off the bed, she was on her feet and facing him. "That's crazy and you know it!"

"No more crazy than anything else we've come up with simply because we refuse to accept the only sane explanation," he said harshly. "I've been keeping my eyes closed just as tightly as you have, Lee, but today I finally saw how it was. Sure, I tried to convince myself that the shooter had to be the Executioner and that for some reason he wanted to postpone our deaths. But the truth was in your eyes at the moment of Watkins's death. You knew I was capable of pulling that trigger, honey—and that washes away the one argument we had against me being the Executioner."

"You intend to turn yourself in."

It wasn't a question, but she kept her gaze on him anyway, as if she still harbored some faint hope that he would refute her statement. When he didn't, she turned away.

"Who to, Malone, the Agency or the police?" She stood by the dresser, her back to him.

"The police." There was no hesitation in his answer. "I won't risk anything happening to you, so you stay with Dare until it's all over."

Lifting her head, she met his eyes in the mirror and nodded slowly. "I get it. This time *I* walk away from *you,* right? This way your conscience is clear, Malone, because you can tell yourself you didn't walk out of my life a second time."

"I didn't walk out on you the first time," he said

sharply. "Not intentionally, anyway. And you're forgetting that I came back to—"

"You didn't come back to me!"

Spinning abruptly around to face him, she flung the accusation at him, her voice high and tremulous. Malone's expression was shuttered, and something inside of her flared out of control as she met that opaque green gaze.

"You *never* came back! Someone who looked like you and sounded like you came back, but the man I loved walked out on me that night two years ago and never returned! You're a complete stranger to me!"

"What the hell are you talking about, Lee?" His tone was tight. "You know me better than anyone, dammit!"

"No, I knew the man I loved and lost." She shook her head in sharp denial. "He may not have revealed everything about his past to me, but he didn't hide away his soul. The man who turned up yesterday calling himself Malone would rather send me away than let me know there's a place inside him so dark and so terrible that from the first he's believed himself capable of the worst crimes imaginable."

"You were the one who thought I'd killed Watkins. That's what finally convinced me—" he began, but she cut him off.

"I didn't convince you, Malone! You've been convinced all along that you could be the Executioner—and some part of me knew there had to be a reason for you to believe that. Do you want to know what really happened today? Just for one moment, I let *you* convince *me!*"

She took a step toward him. "So what is it you're keeping from me, Malone? What do you know about yourself that's too damning to reveal?"

"Nothing." His tone betrayed no emotion. "I told you, I barely remember anything about my past."

"I know what you've told me. I think you're lying," she said unevenly. "I think you do remember something. Is it to do with Joseph Mocamba?"

"I just have the one memory about him." His eyes met hers and she knew he was telling the truth. Then his gaze slid away again. "There's nothing else."

He was only about a foot away from her, Ainslie thought, but he'd just put himself beyond her reach forever. "I was wrong," she said, her voice low and intense. "I thought I threw roses onto an empty coffin. But whether your physical body was in there or not, I really did bury you that day, Malone. You really did die. You didn't come back to me at all."

Chapter Thirteen

She stared at him for a long moment, her vision blurring with unshed tears. "They're going to kill you. The police will hand you over to the Agency, and you'll never be heard of again. The Executioner will see to that. And even if they do hold another funeral for you, I won't be there at the graveside. This time you'll go down into the darkness alone. But that's the way you want it, isn't it?"

She turned away and walked over to the desk. She picked up her shoulder bag and the jacket she'd discarded, and went past him to the door.

Then she paused and turned back to him, the tears no longer in her eyes but silvery tracks on her cheeks. "You were a mercenary, so you must know the legend that Sully once told me—the one about the wild geese. Do you believe it, Seamus?"

He blinked. "That when mercenaries die, their souls take on the form of wild geese and they're doomed to fly for all eternity?" He shook his head. "No, I don't believe that. I never did."

"Neither do I." She attempted a shaky smile. "I wish I did. I'd rather think of you up there with them, than where you're really going."

"And where's that, Lee?"

His tone was less remote than it had been, but his eyes were still unreadable. Ainslie looked at him in faint surprise.

"Why, hell, of course," she said simply. "That's where you think you deserve to go. That's where you've been for the last two years, Seamus, but this time you're going to make it permanent."

She put her hand lightly on his sleeve, and felt his muscles tense under her touch. Rising up on her tiptoes, she brushed her lips against the immobile corner of his mouth, and then stepped back, her anguished gaze fixed on his.

"At least the wild geese seek redemption, however futile their search is." Her words were leaden. "But you believe you're beyond it, Malone. Even I can't convince you otherwise."

She turned back to the door. She put her hand on the knob, pushed it open, and felt the night air rush to meet her.

"They buried me alive, Lee."

His words were low, as if some part of him hoped she wouldn't hear him, but as she froze to stillness he went on in the same flat tone.

"The rest of my reconnaissance party was killed in the ambush, but I was just wounded. The government forces caught me the next day, and they decided to make an example of me. So they buried me alive."

The hair on the back of her neck rose. Very slowly she turned to face him, icy horror washing over her.

"What did you say?"

"They built a wooden box just big enough for me to stand in." A muscle at the side of his jaw jumped. "They put me in it, and five of them lowered it into a hole they'd dug in the ground. Then they filled the hole up again and left me there to die. They wanted it to be slow, Lee. They'd inserted a length of pipe that ran from the box and up through six feet of packed earth as a breathing tube."

Carefully, Ainslie shut the door behind her. She stood in front of him, her stricken gaze on his face.

The eyes that stared back at her were dark and empty, as if the man behind them had gone away a long time ago, leaving only a hollow shell behind. When he spoke again, the illusion was complete. His voice was dead and mechanical.

"Except I didn't die." One corner of his mouth jerked up in a parody of a smile. "I spent the whole of the first day trying to get my hands free from the ropes they'd bound them with. After my wrists started bleeding, it got easier."

"Malone, *don't.*" The cry was wrenched from her. "You don't have to—"

"When my hands were finally free, I took off my belt and started scraping away at the wood of the box with the buckle." If he'd heard her interruption, he gave no sign. "They'd used scrap lumber, so the real problem wasn't in breaking through. It was in making sure that when I finally did, the earth above didn't fall in and suffocate me. In my dreams the last couple of years that's always how it ends—in complete darkness, trying to take one more breath, and not being able to."

He shook his head as if to clear it. "But as I said, that's not how it turned out in reality. Leaving the pipe there was their mistake, because if I hadn't had that as a guide I wouldn't have known which way to dig. It was my lifeline. Even after the delirium took hold, I kept digging up alongside it, even though by then I'd forgotten where I was or what I was doing. Sometime after that I got to the surface. After resting up for a day, I went hunting for the men who'd buried me."

This time when he smiled she saw the brief gleam of his teeth. His eyes were shadowed.

"The details don't matter. The unit they'd been in had been given harvest furlough to bring in the crops, so they'd all gone back to their villages. But one by one I found them. And one by one I killed them." He shrugged. The movement seemed stiff and unnatural. "By that time I was drifting in and out of delirium from the fever I'd contracted, but sometimes my mind would clear and I would wonder what I was becoming. I told myself that they were soldiers, and the enemy that I'd been hired to fight, so what I was doing was no more than I did every day of my professional life. But I knew it wasn't."

"But what kind of men were *they,* to have done what they did to you?" Ainslie said through dry lips.

"Like I said, they were soldiers." He shook his head. "Their unit was known for its atrocities on the area's civilians, which was why the rebels I was fighting with had tried to wipe them out in the first place. But what they were doesn't change anything."

Ainslie wondered if he'd considered whether the future innocent victims of the men he'd killed would have agreed with him—women and children whose lives had been spared because Malone had eliminated at least some members of a death squad. But even as she opened her mouth to speak, he went on, as if he wanted only to get the story over with.

"By the time I found the last of the five, the word had gotten out that a ghost was stalking anyone who'd had anything to do with burying the *Americano,* so he knew I was coming for him. He was standing sentry duty his first night back with his unit when I came out of the jungle and let him see my face."

Malone frowned. "I knew his death would end it all.

But as I stood there in front of him, the fever left me as suddenly as if I'd just woken up from a nightmare, and I knew I couldn't kill him. So I told him it was over between us. I'd taken only a couple of steps away from him when he shot me. The bullet took me high on my left shoulder blade."

"The scar I kissed." Her voice was hoarse. "That's how you got it. What happened then?"

"My shot was better than his had been. I got back to the rebel encampment, and I was flown home to the States to recuperate."

He didn't elaborate, but Ainslie's imagination filled in the details. Racked by some jungle illness and with a bullet-shattered shoulder, it had been a miracle that he'd survived at all, she thought faintly. But he'd paid a heavy price for survival.

"I had a few bad nights when I dreamed I was in the jungle again, but gradually I learned how to stop thinking about it." For the first time since he'd started speaking, his eyes focused on hers. "Eight years later I got shot again in that alleyway and the nightmares returned, although the memory of what had caused them didn't come back until yesterday, along with the one about Joseph Mocamba. His assassination came a year or two after the incident in the jungle, Lee—and about a year before Chris Stewart was killed. Do you see a pattern here?"

"I know the pattern you think you see," she said evenly. "You think that what happened to you at the hands of those five butchers turned you into the same kind of man that they were. You think that's when you stopped being just a soldier, and became the Executioner. I don't buy it, Malone."

She stared at him unwaveringly. "You weren't in your right mind when you hunted them down—how *could* you have been, after what you'd endured? Yes, you crossed a line. But you were driven to it."

"Maybe I was," he said softly. "But Lee, I don't think I ever crossed back. I was in the right place at the right time for two of the Executioner's assassinations we know about—the one in the Balkans and the murder of Mocamba. The only reason I don't know about the others is because of my memory loss."

"But you weren't the only one in the right place at the right time at that airport in the Balkans," Ainslie said slowly. "Didn't you tell me that your driver gave a statement to the police, too, corroborating what you'd told them?"

"He gave a statement, sure." Malone shook his head dismissively. "What the hell does that prove?"

"Nothing, conclusively." Her voice took on an edge of cautious excitement. "But even if you have doubts about everything else, Stewart's is the one murder you can't suspect yourself of committing. There was another man at that airport who knew him, and you've got an independent witness who saw them together. Besides, if you killed him, why would you have insisted on stopping the next morning, when there was every chance that the police might detain you?"

For a moment hope flared behind his eyes. It disappeared, and his gaze became shuttered again. "So I didn't kill Stewart. We've tossed around the theory that his murder was related to the assassination somehow, but that's all it ever was—a theory. He met a friend, they had a falling out and he just happened to be killed on the same night that the country's leader was shot."

His jaw tightened. "You wanted to know why I believed I was capable of doing the things I've been accused of.

Now that you do, Lee, the best thing for you is to just walk away."

As if he couldn't help himself, he reached out and tucked a stray strand of hair behind her ear. "Tell yourself what you told me, honey," he said hoarsely. "Tell yourself that Seamus Malone left you two years ago, and he never came back. It won't really be a lie."

Taking a deep breath, he let his hand drop to his side. "I'm going to go through with this, Lee. It's the only way."

He started to turn away from her, and for a moment Ainslie felt paralyzed with despair. The Executioner had won. He'd studied this particular anthill and then had given it the kick that had destroyed not only Malone's life but hers and had led to the deaths of two decent men in the bargain. If Paul had been right about him, right now he was standing back in the shadows, watching as the events he'd set in motion played themselves out to a tragic finish.

Hot fury rose up in her, consuming the defeated hopelessness like an advancing fire. She threw back her slumped shoulders and grabbed Malone's sleeve before he could take another step, almost throwing him off balance.

He glanced at her in quick inquiry. "What is it—"

"You're taking a *dive,*" she said flatly, her eyes narrowing as she stared at him. "I may not know much about being a mercenary, Malone, but I was a boxer long enough to recognize when a fighter deliberately throws in the towel. You're right. I guess I *didn't* know the real Seamus Malone—I didn't figure any payoff would be enough to make you go down and stay down. It looks like I was wrong."

"Payoff?" His smile was strained. "Come on, Lee, no one's paying me off here and you know it." He attempted to pull away from her, but she didn't let go of his jacket.

"I don't know what else you'd call it." She held his gaze. "You've got a deal going with the Executioner. You take the fall for him and he'll give you what you want. Of course, your deal is going to cost the lives of the thousands he'll go on to destroy, but what does that matter? By the time he sets up his next assassination, you'll be beyond feeling any guilt. *That's* the payoff."

"How the hell could I have a deal going with a man I've never *met,* goddammit?" This time he did wrench away. "For God's sake, Lee, listen to what you're saying. It doesn't make any sense!"

"No, Malone, you listen to what *you* just said," Ainslie shot back. She saw his momentary disconcertion, and pressed home her advantage. "You've never met the Executioner? How could that be, if he's you?"

"It was a slip of the tongue, nothing more," he said tightly.

"Was it?" She shook her head. "I don't think so. I think some part of you knows the truth. But you're not going to let that part of you win."

Suddenly the fire went out of her. He had her on the ropes, Ainslie told herself wearily. She'd hung in for as long as she could, but he was just too good, too determined. And he wanted the prize he'd been fighting for too much to let her to wrest it away from him now, when it was almost within his grasp. She took a deep breath.

"You know, it's too bad you don't believe in the legend," she said quietly. "Because if it was redemption you were seeking instead of oblivion, then putting an end to the Executioner might be the way to buy back your soul, Seamus. But once he gets rid of you he's just going to go on killing—and wherever you are then, *that* blood will be on your hands forever."

Bending, she picked up her jacket and purse from where

they'd fallen to the floor. She straightened and turned to the door.

This time it was Malone's grip that stopped her so unexpectedly that she nearly lost her balance. His hand on her shoulder, he spun her around to face him.

"Once I turn myself in, the blood-letting *stops,* dammit." He ground the words out between clenched teeth. "That's why I'm doing this."

"And if it doesn't? If you've made a terrible mistake, and by giving yourself up you allow the real Executioner to remain at large?" Ainslie struck his hand away and thrust her face close to his. "Maybe I can't convince you you're wrong. But are you willing to stake the lives of innocent people on the certainty that you're *right?*"

For a moment she thought she'd pushed him too far. Then he closed his eyes briefly, as if in defeat. He opened them again, and his gaze met hers.

"One more day." His voice was quiet. "That's all I'll give it, Lee. Twenty-four more hours. If we haven't found anything that points to someone else being the Executioner, then you have to promise me you'll let it go."

Slowly she nodded. "I promise. But we're going to need some outside help. First thing tomorrow morning, we call Sully in on the Chris Stewart lead, agreed?"

His smile was wry. "Agreed. But don't be surprised if he's more interested in taking a swing at me than putting the resources of Sullivan Investigations at our disposal."

She shrugged in mock unconcern, the casual gesture belying her overwhelming relief at his change of heart, however temporary. He'd gone through so much, she thought in sudden fierce resolve. But enough was enough. The Executioner might not know it yet, but she'd won the first round against him.

And she was just getting started.

"STEWART'S COLLEGE records were easy enough to trace. It helped that an ex-mercenary buddy of mine, Quinn McGuire, knew him by his real name a long time ago." Sully spoke tersely, addressing his remarks solely to his sister, as he'd been doing since he'd arrived at the motel a few minutes ago.

Once he and Ainslie's half brother had been friends of a sort, Malone thought. Now the man wouldn't even look his way, and under the circumstances he supposed he couldn't blame him. But they couldn't work together like this.

"I appreciate the help, Sullivan. What did you find out?" He knew his question was the opening that the other man had been waiting for.

Sullivan swung around to face him, his eyes chips of ice. "Get one thing straight, Seamus. Any help I'm providing here has *nothing* to do with you."

Ainslie had been sitting at the desk, poring over a sheaf of documents that Sullivan had handed her, but at his outburst she jumped to her feet. Her hair swung in two dark wings at the sides of her set jawline, and her eyes were suddenly as blue as Malone had ever seen them.

"That's *enough,* Sully," she said tightly. Malone saw Sullivan's quickly disbelieving glance at her as she went on, her voice edged with anger. "Malone and I are on the same side, and if you're not with us—*both* of us—then we don't need your help."

"Dammit, Lee, the man's probably a killer, for God's sake!" Sullivan exploded. "What I'd like to know is how the hell he managed to convince you he's innocent."

"It looks like you and I are on the same side, Sully." Malone pushed himself away from the door frame. "I think there's every chance that I'm the Executioner, too.

But you don't know Lee if you think she's going to let either of us make up her mind for her."

Sullivan narrowed his eyes at him. "You're damn right I think you're capable of everything they say you did. I've done some asking around, and I've heard some things that made even my blood run cold. Apparently you once went on a one-man killing spree in the jungle—stalked and dispatched five victims with about as much emotion as a man-eating tiger going after its prey."

"Did your informants tell you why?" Ainslie's tone was strained, and suddenly Malone didn't want it to go any further.

"I told you, Lee, why doesn't matter. The stories are true, as far as they go, Sullivan. I killed those men."

"Because they buried him in a box six feet under—buried him and left him to *die*." Her gaze was fixed on her brother. "Maybe your informants forgot to pass on that part of the story."

Terrence Sullivan had a reputation for a cool toughness that nothing could shake. It was obvious he was shaken now. His appalled gaze went from his sister to Malone.

"Is that true?"

Malone held his gaze. "Yeah, Sully, it's true. And you and I both know it doesn't make a damn bit of difference. I hunted them down—not like the soldier I was supposed to be, but like a killer. Maybe I found I liked it."

"I've heard of that happening," Sullivan said shortly. "But usually a man who turns killer shows some sign of his inclinations long before. I never saw that in you."

Malone lifted his shoulders. As if sensing his reluctance to pursue the subject, after a last appraising glance, Sullivan picked up the papers Ainslie had been going through.

"Chris—it's easier to just keep calling him that, since that's the name you knew him by—had a pretty privileged upbringing. He was a golden boy—but a golden boy with a tarnished reputation.''

Beside him Ainslie nodded stiffly, her edginess still apparent. ''According to those records, he dropped out of college midterm in his second year. That must have been when his family finally washed their hands of him for good and he became a mercenary.''

''Probably the most unsuitable profession he could think of, just to shock them,'' Sully said. ''But if you're right, in the end it was someone from his eminently suitable past that killed him.''

''Not just from his past. Someone who'd been in college with him.'' Ainslie frowned at Malone. ''That's what he told you at the airport, isn't it?''

''An old school friend.'' Malone agreed. ''But how the hell are we going to find out which one?''

''The invaluable Moira's already working on that back at my office,'' Sully said. ''We're running all his classmates' names through the computer and eliminating anyone who was in the country at the time of his murder. Then we'll check whoever's left against a State Department database of Americans whose passports show them to have been in that particular area of the world on the date in question.''

Malone knew better than to ask Sully how he'd managed to be allowed access to information like that. But he had one question for him.

''And if none of the names pan out? It's likely our man was using a false passport, Sully.''

''Yeah, that occurred to me.'' Sullivan grimaced. ''My sources tell me the best passport forger in the business up until yesterday was a woman who lived right here in Boston.''

"Until yesterday?" Ainslie queried sharply. Her brother's mouth tightened.

"She was shot while taking her morning jog. The police haven't got any leads on her killer yet. It could be just coincidence, but..."

"But it's never a coincidence."

Malone heard the flatness in Ainslie's tone as she repeated his words of a few days earlier, and suddenly the futility of their undertaking struck him anew. He watched as she sat at the desk and started flipping through the documents again. This was tearing her apart, he thought. There were unhealthy shadows under those violet-blue eyes, and the coffee and bagels that Sully had brought still sat, untouched, by her elbow.

"Oh!"

Her exclamation broke into his thoughts. Glancing quickly over at her, he saw the faint question in her eyes as she looked up at her brother.

"I wondered if you'd catch that." Sullivan, now standing beside her, shook his head.

"What is it?" Rousing himself, Malone crossed to the desk. In answer, Ainslie tapped a forefinger on a name halfway down on the typewritten page in front of her.

"'McNeil, Brian Michael,'" Malone read out loud. "Sorry, I don't get it."

"A couple of days ago he came to within half an hour of being Ainslie's brother-in-law," Sully drawled. "Then my sister ran off with you. But having his name show up on this list is probably one of those rare times when it really is just a coincidence."

"Oh," Ainslie said again, this time with a tinge of disappointment in her voice. She looked instantly guilt-stricken. "Not that I want Pearson's brother to turn out to be a murderer, of course,'' she said hastily. ''But I thought we might be on to something.''

''At first glance, so did I.'' Sullivan jammed his hands into his pockets. The gesture betrayed slight frustration. ''At second glance he looked even better—he was on the rowing team with Stewart, and the two of them had the same circle of friends. But he wasn't out of the country at the time of Stewart's death. In fact, he was a very junior member of a committee that was looking into the alleged misuse of funds by a covert government agency—not the Agency, but one similar,'' he added as Malone's gaze sharpened.

''Anyway, he was in the public eye at the time. I've still got feelers out to see if I can pick up any rumors of our Brian ever being suspected of acquiring a false passport, but I think for now we have to scratch him as a possibility, Lee.''

''I suppose I'm glad.'' She smiled crookedly. ''Pearson's always known that his brother wasn't perfect, but that would have destroyed him. He doesn't deserve to have any more bombshells dropped on him.'' She shoved the pile of papers away from her and reached for a container of coffee. ''I haven't had a chance to ask how Bailey and Megan are doing, Sully. Don't they come home from the hospital today?''

''I'm picking them up later this morning. Tara's coming with me.'' Sullivan shot her a glance. ''I'm keeping her out of school for a day or two and I brought her over to my place last night so I could have one of my men with her at all times. She was still asleep when I left the house, but I wrote down the number of the motel and stuck a note up on the refrigerator. You'll probably hear from her yourself sometime today.''

''Thanks, Sully,'' Ainslie said softly. ''I know she'll be

safe with you.'' She fixed a determined smile on her face. ''Now, fill me in on all the fascinating details about my new niece's first day in the world. You have my permission to brag as much as you want.''

Her brother obviously didn't need any further prodding. As he launched enthusiastically into a recounting of all the ways that Megan Angelique had already demonstrated that she was the most adorable baby in existence, Malone saw the troubled lines between Ainslie's brows smooth out.

This had been one of his dreams, he thought heavily, being part of a circle of family and friends, sharing with Ainslie and the people they cared for the daily joys and small setbacks of an ordinary life. But those dreams would never come true. He knew that now.

He closed his eyes and immediately he was there again, the butt of a high-powered rifle snugged up against his shoulder, the scene through the scope jumping into startlingly clear focus....

Chapter Fourteen

It was nearly time. It seemed as if he'd been waiting up here for hours, hiding behind this massive steel girder that provided the framework for the array of powerful floodlights ringing the stadium. In a country where electricity was still a novelty for many of the rural residents, this newly built structure was symbolic of how far the nation had progressed in the five years of peace since Joseph Mocamba had become president. Considering tonight's dedication and formal unveiling was symbolic, too—a declaration to the world that this tiny republic had put its strife-ridden past behind it—Mocamba had insisted on addressing the crowd without a show of armed protectors about him.

The cheers below rose to a crescendo as the slight figure of the man he had been waiting for came onto the field and headed toward the podium, his progress impeded by the television crews milling around him. Malone looked through the scope again, and immediately Mocamba, although partially hidden by reporters, appeared close enough to reach out and touch. It would happen soon, he thought coldly.

It did.

A cameraman on the edge of the group surrounding the

president stumbled, and suddenly the sight line to Mocamba was unimpeded. His finger tightened on the trigger, but even as it did the president looked swiftly around, as if he had somehow sensed the danger coming for him. There was no way he could be visible to the man so far below him, Malone knew, but for a split second it seemed as if Mocamba's gaze, bisected by the rifle's crosshairs, was fixed on his.

And then the view through the scope was obscured by a haze of crimson, as Joseph Mocamba, whose code of nonviolence had set his beloved country on the road to peace, was thrown backward by the force of his assassin's bullet—

"...probably want to go with you and check out it out, right, Malone?"

The query in Ainslie's voice jerked him back to the present. "Sorry, I drifted off there." His voice sounded normal enough, he noted with relief. "Where are we going and what is it we're checking out?"

"When I arrived, Dare told me his friend had brought the car back this morning," Sully said. "It's parked out back. I thought we might take a look at it." There was an odd inflection in his voice.

"Sure." Malone looked at Ainslie. "You mind holding down the fort here for a minute or two, Lee?"

"Hmm, staring at the side of a car or stepping into the shower, turning it on as hot as I can stand it and getting really clean for the first time in two days? That's a tough choice," she said dryly. "But I guess I'll go with the shower option, boys. Go ahead and do your manly stuff without me."

Sullivan dropped a quick kiss on tip of her nose. "Good idea, little lady." He dodged her halfhearted swat. "I'll keep you posted on what Moira and I turn up on Chris's contacts, and if Tara hasn't phoned you, I'll remind her to give you a call. I know you miss the brat, sis."

"You're right. I don't know why, but I do," she replied in mock chagrin. "Now get out of here and give a girl some privacy, bro."

"The car's fine. I had a look at it when I got here," Sullivan said in an undertone as they rounded the corner of the motel to the small gravel lot at the back. "I'm worried about the Chris Stewart connection, Seamus—and the murder of that passport dealer. Maybe it was just a random shooting, but I don't like it."

"Neither do I." Malone looked away. "I think my resurfacing made Chris's murderer nervous—nervous enough to eliminate anyone who might know anything about his existence. That not only includes me, but the one person I might have taken into my confidence." He frowned. "Do you have any contacts on the police force who might be able to give you what they have on the shooting of the forger?"

"Jennifer Tarranova and Donny Fitzgerald," Sullivan said promptly. "Maybe Straub, if he's working the case. I'll make a few phone calls from home before I pick up Bailey." He glanced at his watch. "I'd better get going. I still have to stop by the house for Tara, and there's a couple of errands on my list, too."

He shot Malone a self-conscious grin. "I saw this giant toy giraffe in a toy store downtown, and I said I'd be by today to get it. Plus, the florist is making up a special bouquet that I ordered for Bailey."

Maybe a long time ago their lives had followed similar paths, Malone thought a few minutes later. He let himself into the motel room, the roar of the shower as he entered a noisy indication of Ainslie's whereabouts. But Terry Sullivan's ghosts had been vanquished, and he had become that rarest of beings—a perfectly happy man, supremely content with his lot in life.

Toy giraffes and flowers... Malone sat on the edge of the bed, and for just a moment allowed himself to wonder what his and Ainslie's child might have looked like if things had turned out differently. She—for some reason he was certain that their firstborn would have been a girl—would have come into the world with her mother's same uncompromisingly direct stare, he mused. She would have had the same tough little chin, the same blue-black hair with no hint of a wave in it, just like Ainslie's. But maybe her eyes would have been the same green as his...

He would have liked being a father, he thought. He would have liked that a lot.

The roar of the shower abruptly ceased and he got to his feet, not wanting Ainslie to sense his mood when she came into the room. The papers she'd been looking through were still sitting on the desk, anchored by a slim book. With mild curiosity he picked it up, and just as he did the phone rang.

"Damn!"

Clad only in a towel that was in danger, Malone noted, of coming undone where she'd wrapped it around her breasts, and with another towel towering in a precarious knot on her head, Ainslie came out of the bathroom at a stumbling trot. Strands of wet hair fell out of the loose turban into her eyes, despite her distracted efforts to tuck them in as the phone rang again.

"It's probably Tara. Want me to answer it?"

She looked up through her hair, obviously startled to see him there. Then her eyes narrowed. The note of innocence in his voice hadn't fooled her, Malone knew.

"You were just praying for this to fall off, weren't you?" Ainslie gave him a frosty glare that was ruined when she reached for the telephone and her towel slipped another notch. ''If I even *think* I hear you snickering, you're in a world of trouble, Malone,'' she muttered under her breath.

She picked up the receiver, cradled it on her shoulder, and before he realized what she intended to do, quickly flashed open the front of her towel at him, revealing a momentary glimpse of creamy breasts, heat-pinkened skin, and the tangled and still-damp triangle at the top of her thighs. She closed the towel just as swiftly, and batted her lashes at him before switching her attention to the phone.

''Hello?''

Her innocent voice was better than his, he conceded. Hell, her whole damn trick had been better than his, although if she glanced at him right now and slightly south of his belt buckle, that nonchalant air she was assuming might just be shaken the way she'd shaken him.

Which wouldn't be appropriate at all, he told himself repressively, catching enough of her conversation to realize that his guess had been right and it was Tara on the other end of the line. In an attempt to distract his thoughts from the X-rated vision Ainslie had just tantalized him with, he flipped open the book he'd been holding.

Yeats, he thought as he leafed through the pages. With a name like Malone he'd naturally heard of him, as one of Ireland's most beloved bards, but poetry had never been something he'd made time for. And maybe that had been his loss, he told himself a few minutes later, re-reading the final line of a verse, and feeling something stir in him at the simple resonance of the words.

A handful of poems that would live forever. A man could face death calmly if he knew he was leaving a legacy like that for the world to remember him by. For the first time that day the stabbing pain lanced through his skull, as if to remind him that it hadn't disappeared completely, and his grip on the book tightened as he waited for it to subside.

It did almost instantly, but for once he barely noticed its passing. His fingers unsteady, he felt carefully along the spine of the book, sure that his imagination had misled him. He froze as once more he felt the hard, disklike shape beneath the binding. With a swiftly violent movement, he ripped the gold-stamped leather away and stared in disbelief at what had been hidden there.

"I COULDN'T EVEN go over to Chelsea's last night because of this nut bar who's targeted Uncle Sully's business. On top of that, Uncle Sully won't tell me *anything,* except that you're probably not going to marry Pearson now."

Tara's voice in her ear sounded aggrieved, and Ainslie repressed a smile. To a teenage girl, everything was the end of the world. But this time her dramatics were understandable. She had a right to know at least something of what had been going on, since her future was involved, too.

Malone had been sitting on the bed. Out of the corner of her eye she saw him get up and walk to the window, but she forced herself to concentrate on what her adopted daughter was saying.

"Is it true, Aunt Lee? Is the wedding really off for good?"

"It's true." Ainslie chose her words with care. "I'm not saying what I did was the right way to have handled the situation, but I think going through with it would have been an even bigger mistake. Pearson's a good man. He just wasn't the man for me." She could tell by Tara's indrawn breath that she was readying a flurry of questions, and she cut her off before she could start. "That's all I'm going to say right now, pumpkin. I'd rather tell you the rest of it in person."

"Okay." For once Tara sounded subdued. "I guess I can understand how you feel. I know I said he was boring and all that, and he was, but he wasn't ever mean or anything to me. Not like his stupid brother was," she added.

Ainslie's parental antennae went up. "What do you mean? Did Brian do something that I don't know about?" she asked sharply.

"It wasn't any big deal. That's why I didn't tell you when it happened, but from then on I made sure I stayed out of his way when we were at Pearson's and he came by to visit," Tara said slowly. "Actually it was kind of weird. I was in Pearson's library one night when we were there for dinner, and I dozed off in the big wing chair. Brian must have come in without seeing me there, and when I woke up he was sitting at the desk with his back to me, writing something. He was talking to himself. I couldn't hear what he was saying, but his voice was really creepy-sounding."

She stopped, and gave a little laugh. "I know it sounds silly, but he really scared me."

"I believe you, baby." Ainslie gripped the phone tightly. "What else happened?"

"I thought I'd just try to get out of there without him seeing me. I started edging toward the door, but I must have made a noise because he whirled around and jumped out of his chair with his face all strange and angry-looking. For a minute I thought he was going to hit me." Tara's voice shook at the memory. "He was shouting at me, asking me what I was doing spying on him and how long I'd been standing behind him reading what he'd been writing. I told him it was his own fault for not seeing me when he came in, and that I hadn't seen anything. He stared at me for a minute, as if he was trying to figure out if I was lying. Then he grabbed the paper off the desk, shoved it into his pocket and stormed out without saying anything else.''

''I wish you'd told me.'' Ainslie's voice shook too, but with anger. ''I don't think Pearson would want his brother treating a guest that way. The man must have been drunk, for God's sake.''

''He hadn't been drinking. When he was yelling at me he had his face right up to mine, and I'd have smelled it if he had liquor on his breath. I don't think he ever drank as much as he pretended to,'' Tara said. ''You know how he was the only one who liked bourbon? I saw him topping up a half-full bottle once in the kitchen with cola. I thought that was weird, too, but not nearly as weird as what happened in the library. I don't know what he would have done if I'd told him I really *had* seen what he was writing.''

''You did? What was it, to get him so excited?'' Ainslie frowned.

''That's just it, Aunt Lee, it wasn't anything really. It was just a darn *list.*'' There was a note of confusion in Tara's voice. ''Some of the names on it were crossed out.''

The towel around Ainslie's head fell, unheeded, to the floor behind her, but the strands of wet hair clinging to the curve of her neck weren't the reason for the sudden coldness that gripped her. ''A list of people?'' She tried to keep the edge from her voice, and failed. ''Tell me, Tara, was it a list of *people?*''

''No.'' If Tara had noticed the urgency in her question, she had obviously identified it as motherly concern. ''They weren't people's names, they were the names of *countries.* Half of them I didn't know, and the other half I wouldn't have been able to pronounce. But one of the crossed-out ones was a place that you still hear about in the news sometimes. You know...that country that used to be part of Russia where the terrible war's been going on for so long?''

Afterward, Ainslie never recalled just how she'd managed to wind up her conversation with Tara without revealing her agitation, but somehow she did. Her hand was shaking, she noticed as she hung up the phone. But that was hardly surprising. She'd just been given the proof she needed to convince the man she loved of his—

''Get dressed as fast as you can, Lee. We've got to get out of here.'' His voice cut harshly across her thoughts and she looked up swiftly. He was still standing by the window, his expression grim. ''They know where we are. They've known all along.''

''It's Brian, Malone.'' Her voice was unsteady with excitement. ''He was the one who killed Chris Stewart at that airport. He's the—''

''Brian gave you the book?''

He jerked his head toward the bed. Confused, Ainslie followed his gaze, her eyes widening in shock as she took in the destroyed book and the small metallic object beside it.

''What's that?'' She turned back to him, not understanding.

''It's a tracking device. It's sending out a signal right now, telling him where to find us. It was in that volume of Yeats.''

''That's how Noah knew where we were yesterday?'' Ainslie's voice rose. ''Because I was carrying around a damned *bug?*'' Her lips tightened and swiftly she went to the bed. ''I thought it was from Pearson—Brian knew I'd assume that. He must have dropped it into my purse himself. Let's see how well it signals him when it's in a thousand pieces, dammit!''

''No.'' Malone stepped in front of her as she reached for the disk. ''We don't want to do anything to panic him, Lee. He's already killed one person to keep the secret of Chris's murder safe.''

''One person?'' He was right. This was no time to act on impulse, she thought reluctantly. She grabbed up a pair of jeans, shoving first one leg and then the other into them without ceremony, her eyes dark with anger. ''He's responsible for thousands of deaths, Malone. Killing that forger probably meant less to him than swatting a fly.''

''He killed Stewart and the forger, Lee. Any way you add that up, it only comes out to two murders.'' His tone was even, and Ainslie pulled her T-shirt over her head before answering him.

''I'm including his kills as the Executioner,'' she said briefly, walking over to the desk and gathering up the sheaf of papers. Beside them was her purse, and she stuffed them into it and slung it over her shoulder. ''Okay, I'm ready. Let's go.''

''He was Noah's informant and Stewart's murderer. But he's not the Executioner.''

Malone hadn't moved. He still stood by the window, his eyes on her. She met his gaze blankly.

''Of course he's the Executioner. That's what I was trying to tell you—Tara saw him going over a list of countries, and the one where Chris was killed had been crossed out. It was a list of places where he'd already started a war, or was planning on starting one, Malone. What other explanation can there be?''

''It was a list of places where the Executioner had been suspected of starting wars.'' His jaw was tight. ''Yeah, Brian killed Stewart. Everything seems to point to that.

What his motive was we don't know yet, but he obviously had some reason to want him dead. You say he's politically ambitious, and we know part of his power base comes from the sensitive positions he's held in various government agencies, so maybe it was just Chris's bad luck to spot him with someone from the opposing side. Someone he should never have been seen with. So he killed Chris, probably left the country on the next flight out, and thought he was safe until he heard through his contacts that the Agency had pulled me in and was questioning me about the man I'd seen at that airport.''

''But the Agency was investigating the assassinations, for God's sake. *That's* what had him worried,'' Ainslie said heatedly.

''He was worried because he knew in the course of the main investigation, his unrelated murder might come to light. He had to discredit anything I might say—and fast.'' Malone shrugged tensely. ''After checking into my background, he realized that if he approached Watkins with just enough facts and dates to give the impression that he'd been studying the Executioner for some time, he could convince the Agency that I was the man they'd been hunting, and that in pretending to help them I'd been playing a double game.''

''No. Not even Brian would have taken such a crazy chance.'' Ainslie shook her head. ''All the Agency had to do was come up with a single instance when it could be proven that you were in another place while the Executioner was somewhere else carrying out an assassination. It was too much of a risk.''

''Was it?'' Malone smiled crookedly at her. ''They must have carried out that elementary check, Lee. They obviously didn't come up with an alibi that would disprove Brian's story.''

"You're saying that he inadvertently hit upon the truth without realizing it? That's one hell of a lucky guess, Malone," Ainslie said tightly. "I still think he's the Executioner himself, and I say we act on the assumption that he is. We can't afford not to."

She took a deep breath. "He's lost any control that he once had. Killing that forger right here in Boston is something he never would have done before, and Cosgrove's murder was the act of a man who wasn't thinking straight. Then he shoots Watkins and lets us go free. I think he knows his time is running out, and he doesn't care if the last anthill he kicks over is in his own backyard, as long as he can destroy as many other lives as possible when he does." She stopped suddenly, struck by a terrible fear. "*Pearson!*" she whispered, her eyes wide with alarm. "Malone, we've got to warn him!"

"Phone him right now." His words were clipped. "Even if his brother's not the Executioner, he's still a killer and you're right—he's running scared. From what you've told me of Pearson, he's no dummy. If he gives any indication of suspecting Brian of anything, he could be in real trouble."

Ainslie was already dialling the number. Holding the receiver to her ear, she chewed nervously at her bottom lip. "When I spoke to him last night he said he expected Brian at Greystones today." She switched her attention back to the phone. "It's not even ringing. I'll try the operator."

"Don't bother." Malone's expression was grim. "His phone was working fine last night, and now it's out of order? I don't like that, Lee. Do you know how to get to Greystones?"

"You think Brian's already there, don't you?" Ainslie paled. "You think Pearson's already dead."

"I think Pearson's in danger," Malone said forcefully. "And if we try to convince the authorities that a respectable citizen is a killer, it's going to take time we don't have. We could try to raise Sully on his cell phone, but he's got his own family and Tara to worry about."

"I won't have Sully involved," Ainslie agreed automatically. "But Seamus, if Pearson's..." She swallowed, and then forced herself to go on. "If Pearson's already dead when we get there, what are we going to do?"

"If Pearson's still alive, we get him the hell to safety. If he's dead, you're going to turn the car around and head straight back to Boston. Then you can contact Sullivan and the police."

Malone pulled open the desk drawer, revealing his own gun and the automatic he'd taken from Watkins the day before. Ainslie stared at him as he retrieved both weapons.

"And while I'm high-tailing it out of there, what do you propose to do?" she said shakily. "The property's enormous, and Brian's been hunting on it since he was a boy. You won't stand a chance."

"You're wrong, Lee."

There was a tone in his voice that she'd never heard before, and when she looked at him he met her gaze with no emotion at all.

"He's just a two-time killer," he continued in the same cold tone. "I'm the Executioner. I'd say it's Brian who doesn't stand a chance, going up against me."

Chapter Fifteen

From the winding entrance road that led up to Greystones the estate appeared to be encircled with a high brick wall, but that was deceiving, Ainslie knew. Where the forest began, the wall was replaced with a high-voltage electric fence, and on the few occasions she had visited here Pearson had warned her that under no circumstances should she brush against it.

She told Malone about it now, as they rolled to a stop in front of the estate's imposing iron gates. Except for the most perfunctory of exchanges, the two of them had barely spoken a word during the long drive.

"What about this part? How is it kept secure?" He glanced at the gates and the wall in front of them. "Didn't you say something about an alarm system?"

"There's a code panel. Unless the sequence has been changed recently I should be able to get us in." Ainslie kept her own tone brisk and started to get out of the car, but he put his hand on her arm.

"Give me the numbers and I'll do it. I don't want you walking around outside until we know for sure what the situation is."

Even his touch was as impersonal as a stranger's, she thought, watching him swing open the control panel and punch in the sequence she'd given him. He'd finally convinced himself beyond all doubt that he was the man he'd feared he was, and he was deliberately distancing himself from her.

"How far away is the house?" He got back into the car, but he made no move to put the vehicle in gear. Ainslie frowned.

"About a mile. Why?"

"If I'm not back in half an hour, I want you to leave. Don't wait any longer than that." His smile was humorless. "And don't come in to save me, Lee. I don't need saving, okay?"

"No, that's not okay." Her smile was even briefer than his. "That's freakin' ridiculous, is what it is. I'm coming up to the house with you, and there's no way you can stop me. Get this damned thing moving before the gates start to close again."

"This is between him and me now. You're not part of it anymore."

"Pearson could be lying dead or badly wounded up at that house!" Ainslie snapped. "He's a decent man, and if there's anything that I can do for him, I will. If he's beyond help—" She paused, fighting back the tears that had suddenly welled up. "If he's beyond help, then at least I'll know I tried. I owe him that much, Malone," she finished, her tone low.

For a moment she thought he intended to press his point further. Then he gave a curt nod.

"You still care for him, don't you, Lee?"

"I care for him as a friend," she said quietly. "If you're asking me whether I love him, you know the answer to that. You were the only man I ever loved. You're the only man I ever will love."

"And if it was within my power to change that, I

would,'' Malone said harshly, putting the vehicle into gear and accelerating through the gates as they began to swing closed again.

Ainslie reacted instinctively to his words, needing desperately for that one moment to wound him as deeply as he'd just wounded her.

''Maybe you *are* the Executioner, Malone. Destroying lives seems to be something you excel at.'' Her voice throbbed with anger. ''Especially your own.''

She wanted to take the terrible accusation back as soon as she'd spoken, but it was too late. He glanced over at her, his gaze shadowed.

''I've been trying to tell you that all along, Lee,'' he said softly. A corner of his mouth lifted, but she saw the pain that flashed swiftly behind his eyes. ''I was beginning to think I'd never convince you.''

She stared at him, her eyes wide and stricken. Then the frozen stillness around her broke and she started to put her hand out to touch him, as if only physical contact could bridge the chasm between them. Before she could, Malone swung the car around one last bend in the road and the house came into view.

The house, and the tall, spare figure of Pearson unfolding himself from an armchair on the veranda, pushing his reading glasses up into his hair and shielding his eyes against the lowering sun as he watched their approach.

The scene couldn't have been more mundane or less sinister, Ainslie thought as she saw him carefully tuck a book under his arm and descend the stone steps to meet his unexpected visitors. She turned to the silent man beside her, her eyes foolishly bright.

''He's alive, Malone!'' she said inanely. ''We've been worrying about nothing. Brian must have changed his mind about coming.''

"Then how come there's a Mercedes and a sports utility parked in the garage?" he asked in an undertone.

She followed his glance. He was right, she saw, some of her relief evaporating. The doors of what Pearson had told her had once been stables were open, the last of the autumn sunlight catching the chrome of the two vehicles parked inside.

"If he's in the house he'll have heard us drive up." A muscle in Malone's jaw tensed. "Dammit, Lee, I never should have—"

He broke off abruptly as the sound of a shot split the pastoral peace. As he brought the car to a stop a few feet away from where Pearson stood at the end of the flagstone path, a second shot drowned out the echoes of its predecessor. Ainslie met his gaze.

"At least he's not in the house," she said hollowly.

"Those shots had to come from at least a couple of fields away, so that gives us time to explain the situation to Pearson," Malone added, reaching for the door handle. "Come on, let's get this over with as quickly as we can."

Aside from everything else, this wasn't going to be the easiest of social situations, Ainslie realized as she got out of the car and saw Pearson's smile. But she'd underestimated the innateness of his courtesy. After the slightest hesitation as she introduced Malone, Pearson extended his hand.

"So this is the man who came back from the dead," he said wryly. "There must be quite a story behind that, Malone, although I'm sure that's not the primary reason you two are here. Ainslie, I appreciate your coming in person to give me your decision. I don't think I have to ask what it is, my dear."

His smile was genuine, although his eyes were shadowed. Her heart sunk as she answered him.

"That's not why I came, Pearson. I've learned something about Brian that I have to tell you about. It...it's not good."

"About Brian?" Pearson looked past the house to the fields beyond. "He's out trying to bag a duck or two. If this concerns him, shouldn't we wait until he gets back to the house?"

"We think your brother's a killer, McNeil," Malone said harshly. "Waiting for him to return would be a mistake. I think he came here to kill you—and I know he wants to kill me."

For the first time since she'd known him, Ainslie saw Pearson's composure slip. A flush of angry color stained the light tan of his face.

"I've never heard anything so damned ridiculous," he snapped. "Is this some kind of tasteless joke?"

From the fields came another shotgun blast, and Ainslie's attention was caught by a wavering vee of birds making its frantic way across the pink-streaked sky. Even as she watched, one of their number dropped out of formation and plummeted awkwardly down to earth. Cold dread enveloped her.

"It's not a joke, Pearson, and Malone's right—we should get you away from here before Brian returns." She saw the stubborn disbelief in his eyes and tried a different tack. "Does Brian have access to tracking devices, bugs, things like that?"

"Spy paraphernalia? Of course not!" he answered curtly. Then he paused, and she saw his brows pull together reluctantly. "I suppose he might have had last year. He was on an economic subcommittee looking into the budgetary demands of covert government agencies. One of their suppliers of electronics was examined very closely."

"He gave me a book when I came to see you two days

ago,'' she said flatly. ''Hidden inside it was a transmitter that signalled where I was at all times. Since the people who knew where we were tried to kill us, I don't think Brian was keeping tabs on me out of simple curiosity.''

She'd shaken him, she saw. The skin over his cheekbones seemed to tighten, and his expression was suddenly bleak. He looked once again at the fields stretching away from the house, and then back at her and Malone.

''I'd prefer we retain some sense of decorum and continue this conversation in the house.''

''We don't have time to—'' Malone began, but uncharacteristically Pearson interrupted him.

''The least persuasive of all arguments to use with me, Malone, and the one I grow most weary of in this modern and soulless age,'' he said coldly. ''You're going to have to make time if you hope to convince me my brother is a murderer.''

Without looking to see if they were following him, he preceded them up the flagstone path to the stone steps. Ainslie looked apprehensively at Malone.

''Tara called him stuffy, but he's not really. This would come as a shock to anyone.'' She bit her lip as they took the first of the steps to the veranda. ''Malone, about what I said in the car—''

''I hope you'll forgive the disorder. I usually have a woman in to clean once a day, but since I wasn't expecting company I thought I'd let it go for once.'' Pearson held the wood screened door open for them. ''We'll sit in the trophy room, I think.''

Like the flannel trousers and crisp white shirt he called casual wear, only by Pearson could life at Greystones be considered roughing it, Ainslie had often thought. But today as he ushered them into the paneled room where generations of McNeil males and their guests had smoked cigars, cleaned rifles and exchanged hunting stories and stock tips in equal measure, she barely saw her surroundings, although it was impossible to ignore them completely. Framed photographs, some decades old, of past McNeil athletic triumphs were grouped on the mantel above the fireplace, and on the walls, a veritable menagerie of mounted heads, the long-slain quarry of Pearson's father and grandfather.

Without preamble, Malone began to outline the chain of events that had brought them there. Ainslie was grateful he had taken the lead in the conversation, and not only because she found it painful to watch the slightly chilly courtesy on Pearson's face change gradually to troubled concern, and then to fearful dismay. But although Pearson's trepidation stemmed from what Malone was telling him, hers was based on what he left unsaid.

He mentioned nothing of her belief that Brian was the Executioner, or of his that he was, and she herself kept silent on the topic. Accepting the probability that his brother had killed two people was overwhelming enough for Pearson right now, she thought, watching him needlessly polishing his glasses as Malone recounted how he had found the tracking device this morning. In a way, it would have been easier on him if Brian had died. At least then Pearson would have been able to preserve his brother in his memories with no fear that the image he had of him would ever tarnish.

Even as the thought went through her mind she froze.

Malone left you...and some part of you never forgave him for that. You need him to be dead, Lee. That way he'll always be a perfect memory, and he'll never be able to leave you again.

Malone himself had said those words to her two nights ago at the hospital, Ainslie thought. She'd denied that there was any truth in them. She still denied it. He'd left her, yes—but only because his whole life had been ripped away from him. There was nothing to forgive...

But he was right. Somewhere inside her there still existed a little girl whose father and adored big brother had walked out on her one terrible day—a little girl whose pain had never fully healed. That five-year-old Ainslie had *never* forgiven Malone. And because she was only a child, that Ainslie had sometimes frightened even herself by wishing that he'd remained a memory, rather than coming back into her life and forcing herself to face his all-too-human flaws—and hers.

You told him you didn't trust him because you knew he was hiding himself from you. But it was exactly the opposite. You've kept the walls up since he returned because you knew that this time he was determined to hold nothing back—and that terrified you. You knew that if he revealed himself to you, you would have to reveal yourself to him. When you did he would see that the toughness and strength that you show to the world is just a cover for that scared little girl inside.

"That first murder—the one at the airport. When was that, did you say?" The sharpness in Pearson's voice jolted her from her thoughts.

"Five years ago," Malone said steadily. "There's no record of him leaving the country at that time but—"

"The time fits." Pearson passed his hand shakily across his eyes. "Dear God. It's true, then."

He stood, his spare figure somehow diminished. "I came home one day and found Brian in my library, the whole room reeking of some vile-smelling tobacco. The cigarettes he'd been smoking were a cheap Eastern European brand, but at the time I was more concerned with getting the stench out of the upholstery than asking him where he'd obtained them. There've been one or two other little incidents..."

He raised his head, his gaze bleak. "I'll grab some things, and we'll leave immediately. I've been having trouble with the phone today, so we'll have to contact the authorities from town."

Malone got to his feet as Pearson left the room, and Ainslie rose, too, feeling suddenly weary. She watched as he stood by the fireplace and picked up a silver-framed photograph from the mantel.

"You're coming with us, aren't you?"

"You mean will I leave it to the authorities to deal with Brian?" He looked over his shoulder at her. "Yeah, Lee, I will. If we'd found Pearson here dead it would have been a different scenario, but once Brian's behind bars you'll be able to go back to living a normal life, and that's all I care about. His brother's life won't ever be the same, though."

"I know," she said softly. She walked over to the French doors and looked out onto the lawns at the side of the house. It would be the second time in as many days that her happiness had been bought at the expense of Pearson's, she thought somberly. With Brian in custody, the Agency would be forced to reexamine their case against Malone. Once they started looking into their unimpeachable source's own movements, it wouldn't be long before they found out that Brian was the Executioner himself.

Malone would be completely exonerated, she thought, the scene in front of her suddenly blurring. She blinked her tears away and the lawns and gardens came back into focus again. At long last he'd be free to come back to her, with no shadows between them.

She had her own shadows to confess to him too. Although it had taken her too long to acknowledge their existence, now that they had come out into the light she could see them for what they were, and put them behind her.

It would work out. She would *make* it work—

Pearson appeared from around the corner of the house, carrying a rifle in one hand, the barrel pointing at the ground.

Ainslie turned in confusion to Malone but he was already at her side, frowning down at a photograph in his hand. "This picture of the rowing team, Lee—there's Brian and Chris, but take a look at the older student wearing the coaching sweater. It's Pearson."

At his words the final piece of the puzzle suddenly fell into terrible place. Icy fear trickled down her spine as the full enormity of what she'd just realized slammed into her.

"Dear God, Malone," she whispered in cold horror, lifting her gaze to the man walking across the lawn. "We got the wrong *brother!*"

Beside her he stiffened. From the fields beyond Ainslie saw a second figure approaching, a brace of ducks in his hand, his rifle slung across his back.

Even as she watched, Pearson shoved his glasses up into his hair and brought the rifle to his shoulder, but by then Malone was pushing open the French doors and racing across the grass toward Pearson, reaching for his gun as he ran. A heartbeat later Ainslie sprinted after him, her eyes wide with shock.

The explosion was deafening.

Her stunned gaze flew to Brian just as his disbelieving expression turned to comprehension. Slowly he looked down at the bright scarlet stain already covering the left half of his khaki hunting vest. He put his hand gingerly to it, as if he still hoped there was a chance that it wasn't real, but even from a distance Ainslie could see the blood pumping through his outspread fingers.

He started to look up toward the brother who had just killed him, but before he could complete the movement he crumpled bonelessly to the ground. Around one wrist a leather thong secured the two mallards to him.

"Pull that trigger and she'll be the next to die, Malone." Pearson sounded unconcerned. "Believe me, I'd much rather give the pair of you a sporting chance at survival. Put your guns on the ground, please—the one in your hand and that spare you have shoved into your waistband at the back."

The rifle was pointing at her now, Ainslie saw. Sharp fear ran through her and she remained motionless, hardly daring to breathe. Malone's jaw tightened. After what seemed an eternity he slowly lowered his arm and set the gun he was holding on the ground. He reached around to his back and put the gun he'd taken from Watkins beside his own before he straightened again.

"I just saw what you call a sporting chance." He moved closer to her and away from his weapons as the other man, his rifle still unwaveringly aimed at Ainslie, scooped up the guns and deposited them in the khaki bag at his hip. "Brian didn't even see that coming, McNeil."

A look of distaste crossed Pearson's patrician features. "My brother never appreciated the aesthetics of the hunt."

"He'd begun to suspect something, hadn't he?" She heard the quaver in her voice and tried to control it. "That's what that list was all about—he was putting two and two together. Only he couldn't bring himself to believe that his own—"

"Don't spoil it for me, my dear. Not when I've waited so long for this moment."

Was it her imagination, or had his finger tightened on the trigger? Ainslie swallowed, her throat suddenly dry.

"When I learned that the Agency was questioning you

about—what was the name he was going under? Stewart?" Pearson shrugged. "About Stewart's death at that godforsaken little airport, I made it my business to find out what kind of a man you were, Malone. I needed to know if anyone would take you seriously—after all, there was a chance you might run into me and recognize me, since I was called in quite often by the Agency to analyze certain trends in volatile world situations. I learned that you had once risen from the dead, and taken your vengeance on the men who had buried you."

He paused thoughtfully. "Let's stroll a little as we talk, shall we? This is my favorite time of year. Besides, Ainslie, the last time you were scheduled to walk with me you ran out on me rather abruptly, I recall." His tone didn't change. "You ceased to exist for me the moment you left that church, my dear."

"I never existed for you." Numbly she put one foot in front of the other. At the periphery of her vision she saw Malone's eyes narrow as he scanned the field they were entering and the heavily wooded area farther on. "From the start you must have seen me as a possible pawn to use if the situation arose."

"At the start. But then I saw you fight." Pearson's voice came from behind her. "You didn't know that I'd attended one of your boxing matches, did you? I recognized in you the same killer instinct that I'd recognized in myself years before. Yes, when I first saw you at Malone's funeral I thought you might be the bait he would eventually come back for, but after a while I realized that I wanted you for myself. You disappointed me in the end, though."

Ahead of her the sun was setting the clouds on fire. A faint honking came from somewhere high above, and beside her she saw Malone tense.

"But enough of the hearts and flowers." Pearson's tone

gave no indication that he had just walked past his dead brother. "As I said, I learned about your episode in the jungle, Malone. It occurred to me that our lives had followed parallel paths, and from there it wasn't much of a leap to consider that you would make a perfect Executioner.

"Watkins had become obsessed with the case. All I had to do was point him in your direction and unleash him, but even I hadn't hoped that you would come to believe it yourself."

"I believed it because of Joseph Mocamba. But he wasn't one of the Executioner's kills, was he?" Ainslie had expected to hear some sign in Malone's voice that the burden of guilt he'd carried so long had finally lifted, but if anything the self-loathing was more pronounced. "Everyone assumed he was. But like you say, it was just that our lives were following parallel paths. The only real difference between us is the body count, McNeil."

"You're wrong! You *have* to be." She couldn't allow him to go to his death believing that, Ainslie thought sharply. She stopped and turned to him, her body rigid and her hands clenched at her sides.

"You didn't kill Mocamba. I don't care what proof you think you have—you *couldn't* have killed him. I know you better than you know yourself, Malone, just as you always knew me better than I did. You're the man I love, and I know you didn't do it."

"No, Lee," he said forcefully. "I'm the man who walked out on you. That's the real Seamus Malone."

His expression was bleakly distant. He would never believe her, she realized hopelessly. Nothing she could say would refute the memory he had of seeing Mocamba targeted in the sights of his gun, and seeing the man die at his hand. But there was one crushing burden it *was* within her power to take from him.

"Dammit, Seamus, you're talking crazy again," she said softly. "You never walked out on me. How could you, when I kept you safe in my heart the whole time?"

A corner of his mouth lifted reluctantly. "You'll go down fighting, won't you, champ?"

"I retired undefeated." Her gaze was steady on his. "I intend to keep it that way."

"You took up a position in the steel girders above the stadium. When Mocamba was nearly at the podium, you squeezed off a single shot, Malone. I couldn't have done better myself." A few feet away from them Pearson shook his head admiringly. "I told you I'd researched you. You were good—maybe even good enough to beat me. That's what we're here to find out."

The brief spark of emotion in Malone's eyes died. "So I was right. It's hunting season."

"It's hunting season," Pearson agreed. "But unlike my late father and my brother, I never found much sport in pitting my skills against dumb animals. Man is the ultimate prey, the ultimate thrill." He frowned thoughtfully. "I'll admit that as a scholar there was an added challenge in knowing I'd actually had a hand in shaping the history I wrote about, although Brian seemed to think I would be content with helping him fulfill his insignificant ambitions."

"How much of a challenge was it to kill Paul Cosgrove, Pearson?" He was a monster, Ainslie thought. It seemed wrong that he should still look like the man she'd once thought she'd cared for, right down to the slightly chilly smile he now gave her.

"Don't you ever just do something for fun, Ainslie?" he asked softly. "I know Tara calls me stuffy, but I've got my impulsive side. Who knows, maybe one day the child will find that out for herself.''

An icy shard of fear lodged inside her at his words. Then her internal temperature reversed itself, and hot fury rose in her. She fought down the almost overwhelming desire to launch herself at him, to rip the smile from his face, to see his blood on her fists. Malone put a warning hand on her arm, but it wasn't necessary.

''You just made the mistake that's going to kill you, Pearson,'' she said thinly. ''Didn't your father teach you never to get between a mother bear and her cub?''

''Now *that's* the spirit that once attracted me to you, my dear.'' Pearson sounded gratified. ''I was planning to kill you first, but going up against you might prove to be more challenging than I thought.''

He frowned. ''But we're wasting daylight. Let me outline the rules, and then we can begin. I'll give the two of you five minutes lead time. After that the hunt is on. Malone, I've decided to track you down first. Of course, the two of you can take your chances together if you wish, but that only makes it easier for me. Oh, and if either of you has considered doubling back to the house and making your escape that way, you should know that I've recently had the entrance gates and the brick portion of the perimeter modified. I turned on the power before I left the house, so I wouldn't advise trying that route. I think that's it. Any questions?''

They'd suspected the wrong brother, but they'd been right about everything else, Ainslie thought. Pearson had lost it. If they could only elude him until the sun set completely, his chances of finding them in the dark would be—

The harsh cries high above her sounded like a warning. She raised her eyes, looking past the skein of geese arrowing across the sky to the pale disk already climbing into view.

It was a full moon. At this time of year it was called a hunter's moon, she thought leadenly. He would have no trouble tracking them by its light.

"Just one, McNeil." Malone's voice was expressionless. "I've come back from the dead twice. What makes you think that I won't come back a third time, looking for vengeance?"

"Because I'm a romantic at heart. I believe in the legend of the wild geese."

In a blur of movement Pearson aimed the rifle skyward, pulled the trigger and brought it back down again, levering the weapon's bolt even as the shock wave of sound was still rushing at Ainslie's ears. A second later something brushed heavily by her to crash at her feet, and to her horror she saw the broken body, mighty wings still outstretched in its final flight, on the ground in front of her.

"You see? Even if you do come back, you won't stand a chance," Pearson said smoothly. "If that's everything, let's start the clock running now. You have my word that I'll give you your five minutes."

"Lee, head for the trees." Malone didn't look at her as he spoke, but kept his eyes on Pearson. "Go on. As soon as you reach cover I'll follow."

Slowly, Ainslie turned, and took a few hesitant steps. She looked back over her shoulder at him.

"Malone, I—"

"*Now*, Lee."

The sharpness in his voice galvanized her into action and she started running toward the wooded area surrounding the field, expecting at any moment to hear the flat, deadly crack of Pearson's rifle taking down the man in front of him. She slipped behind the concealing trunk of a massive oak, and saw Malone look over in her direction. He took a step back from Pearson, and then another, the dead bird seeming to mark some dividing line between them. He turned and began jogging toward the trees.

She knew what he would be feeling—the bullet smashing through his spine, himself falling, the blood exploding from his heart as he died. In her own imagination he died a dozen times during the seconds it took him to cross the hundred yards or so of open field to her.

He caught her as she flew at him, his arms tightening around her. For the briefest of moments they stood locked in a silent and desperate embrace, Ainslie feeling the tenseness in his biceps as he clasped her to him. Then he released her.

"You're going to get out of this alive, Lee," he said quietly. "I'm going to make sure of it."

"*We're* going to get out of this—" she began, but he put a finger to her lips.

"No, honey." He shook his head. "This is the end of the line for me, and that's how it should be. Last night you told me that if I was looking for redemption I could find it in stopping the Executioner. I *can* stop him, Lee. But he's going to take me down with him. There's no other way, and even if there was it wouldn't matter. He was right. I'm no different than him—except for the fact that I always had you, and he never did."

"You didn't kill Mocamba, Seamus. He lied about that. He knows you're the only man who can defeat him—he's always known that—and right from the start he's used your doubts as a weapon against you. Don't you see that?"

"I see a good man in the crosshairs of my rifle." Malone's voice was edged with pain. "Maybe after today I won't see that anymore."

He shook his head. "But we don't have time for this.

I'm going to lead Pearson away from this area, and while he's tracking me I want you to make your way back to the house."

"His gun room." Ainslie's eyes widened. "Of course! Circle around and end up back here, Malone. I'll meet you with whatever weapon I can find and—"

"He would have thought of that. He wouldn't have left anything lying around that we could use and anyway, I want you as far away from him as possible. Burn his house down, Lee."

He was speaking faster now, his words low and hurried. "Get a rag and stuff one end into the Mercedes's gas tank. Light the other end and run like hell because it's going to blow sky-high. That wooden veranda's going to catch, and then the house will start blazing. It'll be seen for miles, and every fire department in the county will send out trucks. All you have to do is find a place to hide until they come."

"It's a great plan except for one thing." She looked at him stubbornly. "You're coming with me. We'll do it together."

"Yeah, that might work." A shadow crossed his features. "We might even get away alive, but so might Pearson, Lee. I can't let that happen, and you know it."

"No more barriers, Malone." Ainslie felt suddenly immensely tired, as if she had gone through ten gruelling rounds with an opponent who had finally proved too tough for her. She felt the tears come to her eyes, but with the last of her strength she managed to bring a shaky smile to her lips. "Not anymore. Not between us. It's not only Pearson you can't allow to leave here alive. It's yourself. Even if you could stop him and still survive, you wouldn't, would you?" She didn't need to hear his answer, she thought. It was there in the brilliant green gaze meeting hers.

"Two weeks and two days," she whispered, raising her hand to his cheek and laying it lightly against the roughly stubbled jawline. "How incredibly lucky I was to have had even that much."

She brought her face close to his, and then, as if he needed to obliterate for this one final time any distance between them, his mouth came down on hers. His hold on her tightened almost painfully, but all Ainslie was aware of was the taste of him, the feel of him, her own breaking heart. Malone lifted his head, and gently put her away from him.

"I love you, Lee." He let his hands slip from her shoulders. "Don't go to the funeral, champ. Remember me this way, okay?"

She nodded mutely. He looked at her one last time, and then he turned away, slipping between the trees and melting into the deepening shadows until she could no longer see him.

Chapter Sixteen

Time was of the essence, Ainslie thought. She had to make her way to the house, find material and matches to ignite a fire with and then deliberately start a conflagration that the most insane arsonist might envy. And after that she had to come back here to find Malone.

She had no intention of letting him go up against the Executioner alone.

She didn't want a dead hero, she told herself with a quick spurt of anger. She wanted a live Seamus Malone to make a family with, to build a future with, to grow old with. No matter how well Pearson had covered his tracks, once the investigation into his killings began his deceptions would start to unravel. There would be *some* scrap of evidence to prove he'd assassinated Joseph Mocamba.

She glanced nervously up at the moon, still low in the sky, but so full and bright that the landscape was bathed in its glow. Leaving the cover of the trees, she moved swiftly across the field, keeping as low to the ground as she could. She'd almost reached the lawn when she tripped over something and fell heavily to the ground.

She found herself staring into Brian's sightless eyes, only inches away from her horror-stricken gaze. Her outflung arm was lying on one of the mallards bound to his wrist.

Nausea rose in her throat. She scrambled to her feet, almost falling again in her haste, and all of a sudden the night around her seemed crowded with the ghosts of the Executioner's victims. She could feel their hopeless gazes on her, as if they were trying to tell her that she wouldn't succeed, that no one could succeed against the man who had destroyed them.

Ainslie shook off the hysteria that threatened, knowing that to give in to it, even for a second, would be fatal. She ran the last stretch of field without even bothering to stay low, diving into the shadowy bulk of some shrubbery as she got to the edge of the lawn.

From then on it was easier, although she had one bad moment when she realized that the Mercedes's gas cap needed to be unlocked with a key. But the SUV gas tank was accessible, she found after a few minutes of fumbling around in the dark. It would do just as well.

She didn't dare switch on a light, and at one point she was about to open the sports utility's door to look for something to use as a fuse when she stopped herself just in time, her palms damp with nervousness. Even the briefest sliver of light would be visible to Pearson if he was anywhere in sight of the house, she told herself. It seemed to be an eternity before she came across a single greasy piece of rag on a low shelf at the back of the garage.

She hurried back to the car, wadded the rag up into the open gas tank and let as much of it trail down the side of the vehicle as possible. She would have to move fast once she lit it, she thought apprehensively. The rag itself would flare up instantaneously, and the resulting explosion would follow almost immediately.

But first she had to light it. Ainslie bit her lip in frustration as she realized that the one thing she didn't have was a match.

There would be matches somewhere in the house. But in the dark it would take her far too long to locate them, she thought, feeling a thin bubble of panic begin to rise up in her. And using the car lighter from either of the vehicles would pose the same problem that she'd faced when she'd been looking for the rag.

She knew exactly where she *could* find a lighter—somewhere on the body of the dead man lying not more than a hundred yards from where she stood, wasting time.

"You have to do it," Ainslie said out loud. "There's no other way. Malone's out there with a killer stalking him. You *have* to do it, dammit."

It was as terrible as she'd thought it would be. Brian's body had already started to stiffen, and she had to roll him over onto his back to get to the front pockets of his vest. Her hands were shaking so badly when she finally felt the heavy shape of his gold lighter that she nearly dropped it. Just as she stood again, wanting only to leave as quickly as she could, she thought she heard the faintest rustle of movement from the edge of the woods, and she felt her limbs turn to water. She held her breath, waiting for the sound to come again.

But it wouldn't, she told herself impatiently a moment later.

She sped back to the garage, the lighter clutched tightly in her hand.

She was almost certain it had been St. Augustine who'd asked God to make him good, but not yet, Ainslie thought disjointedly, holding the lighter to the end of the grease-soaked rag. Right now her prayers were running along similar lines.

"Make it catch, God," she muttered through lips that

seemed suddenly dry. "Just don't let it go up too fast, okay?"

She flipped back the top of the lighter, put her thumb on the tiny wheel, and spun it. The small flame flared up immediately and, already on the balls of her feet ready to run, she touched it to the end of the rag.

She wasn't going to make it.

Shock tore through her as the rag burst into an immediate sheet of flame, and she sprinted toward the open doors of the garage, the toes of her sneakers digging into the dirt floor in a frantic attempt to propel her to safety. She put on a final, impossible burst of speed and then it happened.

It was as if a giant hand had come up behind her and dealt her a massive blow between her shoulder blades. She felt herself being lifted off her feet, felt herself cartwheeling crazily through the air, felt the super-heated rush of air blasting through the thin material of her T-shirt.

And then she slammed heavily into the earth of a nearby flowerbed, her fall partially broken by the leafless branches of a bush. She got to her knees and looked back.

The garage was a ball of fire. Flames were already running along the overhanging limbs of the maple tree that grew between it and the house, and even as she watched Ainslie saw a flurry of sparks settle on the shingles of the larger building's roof. Belatedly she remembered that there had been two vehicles, not one, in the garage, and she got to her feet and staggered a little farther away—just in time, she realized a moment later.

The second blast was even more forceful than the first. The mullioned windows on Greystones's ground floor shattered in the aftershock and fell, with a sound like a thousand icicles breaking, to the veranda. The roof was now blazing away merrily, Ainslie noted, backing up a few steps as the heat reached out for her. Malone had been right. The fire would be visible for miles.

There was nothing more she had to do here. She turned and began running across the lawn to the field, trying to ignore the throbbing pain in her ankle.

Reaching the cover of the woods, she halted, momentarily disoriented by the contrast between the unobstructed moonlight of the open field she'd just left and the zebralike striping of silvery illumination and black shadows here among the trees.

Everything happened at once.

"*Pearson!* Over here, damn you!"

Turning in shock toward the sound of Malone's voice, Ainslie felt herself being wrenched back by a crushing grip around her neck even as something cold and hard pressed painfully against her temple. At the same moment the very shadows themselves seemed to take shape just in front of her, and with horror she saw the shadows turn into Malone himself, Brian's shotgun steadied against his shoulder and aimed at her.

"Malone, *no!*" she screamed as Pearson pulled her completely in front of him. "Don't shoot—it's *me!*"

Only the arm across her neck kept her from falling. Pearson jerked her head farther up as Malone froze, his finger still on the trigger.

"Put it down, Malone," Pearson rasped, pressing the barrel of Watkins's automatic even more firmly against her skull. "I said I'd kill you first, but under these circumstances I might reconsider."

"Let her go, McNeil."

Malone's features were impossible to make out. Through her half-closed lashes all she could see was a mottled pattern of moonlight and shadow, accentuated by the flickering glow from the blaze beyond the trees.

"It's me you want. It's me you always wanted, isn't it? I only wish I'd stopped you years ago, when you killed Joseph Mocamba. You were the cameraman, weren't you?" Malone lowered the shotgun carefully. Even more carefully he bent and placed it on the ground at his feet.

"So you finally remember." Pearson sounded amused. "Yes, I was posing as a cameraman. And you and several other snipers had been brought in by Mocamba's security advisers, who'd heard a rumor that the Executioner might be at the stadium that day. How close did you come to taking me out?"

"I had you in my crosshairs," Malone said evenly. "But I had no way of knowing who you were until it was too late. Mocamba was jostled by the crowd into my sight line and I couldn't risk the shot. You must have pulled your trigger just as I held my fire."

His eyes met Ainslie's. "You were right, champ. I'm probably not all I should be, but I'm not the man I thought I was." One corner of his mouth lifted in a tired smile. "That's a candle to take with me into the darkness," he said softly.

Slowly he raised his hands and locked them together at the back of his head. He looked at Pearson, his gaze steady and unafraid.

"Take me for her," he said quietly. "I'll give you my word that I won't try anything, McNeil. You still have time to get away, and I'm sure you set up a new identity to vanish into a long time ago. But let her go."

"You know, Malone, I think I believe you." Ainslie felt Pearson's arm slacken its hold across her throat. Keeping his eyes on Malone, he released her completely, and then stepped slightly away from her.

"Her for you," he said, the gun still inches away from her neck. "It's a deal, Malone—but only because I know that letting Ainslie live without you for the rest of her life is much worse than anything else I could ever do to her. Goodbye, my dear," he said to Ainslie without looking at her. "I doubt our paths will cross again."

"Don't *do* it, Malone," she croaked desperately, her throat raw from Pearson's chokehold. "He's right—I *can't* lose you a second—"

Pearson swung the gun away from her and fired. Malone staggered backward from the force of the bullet and fell.

Unconcernedly Pearson pocketed the weapon in his hand and bent to pick up the shotgun Malone had surrendered. "I'll send roses to his funeral," he said lightly. "Red ones, weren't they? Go on, Ainslie. I meant what I told him. I have no intention of killing you."

His hand reached out. His fingers touched the stock of the shotgun. The silent screams inside Ainslie's head suddenly tore from her throat.

"*No!* Dear God—*noo-oo!*"

She launched herself at Pearson, knocking him off balance and falling with him to the ground, her left hand grasping at the collar of his shirt and her right hand already tightened into a fist. She felt her knuckles land with such force at the side of his jaw that his head snapped backward from the blow.

He was as quick as a cat. Twisting away from her, his hand went swiftly to his jacket pocket as Ainslie lunged at him again. This time her punch landed high on his cheek, and she followed it up with a punishing left jab that knocked him back down. His hand came from his pocket empty, and she saw the gun he had been looking for lying a few feet away in some leaves.

"You bitch!" His voice was thickly slurred, and she saw the blood running from the side of his mouth. "I'll send you to hell!"

"You're the one who's going there, Pearson," Ainslie grated. "For killing Malone, for killing Joseph Mocamba, for killing your own brother and all the other thousands of innocent victims whose lives you snuffed out." The sound she had been hearing for the last few seconds grew louder, and she smiled tightly at him. "*You're* going to hell. I'm going to send you there and the wild geese have come to escort you down. Do you *hear* them, Pearson?"

He made a desperate grab for his gun, and she hit him again, this time sending him smashing facedown into the fallen leaves. She wanted to see his face turn into a bloody pulp, she thought coldly, pulling him up and hitting him again, and then again. She wanted to hear him scream. She wanted to stop this pain inside her that was tearing her apart.

She wanted to bring Malone back.

Her arm was already drawn back for the next blow, but she stopped herself before she could send her fist crashing into his face again. She looked down at the unconscious mask that had only seconds ago been the coldly patrician features of Pearson McNeil.

He was a monster, she thought dully. If she killed him like this, she would be one, too.

And it wouldn't bring Malone back. Nothing would bring him back this time.

She shook her head, as if to clear it, and realized that the sound she had heard was the thin wail of sirens from approaching fire engines. It was over, she thought. It was all over.

She got painfully to her feet, averting her eyes from Malone's still body. She didn't want to think of him as dead anymore, she told herself unsteadily. She'd done that for two long years, and she didn't want to do it anymore. From now on she would think of him as he'd wanted her to remember him—as the man she loved, who'd held her in his arms and taken her to the stars.

She took a limping step away and heard the click of the automatic's safety behind her. Slowly she turned around and saw the Executioner facing her, his gun in his hand.

"I hear them too, Ainslie." She could barely make out what he was saying through his shattered jaw. "You're right—they're coming for me. They're all around me. They know I killed one of their own back at that damned airport." His broken lips stretched into a madman's grin. "But if I'm going to hell anyway, I might as well make one last kill."

The gun in his hand came up. With dreadful clarity she saw him take aim.

And out of the corner of her eye, she saw Malone rise to his full height, the shotgun held loosely in the crook of one arm as he pulled back on the trigger and discharged both barrels straight into the Executioner's chest.

A terrible sound came from Pearson's throat as he slammed backward against a nearby tree trunk. The gun flying from his hand, he frantically beat at the empty air around him as if to ward off something that only he could see.

His terrified eyes suddenly opened to their widest, and then all life disappeared from them and he slid slowly down to the ground.

"Are you okay, Lee?" Malone's voice was a hoarse rasp.

Ainslie looked at him, her gaze filling with tears.

"You're dead. He was the Executioner and he killed you. Malone's dead." Her hands hung uselessly at her sides and her shoulders were bowed. She shook her head. "You're a ghost. This time he didn't come back."

"This time I didn't leave, Lee." He was beside her, and

he turned her to face him. ''The Executioner's aim was off. Maybe he'd started to need those glasses for more than reading, or maybe the geese had something to do with it. But he didn't kill me. I think my shoulder might be broken, though.''

The wry smile was Malone's. The eyes were the same brilliant green as his. And no other man had ever gazed at her the way he was doing now—as if she was the first, the last, and the only woman he would ever love.

Ainslie looked up at him, the tears streaming heedlessly down her cheeks.

''Malone, is it really *you?*'' she breathed in incredulous joy.

She didn't give him a chance to answer. Her lips opened under his, her arms went around his neck, and Ainslie O'Connell held onto Seamus Malone as if she would never, ever let him go…

…and somewhere high in the sky above them, a ragged vee-shaped flight of wild geese, moonlight on their wings, flew into the night to eternity, and redemption.

Epilogue

Maybe ''Danny Boy'' wasn't the most traditional song for a newly married couple's first dance, Ainslie thought as Malone took her hand and drew her into his embrace. But the hauntingly plaintive air held a special meaning. She tipped her head back and met his gaze.

''Have I told you tonight how beautiful you are?'' he asked softly, as they circled the floor. ''With that dress and those violets in your hair you look like something out of a fairy tale, Lee.''

''I told the saleswoman absolutely no frills,'' she said, smiling. ''When I saw this, my only worry was whether the aunts could arrange a wedding soon enough so that I would still fit into it. Plain satin and a bias cut don't hide much, Malone.''

A corner of his mouth lifted. ''I know you can eat like a stevedore and not put on an ounce. You'll probably be able to wear this at our fiftieth anniversary, honey.''

''Maybe.'' She gave him a wide-eyed look. ''But it's a good thing you accepted that job Sully offered you running the security division of his firm. You'll be able to keep me in all the new outfits I'm going to need in the next few months.''

Around the dance floor she glimpsed the faces of her

aunts, Kate escorted by Billy Dare and Cissie and Jackie beaming as they watched her. Sullivan, a two-month-old Megan cradled in his arms, was sitting at a nearby table with Bailey and Tara, and even as Ainslie's gaze met her brother's he closed one eye in a wickedly slow wink.

He knew, she realized with a small start of amused surprise. And any minute Malone would put two and two together, but for now she was content to just stay here in the circle of his arms and let the song play to a finish.

True love never died, she thought, feeling Malone's heartbeat beneath her outspread palm as he maneuvered her one last time around the floor. That's what the song really meant. That was why she had chosen it. The final strains of the violin echoed in the hushed room and Malone pulled her closer, bending his head to kiss her.

She felt him stiffen. His head jerked up suddenly, belated comprehension spreading across his face.

"A few months? You mean you're—you mean we're going to have—" He broke off, his gaze searching hers.

Once she'd seen ghosts and darkness in those emerald eyes, Ainslie thought, nodding up at him and feeling her throat tighten foolishly. But after two long years, the ghosts and the darkness were finally behind them. She saw the incredulous joy spread across his face, and then his mouth came down on hers. His arms tightened around her as if he would never let her go.

And then, like wine and perfume and a lover's kiss, the faint scent of violets swirled around Ainslie O'Connell Malone and the last man she would ever love...